THE SECRETS OF THE GREASER Hotel

WRITTEN AND ILLUSTRATED BY
J. SCOTT FUQUA

Published by Bancroft Press
"Books that Enlighten"
P.O. Box 65360
Baltimore, MD 21209
410-764-1967 (fax)
www.bancroftpress.com

illustrated by J. Scott Fuqua.
written by J. Scott Fuqua.

design by Susan Mangan.

978-1-61088-130-2 (hardcover)
978-1-61088-131-9 (paperback)
978-1-61088-132-6 (mobi)
978-1-61088-133-3 (ebook)
978-1-61088-134-0 (audio)

First Dedication

This book is dedicated to my children:
To Gabriel, whom I love and have spent long parts of every
day with for years; it's mostly a pure and unfettered joy.
To Calla, whom I love unconditionally, and whom
I've watched grow into the loveliest young woman.

Second Dedication

A smaller but sincere dedication goes out to the Voos family,
who really had no idea what I was doing but participated anyway.

Third Dedication

To David Simon, who doesn't know me but is an artist
I respect so much for speaking truth to power.
He interprets the world for others in ways
I am incapable of doing.

The immense Greaser Hotel was located amidst the once famous and now bankrupt department stores and theaters of downtown Baltimore. A monstrous hulk of brick and stone covering an entire block, The Greaser was plastered with a hodgepodge of architectural

J. Scott Fuqua

details, pieces of which had been coming off in flakes and chunks for the last two decades. For fear of getting struck dead by a plummeting Italianate bracket or medieval gargoyle, pedestrians strictly avoided using the sidewalks adjacent to The Greaser, a fact that suited the caretakers just fine.

Opened by the mysterious Marvin Greaser in 1880, the once posh hotel was leased to the city seventy-five years later. Thereafter, for three decades, it served as public housing, after which time, and due to the fact that it was considered unfit for human habitation, the lease expired and the building became a chemical warehouse for Greaser Consolidated Enterprises until the day a nosey fire inspector (now deceased) pronounced the facility a terrible fire hazard. Following that, the old hotel was emptied of chemicals and assigned an on-site property manager.

Greasy Blight, which is what the building was called by locals, was a stain on an already stained landscape of failed Baltimore businesses. It was a monument to a once prosperous Baltimore. Most every resident of the city wanted it torn down, presuming it abandoned and an obstruction to downtown redevelopment.

But the building wasn't vacant at all. It was occupied by the wicked, unlikeable Friendly family, a clan consisting of a wildly tough mother and her five adult boys.

A young girl named Allie Argos, as well as three other forlorn and desperate individuals, also inhabited the building, but they weren't there by choice.

Allie had moved to The Greaser Hotel when she was only six. She'd come to live there after her parents, Gordon and Melinda Argos, were sent to prison for kidnapping one of the Gristles of Gristle Brand meat fame. Of course, being so young at the time, Allie had only vague memories of the incident. She recalled that the

victim had been a child born to the Gristle family empire. That was all. One week after Allie's parents were condemned to twenty years of hard time, Mrs. Friendly, the caretaker of The Greaser Hotel, swaggered into the Children's Welfare Office, sidled up to a caseworker, and declared that she wanted "that dear, unfortunate Argos girl" to grow up in a caring environment.

"You're looking to be her foster parent?" an employee asked.

"Yup. Exactly."

"Don't see why not. Fill this out," he instructed, and Allie's fate was decided.

Greasy Blight became her home. In fact, she'd spent nine years imprisoned behind the old hotel's chipped brick and its boarded

J. Scott Fuqua

windows, never once leaving. It was her job to clean 460 of the building's dilapidated apartments, from the fifty-fourth floor down to the fourth and back again, without a day off. The mammoth hotel was in fact a prison camp, with six guards—Mrs. Friendly and her five creepy boys.

It was not a hospitable place. It was not a welcoming place. It was an ever-changing environment run by the whims and will of people whom Allie had learned to both hate and fear, depending on the situation. Sometimes, when Allie stopped for a moment to gather in her environment, a heavy helplessness settled upon her narrow

shoulder blades, making her weak. In the bleakest of moments, her bony knees trembled so hard against one another that they sounded like chattering molars.

Truly, if Allie hadn't had Jerome and the company of her fellow prisoners, she was sure she'd have gone insane.

☙❧

By six in the morning, all four Greaser Hotel detainees were, as usual, hard at work. Allie Argos, Arnold Armstrong (the former millionaire and frozen food titan), Midge Darlington (yes, the very Midge Darlington once known nationwide as North America's homemaking diva), and Rena Duchamp (the missing daughter of Harold and Louise Duchamp, the founders of Du It! Software and Internet Systems), busily prepared breakfast for the Friendly clan, then tended to piles of dirty dishes. When all was spic and span, they were immediately escorted to their menial jobs.

By eleven in the morning, Allie had progressed to her third apartment unit. As was her custom, she began by cleaning the bathroom. Even more than kitchens—with their drippy pipes, mildew slicks, and ancient grease residue—she disliked bathrooms. Peering into the ancient toilets and tubs, especially the ones marred by permanent brown stains left by deposits of minerals and gallons of disgusting biological matter, made her queasy.

After a few minutes, Allie finished the toilet and began scrubbing the claw-foot tub. She exhaled, blowing her hair from her face and pinning it against her head with a wrist. "Got you," she told her hair, but when she let go, it fell back across her eyes.

She raised her sponge and labored at the chipped tiles surrounding the tub's old metal faucet when, from the corner of her eye, she saw something move inside the drain hole. Uneasy, she backed away, worried that some sort of pest might race out of the

J. Scott Fuqua

opening, its teeth or pincers chomping wildly. She had good reason to be concerned. Once, while cleaning a crumbling kitchen cabinet on the seventh floor, she saw a rat scuttle from behind a box of petrified grits and latch onto her finger. It took her at least a few terrified minutes to remove it from her hand. Ever since then, rats, mice, bugs, and spiders terrified her, and The Greaser was swarming with all of them.

"Here creepy, creepy, crawly," Allie said, snapping her fingers softly to get whatever it was to rise from the drain. She stepped forward, leaned, and cranked a faucet handle so that orange rust-water flooded into the tub. After counting to twenty, she turned the spigot off. To make sure she was safe, she squinted and searched the dark hole. *Nothing.*

To get a better view, she placed her hands against the far wall and stretched over the tub like a tiny bridge. She blinked. "Is—is something in there? Come out, you nasty little . . . oh—!"

A gargantuan bug stepped out of the drain and, without a moment's

The Secrets of the Greaser Hotel

hesitation, flew at Allie's face. "No!" she screeched. "Stop!" She tried to block the pest with flailing hands. Unfortunately, she'd been using them to prop herself over the tub and, like a chair with two legs missing, she toppled forward, her skull whacking against the tiled wall.

Confused and frightened, Allie landed in the tub and squirmed onto her back, kicking over the container of Bon Ami cleanser in the process. A storm of white powder drifted about. Her vision swam before zeroing in on the big black insect resting atop one of her shins. Screaming, she thrashed her legs, dislodging the monster so that it landed on one of her knees and ran beneath her dress.

Allie let out a howl so loud that the Friendly boy guarding the door began laughing uncontrollably, which he always did when one of the captives screamed.

As for Allie, she fainted.

Not ten minutes later, Jerome serenely padded into the bathroom. He was greeted by two legs dangling indelicately out of the tub. He stopped, listened for Allie's breathing, and allowed himself to exhale. Calmed, he carefully nudged one of her unraveling boots. "Allie, sweetheart," he said. "Wake up. Wake up. You don't want your dear foster mother to catch you this way."

Allie groaned.

"Wake up, child."

Allie raised her eyelids, confused.

Jerome jumped onto the big tub's battered rim and looked at her. "Dear," he said, "you're a mess. You split your head wide open and your dress is covered in Bon Ami."

To Allie, it seemed the old building was swaying back and forth. "What . . . happened?"

"Well," Jerome said, "I'm no expert. I don't know much about human injuries, since I'm a cat, but I believe you cracked your noggin."

"I knocked myself out?" she asked, surprised.

"That's my guess. I was five floors down." He licked around his mouth.

Allie studied the narrow band of green tile encircling the bathroom walls. Disoriented, she lowered her eyes and gazed at the tub's black drain. There was something odd about it.

Then she remembered what had happened and commenced to thrashing like a family of netted rats she'd once caught on the forty-second floor. She jerked and scrambled and somehow flopped out of the tub and onto the bathroom floor. Standing, she furiously shook her floral-patterned dress before sighing and leaning against the wall.

"Ah . . . what?" Jerome asked.

"There . . . there was an insect, like a giant flying roach. It attacked me and ran up my dress."

Jerome smiled, which is hard for a cat to do. He sat down stylishly. "A giant, flying cockroach, eh? Sounds like a palmetto bug to me, which is basically the same thing as a roach, only bigger and uglier. They usually live down south. They were all over New Orleans when I resided there. Guess they're migrating north, what with global warming and all. They won't hurt you, though. I know that for a fact."

"It flew at my face!"

"It's stupid is why." He tilted his head and licked a shoulder. "Bet it didn't want anything to do with you."

"Seemed like it did."

"Allie, palmetto bugs do not attack people. They are primitive little beasts. They can live for a week with their head cut off. What does that say? It tells you their brain doesn't mean squat. So, I promise, it didn't plan an assault."

Allie wasn't so sure. She pushed at the hair drooping in her face but found it glued down by something sticky. She looked at her fingers and realized she'd been bleeding. Pinching her lips together, she said, "I must look terrible."

Jerome made a show of sizing her up. "Yeah. Not so hot."

"How bad is my head?"

"Probably fractured your skull, ruptured your eardrums, and severed your spinal cord." He stared at her. "You'll live, dear. I promise."

She nodded and beat the powdery cleanser off her dress. Turning, she ran water into the ancient sink and rinsed the blood from the bump on her forehead. When done, she sat down on the rim of the toilet and slumped forward. Throughout the years she'd lived at the hotel, she'd tried to train herself not to expect much from life but always wished for more, which got her angry at herself, her parents, and everyone in The Greaser except her three friends and Jerome. She asked herself aloud, "What would I be doing if I was out in the world right now?"

"Let's see. It's Friday," said Jerome. "You're fifteen, intelligent and attractive, small for your age and very naive, what with living in here for so long. Hmm, I guess you'd be at the mall."

"Mall? What's that?" She sat forward.

"A large building with a bunch of shops inside. Human kids like to walk around in them buying shoes and big soft pretzels."

She kneeled and picked up her sponge.

"Your life is better than that, huh?" Jerome said.

"Oh, it's everything I've ever wished for," Allie played along, wondering if it was all she *should* wish for, because, surely, she'd never leave.

He watched her work a moment or two. Unexpectedly, he made a retching sound.

She looked at him. "You okay?"

He nodded and gagged again.

"You sure?"

"Y . . . you know cats," Jerome said. His furry throat spasmed, and without further ado, he opened his big cat mouth and out came a glob of something that had been in his stomach.

Allie turned away. "I suppose you're not going to clean that up, are you?"

Ignoring her, Jerome shuddered in disgust. "Musta been the Chinese food I had for breakfast. Kung Pao Chicken never hits me quite right, especially when I find it in a dumpster."

"You think it might've gone bad?"

"It must have, sister. Lord knows that restaurants don't throw away perfectly good food. But that's not the problem. It's the spices my stomach doesn't get along with."

Sometimes Allie felt so much affection for the cat that tears came to her eyes. She wiped at them and said, "You're so strange."

"You have no idea."

"Are you going to stay till I'm done in here?"

"In case you see another pesky palmetto bug?"

Allie nodded. "Yeah."

"Sure. Why not?"

Leaning over, Allie grabbed the Bon Ami container. "Um, I didn't know you lived in New Orleans."

"Love," Jerome said, "I'm a world traveler. Back when I was younger and not nearly as smart, I climbed onto the warm engine block of a refrigerated seafood truck and rode it here by mistake. Until then, I was a New Orleans kitten born and raised."

Allie sized up the cat, cocking her head to the right. "It's funny, but I can't imagine you as a kitten," she said.

"Everyone starts somewhere. When I was first born, my mother, who was a stray, kept me and my four siblings in an empty dentures box behind a dentist's office. I'll never forget. Smelled like peppermint toothpaste. At first, when I was really little, I thought my mom actually smelled that way, but whenever we left the box, the smell was gone, so I learned."

Allie stopped. "What are dentures?"

J. Scott Fuqua

"Fake teeth. Choppers. Fangs. Grinders. A person slides them into their mouth when all or most of their real teeth have rotted out of their heads."

Allie said, "People really have those?"

"Yup. Just humans, though."

"Man," Allie said. "I sorta think the Friendly boys should get some."

At dinnertime, after Allie served the Friendlys their baby-back ribs and heaping spoonfuls of Hamburger Helper, she quickly started a pot of water for oatmeal, which is what the four detainees of Greasy Blight consumed for breakfast and dinner (they didn't get lunch). She bent and watched the blue flame flicker against tarnished metal, nearly hypnotized by its beauty. She wished there were more beautiful things in her life—more vibrant colors, soothing smells, and even pretty sounds. She yearned for it all the way a person might yearn to remember the details of a dream.

Ten feet away, Arnold Armstrong scrubbed pots and pans, and Midge Darlington swept the floors in preparation for mopping. When she arrived beside Allie, Midge stopped and lifted a hand, sweetly palming the young girl's cheek. She studied the smallish bruise on her forehead. She touched it and mouthed the word, "Ouch."

Allie shrugged, noting that each and every finger on Midge's hand was as scratchy as steel wool. "Are you okay, sweetheart?"

"Just a little dizzy from whacking my head."

"Probably have a small concussion. You should sneak a break. I'll cover for you."

Allie looked at the door to the dining room. She took a deep breath and carefully sat down on a large box containing canned

meat. Placing a hand under her chin, she rested her elbow against her knee and waited to fetch her foster family's dishes from off the dining room table.

It was at that very moment that Oda Friendly stormed into the kitchen. Spotting Allie, she froze in her tracks and scowled frighteningly. "Rat, my God!" she shrieked. "Slacking off on the job!"

"I wasn't, ma'am." Allie stood.

"Caught ya nappy-napping. Well, missy, no supper for ya tonight! Don't even entertain the notion."

Allie stared silently, shocked.

Oda smiled and glanced about the kitchen. "So where's Hammerhead? Hammerhead, where are ya?" she yelled. "Come out here, now, girl!"

Hammerhead was actually Rena Duchamp, who was only nine years old. Scared, she scurried out from the walk-in refrigerator. "Yes, ma'am, Mrs. Friendly?"

"There was a stain on one of the boy's napkins. Was like a dark spot. Disgusting!"

"I'm—I'm sorry, ma'am."

"Sorry don't take stains out, now does it? Nope, it don't. And ya call your ownself a laundress. You're a slacker giving us dirty napkins! Ya won't be getting no dinner tonight, neither. Ya get ta join our little Allie Rat in today's hunger parade. Break out the fiddles, huh?"

"Yes, ma'am."

Oda scrunched her nose and inspected a few of Arnold Armstrong's pots and pans.

He grinned up at her. "Hope they're to your satisfaction, ma'am."

"Shut your trap, Arnold," she said.

"Sorry, ma'am."

"I said hush it!" Oda Friendly pivoted to study Midge Darlington's

progress on the kitchen floor. "Spotless, Midge. Best be spotless."

"Yes, Mrs. Friendly," Midge said.

Oda's head pivoted around like a tank's cannon. "Now listen here, Allie Rat. When the boys and me are finished with supper, ya come hurry and fetch our dishes right away, 'cause we got bad moods all around out there, what with getting a dirty napkin. Ain't nobody feeling charitable tonight. Ya understand me, girl?"

Allie peered into her foster mother's torch-red eyes. "Yes, Mrs. Friendly."

"Course, if there's anything left on the bones of our baby-backs, ya and Hammerhead are welcome to it. But don't either of ya dare sneak one bite from the oatmeal trough, not unless ya wanna meet the working end of my new belt." Oda grabbed her belt's big shiny buckle, which was the size of a butter plate and decorated with the word "KISS."

Rena nodded.

Allie didn't move.

Oda sauntered back into the dining room.

Midge Darlington stopped sweeping and glowered at the door as she twisted her hands around the handle of the broom. "One day," she whispered, "I will get that woman back. I'm patient. I'll get my chance, and I won't be kind."

From the sink, Arnold Armstrong giggled softly. He was no longer the proud, elegant millionaire. Twelve years of grueling work and poor treatment had defeated him. His cheeks were sunken and dark. The skin surrounding his faded-blue eyes was creased like the hide of the small stuffed alligator Allie had found in an apartment on the thirty-third floor.

Allie's water began to boil, and she longingly deposited two cups of oatmeal into it and stirred. Shortly, one of her foster brothers hollered, "We's done, Rat!"

Still angry at Mrs. Friendly for taking away her dinner, Allie walked out to the fancy dining room. For some reason, back when the hotel had been converted into public housing, the top floor (or what Allie believed to be the top floor), which had been Marvin Greaser's private residence, hadn't been touched. Not even in the days when it was a chemical depository. Somehow, even the old furniture remained. Throughout, built-in mirrors ran floor-to-ceiling, as if Marvin Greaser had enjoyed admiring himself from every conceivable angle. In the dining room, directly over the expansive dinner table, was a huge chandelier comprised of five pale buffalo skulls. The fixture's strange, broken light flickered like a flame.

"Take these plates away," Oda said, snapping her fingers brusquely. "We'll be wanting our desserts now."

Allie grabbed up the plates and platters, stacking them atop one another. As usual, the spare-rib bones looked as if they'd been picked clean by jackals. Not one had a nibble of meat left on it.

Caskey, the oldest boy, said, "I'm wanting whipped cream on my dessert."

In the kitchen, Allie placed the dishes on the steel table beside Arnold Armstrong. In one fluid motion, Rena handed her a bowl of Gristle Brand Blood Pudding, which wasn't considered a dessert by most standards, since it was made from pints of jellied cow blood. Regardless, the Friendlys loved the stuff. They sucked it down like it was ice cream.

Allie spooned out large slabs, slopping them into bowls. Rena placed the bowls on a waiter's tray and handed Allie a can of pressurized whipped cream. Allie squirted mounds of the stuff into Caskey's dish and carried it all into the dining room.

Spotting her, one of the boys, Scratch, said, "You can't expect me to eat dessert with the Hamburger Helper still on the table."

Annoyed, Allie replied, "Just hold on. I'm getting it."

J. Scott Fuqua

"Don't give us no guff, girl," Oda Friendly snarled.

Allie finished serving everyone and took hold of the bowl of Hamburger Helper, heaving it atop her tray.

A half hour later, in the kitchen, Allie wiped the dessert plates while Arnold completed washing the other dishes. The four detainees dried and stored the set. Then they lined up, shoulder to shoulder, as the Friendly boys came in to escort them back to their tiny rooms for the night.

It was always the same.

Following behind Allie, Shoat Friendly picked his teeth and minced his moldy mouth. Of all the boys, he was the most attractive, which said absolutely nothing. He was tall and lanky and shared the family complexion, in that his skin resembled a clear rubber membrane blotted with tan hues. Akin to a leaky automobile engine, his nose constantly dripped oily liquid.

He snickered, "Ya hungry?"

"I'm okay," Allie responded.

"We'll see how ya feel when ya don't get no breakfast in the mornin'."

"Why won't I get breakfast?" Allie asked.

"'Cause I just now caught ya talking back." He snickered as they exited the stairwell and passed down the crumbling

hallway. They arrived at a room with four enormous padlocks on its metal door. Shoat selected keys from a large round ring and unlocked each door. Pushing Allie in, he slammed the barrier closed.

❧

Huddled in a corner, Allie rested against a chalky wall and absentmindedly touched where she'd hit her head that morning. Aside from the small bruise Midge had noticed, the area was almost healed. She'd always gotten over injuries faster than most people.

Crossing her arms, she tried to think of nothing, but instead, visions of Rena played across the movie screen of her mind. The girl had arrived only about four months back. She was sweet and soft-spoken and not a lot of help. Mostly, she was too young to do anything. She was young and scared and, for that reason, quiet—so quiet that Mrs. Friendly thought she was stupid. That's why she called Rena "Hammerhead," as in a head so hard it was like the head of a hammer.

As much as possible, Allie tried to be nice to Rena. In fact, some days and most nights, her heart ached for her. How could such a young, fragile girl survive such cruelty?

How had *she*? She wasn't exactly sure anymore. When she'd first arrived, life in The Greaser was such a shock that she actually thought, for the first few weeks, that she was dreaming—that it was all a long, ridiculous nightmare.

It wasn't and never had been.

During mealtimes, Allie and Midge, who seemed to feel the same way about Rena, gave the small girl the relatively easy job of food storage. They had no say in her workday, though, when she was assigned to wash, dry-clean, iron, and sort the Friendlys' laundry, a task that had gotten too difficult for the age-stiffened

Arnold Armstrong.

Allie breathed out. Her thoughts traveled back to her first awful months in Oda Friendly's care, when she didn't know how she'd even survived. Day after day, she had blathered, "I just wanna see Momma."

Week after week, she had cleaned, waiting desperately for a day off that never came. While making dinner, Midge Darlington and a still-sane Arnold Armstrong had told Allie to be strong. They soothed her, straightened her dress, and untangled her oily hair. They held her when she broke into tears from loneliness and exhaustion, at least as often as they could without getting spotted by Mrs. Friendly. They squeezed her hands, contorting their dirty faces into kindly expressions. And still she grew hopeless. Over time, her mind began the sad process of adapting to the artless art of survival.

Then Jerome saved her.

Recalling their first meeting still made Allie smile.

At the time, she had been mopping a kitchen on the twenty-sixth floor. Back and forth she went, trying to loosen the ground-in dirt on the linoleum tiles, which was the result of a partially collapsed ceiling. Then she heard an animal pad across the apartment's living room. Nervous, she peeked around the doorframe and spotted an oversized tan tabby standing by the locked door to the hallway.

Allie approached it in a distant emotionless state. But peering into the cat's large, somehow familiar green eyes, she felt her detachment wash away. Sniffling, she said, "Oh, kitty, you . . . you shouldn't be here. I don't know how you got in, but you've got to leave before the Friendlys catch you."

The cat seemed to wink at her.

Allie kneeled down and rubbed the cat's head. "Run for your life, little one," she whispered. "If one of the boys finds you, he might use you for target practice, or . . . have you for dinner. I'm not kidding. They eat a lot of meat."

The cat yawned sleepily.

"Do I have to chase you off?" Allie asked. "Do I, little mister? Don't make me."

The cat stared at her. "Oh, Allie, I promise you I can handle myself," he said. "Those Friendly boys won't catch me. There isn't a chance."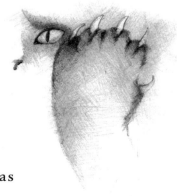

Allie stood up and backed away, her foot kicking over a spray can of Lysol. "You . . . you can talk?"

"Of course I can talk. And call me Jerome." The cat's tail hovered as if weightless.

J. Scott Fuqua

"I never heard of a cat who talks," said Allie.

"Now you have."

She broke into her first smile since arriving at The Greaser. "Say something again."

"Meow," he joked.

"Wish I had a treat for you."

"A treat for me, Ms. Argos? You're the one who's in need of a treat," said Jerome. "Believe me, if I had pockets and money, I'd go buy you a sardine sandwich straightaway."

Allie smiled even wider.

"I was sent here by someone who loves you very much, Allie. Is that okay?"

"Wh—who was it?"

"I really can't say. But I wouldn't lie to you. *Capiche*?"

"*Capiche*?"

"It's a word from the Italian language. It means, 'Get it?' So, be honest: Can I be your friend?"

She nodded hesitantly. "Doesn't being friends take time, like when kids play together for awhile?"

"Well, due to the circumstances, I'm trying to be more straightforward."

"Uh-huh," Allie said. "I guess we can be friends, Mr. Jerome."

"Just Jerome, please."

Since that day, nine dismal years had passed, and Jerome remained, along with Midge Darlington, as Allie's closest friend and confidant. He somehow wormed his catty way into whichever locked apartment she was cleaning, providing her with company, entertainment, and a window to the outside world.

Seated silently in her room, hands aching and feet sore, Allie twisted the overhead bulb till it went out. Then she collected the stuffed alligator she'd found years before, curled up on the bare floor, and pulled some old curtains over her narrow shoulders. The fabric had a faded lobster pattern, but the material was thick enough to cut the damp chill of The Greaser Hotel.

Her mind still buzzing with worry for Rena, Allie closed her eyes, her stomach rumbling loudly, and fell asleep.

J. Scott Fuqua

3

In the morning, Jerome woke Allie by nudging her cheek with a paw. "Allie. Allie dear," he said. "We need to talk."

Confused, Allie cracked her lids and raised her head from the floor. She massaged her eye sockets with the heels of her palms and slowly focused on Jerome. He stood in a brilliant shaft of sunlight issuing from a gap in the splintery boards that sealed the windows. "What time is it?"

"Early."

Allie nodded and her stomach roiled like that of a baby lion.

Jerome said, "Dear, you don't look well."

"I'm starving is why. Mrs. Friendly wouldn't let me have dinner last night."

Jerome's brow tensed into a strange cat version of a frown, causing the wavy black stripes on his head to pinch together above his nose. "If I could, I would give her a scratch she would never forget," he said, lifting a paw and curling it like a fist, exposing claws that resembled five tiny scimitars, "from head to toe and back again."

"I wish you could," Allie said.

"One day." Jerome stretched his neck as if he was wearing a tie that was too snug. He inspected Allie's room by rotating his large head from side to side, as if it was a screw top on a bottle. "This place is worse than I remember."

"It's not so hot."

"No, it's not."

Allie sat up, leaned against the wall, and untied the fabric holding back her hair.

Jerome twitched a rectangular ear. "So, about why I'm here."

"Yes," Allie said.

"Brace yourself."

"I'm braced."

Jerome cocked his head to one side. "There are visitors coming. Today, Oda will have you, Midge, Rena, and Arnold clean the upper floors for those two visitors and their ancient, oversized entourage."

"Entourage? What's that mean?"

"It means group."

"Oh. Group," Allie said.

"This group is comprised of very different sorts of men, dear. They are large and powerful individuals, plucked, seemingly, out of time. As for the two men whom they serve, both fellows have hair-raisingly bad breath. Plus, both are very shifty, very persuasive—beguiling when they want to be."

Allie shivered. "I'm . . . I'm used to bad breath. All the Friendlys got it."

Jerome seemed to shrug. "Anyway, they will all arrive sometime tomorrow, and I hope to be here when they do. If I'm not, you should know that out of curiosity, they will want to meet you. Distrust anything they say. Truth is pliable, especially to them."

Allie stared at the cat and shivered. "Who are they?"

J. Scott Fuqua

Jerome thrashed his mouth distastefully. "Marvin Greaser the Third and Herman Gristle, a.k.a. the King of Cartilage."

Allie rocked forward. "Marvin Greaser. Is he related to the person who built this place?"

"Very related, dear." Jerome stepped from the shaft of light, completely disappearing into the inky darkness of the room. A moment later, he reappeared in a second streak. His eyes flared brilliantly, as if yellow gems gleamed behind them. "Do you recognize the name 'Gristle'?"

Allie sighed and lifted one of the curtains from the floor. "Not really," she said, though it was slightly familiar. She wrapped the fabric about her trembling shoulders like a shawl, so that faded lobsters seemed to be scuttling in all directions across her.

Jerome said, "That's strange, seeing as you see the name daily."

"Where?"

"In the kitchen, love."

She considered the kitchen, her mind's eye scanning walls and floors. Then it hit her. "On the Friendlys' meat containers?"

"Precisely."

Confused, she said, "Why is he here?"

"Because you are of interest."

Allie dropped the curtain from off her shoulders, wondering about the man she'd only known through his massive and gluttonous slabs, blocks, and mangled bolsters of meat, from bison to possum, swaddled in sheets of rubbery, clear plastic wrap and Styrofoam meat trays, complete with a large, diamond-shaped label that announced, "Gristle Brand Meat Products." The name left a horrible taste in her mouth.

"He'll be looking for signs that you are a threat, but I don't believe you'll provide him any."

"A threat?" She peered at the cat. Jerome seemed to think he had made everything clear to her, but he hadn't. Not in the least.

"I have much to do now," he said, disappearing into the darkness. "*Sayonara*, Allie. Back soon."

☙❧

In the kitchen, Arnold Armstrong squeezed out large tubes of Gristle Brand sausage as Rena opened packages of the company's scrapple and bacon. Allie ignited the expansive steel griddle and began frying everything up, but when Arnold Armstrong's back was turned, sabotaged it with hairballs and grit from the floor.

Meanwhile, Midge Darlington worked in the dining room, where she artfully set the table with linens, candles, silverware, and bone china decorated around the edges with a wreath of poison ivy and stylized images of hyenas that appeared to be foaming at their toothy mouths. During her days of homemaking notoriety, Midge had seen a good deal of fine china, much of it wonderful, some of it obnoxious, but not a single piece had sported a pattern as odd as Marvin Greaser's finest.

When Allie finished cooking, Midge carried everything out to the dining room, where Oda and the boys waited impatiently, holding their silverware in their fists, fork prongs and knife blades pointed upwards. It was their thrice-daily display of poor manners.

Allie started the water for the detainees' oatmeal, confident that Shoat, who lacked even a modest count of brain cells, had forgotten his declaration the night before that she was to go without breakfast.

J. Scott Fuqua

Thankfully, she was right.

Less than an hour later, the meal was complete and the kitchen spotless.

The four detainees were marched out of the dining room by Caskey and Privet Friendly. Without uttering a word, the two boys directed Allie to her cleaning cart, then gave all four of them a hard shove away from the elevators that had conveyed them, excluding Rena, to their jobs for so many years. Instead, they were directed down a lengthy, twisting, turning hallway none of them had ever noticed before, which was not uncommon. All of the time, strange hallways and residences seemed to appear and disappear in the 460-apartment Greaser. Passing intersections, they veered, veered again, and took several turns before arriving at a thick steel door, like a bank vault, that they'd also never come across until that moment.

Caskey stepped forward and opened it by turning a large key and spinning the dial of a combination lock.

"Wonder where they're taking us," Midge whispered.

Allie thought about what Jerome had said.

The Friendly boys pushed them all through the open door, whereupon Arnold began whimpering. Tears rolled down his hollow cheeks, and he said, "Boys? Oh, boys? I—I gotta tell you something. Okay? Okay, boys?"

"What?" Caskey asked, his thumb rubbing the silver hammer on the backside of his handgun.

"Don't change up my schedule, boys. No sir. I love my schedule, boys. Please."

"Zip it, old man!" Caskey said, locking the massive steel door behind them.

Arnold Armstrong swallowed and nodded, childlike. "Yes, sir. Yes, sir. That's exactly what I'm gonna do. I'll zip it."

Worried that Arnold had become delirious, Allie gently took his arm and, when they started walking, she led him along, trying to soothe him by patting his hand the same way he  had once soothed her early sadness. She missed Arnold's company and wondered if, of all the feelings a person could feel, she felt "missing" the most. She missed her parents and Arnold. She missed neighborhoods, movie theaters, friends, and ice cream. Lately, she even missed boys, though not the type that the Friendlys were. She missed the normal ones she vaguely recalled from years before—boys like the ones in superhero comic books or on television.

They headed down a narrow passage and came to an elevator with gleaming copper doors bordered by detailed engravings of poison ivy vines, set off in the middle by a coat of arms that included a moon and a large image of a growling, foaming hyena. Caskey pressed a button and the doors drew back, exposing the bright red upholstered interior of the elevator car. They entered and were carried upward. When the car stopped, they stepped out and into a gargantuan living room surrounded by furniture draped in white sheets. All of it was offset by grand glass doorways that opened onto a series of elegant balconies overlooking the city.

Caskey pulled a pad of paper from the back pocket of his purple leisure slacks. He squinted at it and read, "You'll find twenty-two

J. Scott Fuqua

bedrooms, twenty-five bathrooms, a library, a ballroom, a lounge, and a holding tank, and they all got to be spit-polished by dinner. If they ain't clean, there'll be severe . . ." He tried to sound out the next word: ". . . con—con—seequen . . ." Giving up, he showed the word to Midge.

"Consequences," she told him. "It means penalties."

Privet spit on the floor. "We'll be back here in about six hours."

The Friendly boys took the elevator down, at which time Arnold threw himself onto a carpet decorated with a bronze lion being eaten by a gigantic, savage dog. Face down, covering his head, he said, "I . . . I loved my old schedule. I want my old schedule."

Rena looked nervously at Allie and Midge.

Allie bent down and touched Arnold. He'd once told her jokes and even sung her lullabies and nursery rhymes when she was upset. Now it seemed like she should do the same for him—a fact she found devastating. "It's okay, Arnold. It's okay. You rest. Just rest." Allie studied the old man. He had changed so drastically over the previous few years, but she was still caught off-guard sometimes by his behavior.

Midge yanked a sheet off an old chair.

Allie patted Arnold's bony kneecap. "Midge, do you think we can ever get him back?" she asked.

Midge, who was folding a white sheet, paused before replying, "I suppose it's possible, but not in here. Not living like we do."

"If somebody got him out, though, could he be fixed?"

Midge said, "I don't know for sure. But . . . maybe."

"Then we have to try to get him free, don't we?"

"How?" Midge asked. "How, sweetie?"

Allie shook her head. "I don't know, but he makes me so sad. He really does."

Midge breathed out, her gaunt cheeks pale where they scraped across the sharp bones of her face. "He was my friend, too, Allie. I miss him, too."

Sad, Allie caught her breath and walked past Midge. She whipped the covering off a sofa, exposing an ancient and ornate piece of furniture with gleaming wooden legs shaped like fierce snakeheads. "Wow."

Midge grinned sullenly. "Yeah, wow. Rather a gruesome piece of furniture. I'd say that somebody had no class."

J. Scott Fuqua

It took an hour to remove every sheet from the penthouse's exotic furnishings. When they were done, they checked on Arnold, who'd crawled into a corner and was now playing with a small, dead housefly. "His name's Artie," Arnold said, grinning like a little boy. "He likes cake and opera in the evenings."

Allie forced herself to smile. "He's really very . . . cute," she told him. "Isn't he?"

Allie felt something inside thump, so she hurried off to dust the floors.

Three hours later, Midge took to vacuuming the various rugs and carpeting as Rena made the beds and Allie cleaned the twenty-five bathrooms.

By the end of the day, Allie, Rena, and Midge were exhausted, bathed in layers of sweat, their hands infused with the smell of harsh cleansers. Regardless, they'd been lucky. If even one of the rooms or chambers had remotely resembled the rest of The Greaser's crumbling stairs, their assignment would have taken weeks. But, truthfully, the upper-upper level of the old hotel seemed to be in wonderful condition, the plaster still intact, the wallpaper crisp, the floors highly polished, and the paint gleaming.

Midge wiped a hand across her head. "Never thought we'd be done in time."

Rena nodded.

Below them, the elevator rumbled to life. Allie got up and shook Arnold Armstrong, who'd spent the last hour napping fitfully. "Wake up," she said, patting his frail, twig-thin shoulder. "Wake up, Arnold."

Arnold's old eyelids reeled back suddenly. "Mrs. Friendly?" he gasped. "I—I wasn't sleeping. No, ma'am." He sat up stiffly, like a soldier at attention.

"It's not Mrs. Friendly. It's me," Allie told him.

At a loss, he blinked.

"It's Allie," she said. "I live with you at The Greaser."

He stared at her. "The Greaser? The Greaser . . . Oh—oh, yes. Oh, The Greaser." He glanced away, pained.

Behind Arnold, three Friendly boys, Caskey, Lesion, and Privet, exited the elevator. Sunlight bathed the room, illuminating their ugly faces so that each appeared to be suffering advanced jaundice.

"How'd it go?" asked Lesion.

"We finished," Midge said.

He scoffed. "I'll be the judge'a that, Midge Fly." He motioned to the other two brothers. "I'm gonna check the bedrooms and crappers, see if they's clean."

"I'll give the rest a once-over," Caskey said.

Privet sneered. "I s'pose I'll stay here with these losers," he said. He casually hooked a big thumb over the handle of his holstered pistol and studied Midge, looked at Rena, ignored Arnold, and ogled Allie. Straightening, he held out his hands and framed her

like an artist about to paint a picture. With a wag of a finger, he motioned for her to step away from the others.

She did.

"Now, you three, sit on the floor," he instructed.

Rena, Midge, and Arnold sat.

Privet licked the dirty palm of a hand and used it to wipe back the patchy straw-colored hair on his head. Done, he carefully picked the filth from beneath a few of his fingernails before strutting slowly over to Allie. He smiled at her, exposing teeth that seemed more like blackened and tarred boards. "Hey now, Rat, I ever tell ya how much pull I got with Momma?"

"No."

"Well, I got me some. A lot. One word from me and ya'd be getting extra oatmeal for a whole week. Whatcha think of that?"

Privet grinned broadly, then, using the hairy knuckle of a finger and the flat of his thumb, reached over and pinched her chin.

Uncomfortable, Allie stepped away.

"Don't be scared, Rat. I ain't looking to hurt ya."

Midge, seated on the floor beside Rena and Arnold, said, "Come on, Privet. Leave her alone. You already bother her enough. She's a kid."

Privet spun around on her. "How 'bout ya shutting up, Midge Fly? How 'bout that?" He licked his palm again and ran it across his hair once more. Casually, he straightened the white belt of his slacks and turned back to Allie. "Well, now, ya want more oatmeal, all ya gotta do

The Secrets of the Greaser Hotel

is tell me, 'cause I can get it for ya. Momma'd listen to me if I said ya needed it. Yes she would."

Allie glanced sideways at Midge, who shook her head and mouthed the word, "No." In turn, Allie told Privet, "I'm okay. Thanks."

Privet bent down. "Come on now, Rat. Look at me. Ya like what ya see, don't ya?" He turned his chunky head as if he was modeling for an artist. "I'm offering ya a chance to get close to me. I might could let ya kiss me on the mouth, Rat. Whatcha make of that?"

"Privet, I'm—I'm sorry, but—but I breathed in a lot of cleanser today and I'm feeling a little . . ." She feigned a gag. "Well, very nauseated, and—"

"Not on the shoes," Privet said, jumping back.

Allie wrapped both hands around her stomach. "I'm—I'm sorry, Privet."

Backing away, he pointed at her. "Well, fine. When you're feeling better, ya just call for old Privet. Ya just give me a call." He spun about and strutted quickly away, stood by the elevator, and lit a cigar. Taking a puff, he twisted and winked at Allie with a bloodshot eye.

Allie sat down beside Midge and whispered, "What's he really want, do you think?"

"What he *really* wants is for you to be his girl. That's what he *really* wants."

Allie blushed. "Why?"

"Because you're lovely, dear."

Allie wondered if that was true—if, beneath the layers of grime, she might truly be "lovely." Of course, the last folks in the world she wanted to appeal to were the Friendly boys, who might, on a good day, attract a desperate female baboon with mange and pinkeye (though desperate female baboons, even those with mange and pinkeye, were probably more discriminating than that).

4

The next day, Scratch Friendly, who had a nose like a pig and one sleepy eye that seemed to melt down across a cheek, read out a list of apartments Allie was supposed to clean, then led her down a long hallway and pulled out his keys. The apartment door swung open, and they were greeted by the sound of water spewing from cracked overhead pipes. Even in the shadowy light, the place was clearly destroyed. Plaster was bubbling and lumped, and all of the wood surfaces were shaggy with curled paint. Also, the apartment's electricity had malfunctioned so that the room was unlit except for the light creeping in from the hallway.

Allie glanced at Scratch. "How can I work in here?"

"Momma says you gotta."

"But, sir, I can't see anything."

Scratch went to the window and tore off two boards so that a bit of daylight illuminated the wrecked room.

Allie said, "Sir, I—I don't think anyone can clean a room like this without turning the water off."

"Well, I got no idea how to do something like that." Sucking at the remains of his teeth, Scratch turned, walked out, and slammed the door so hard that a large patch of the apartment's waterlogged plaster slithered to the floor like snow.

At a loss, Allie glanced around. She passed through and around waterfalls to peer out the open window, where a clean breeze caught her cheeks and rustled tufts of her dirty hair. Feeling better, she tilted her head and gawked happily at the radiant blue sky. Flat, majestic clouds swept eastward, their leading edges churning like a crest of breaking waves. She smiled. It was so beautiful. When or if she was ever freed, she thought that she'd just spin and spin on her toes, allowing the soft air to wisp against her face.

Allie splayed her fingers wide and felt desperation nearly drown her. She wanted to leave so badly. She wanted to look up at the

J. Scott Fuqua

clouds and stars whenever she chose. She wanted to be a girl who did girl-things, as in the princess cartoons she recalled from long ago. But she was caged.

Eventually, fearful of Scratch and Oda, she stepped back from the window and drew her mop and a bottle of Pine-Sol from her cleaning cart. Head lowered against the cascading water, she splashed across the floor and began working in the miniscule bathroom.

Hours passed. Cold and wet, Allie scrubbed away. Not wanting to go without dinner again, she was desperate to finish the job here and move on to the other apartments.

Then came an unfamiliar rumbling of motors and pulleys, and the ancient building shuddered. Curious at the elevator's irregular usage, she propped her mop against a wall and rushed into the living room. Pushing wet hair away from an ear, she placed her head against the door, where, as well as she could, she listened to the elevator descend and descend all the way to the ground. After a few moments of silence, the building shook once more as the pulleys and motors groaned back to life and began hauling up the weighted-down elevator.

"Amazing."

Startled, Allie jumped about, her feet splashing water. She found Jerome standing on the sagging dining room table. "You—you scared the wits out of me," she told him, holding her heart.

"Sorry, dear." Amused, he raised the whiskers above his eyes.

Allie sighed. "What do you think of this place?"

"Miserable."

She nodded. "Nobody could clean it, except I have to."

"But nobody can," Jerome stated clearly. "So they want you to fail." He came to the edge of the table.

Allie reached down and ran a tattered sponge across the door she'd already cleaned twice. From the tiny kitchen, there was a sudden series of slams and crashes, like metal garbage cans falling down some steps. Concerned, Allie ventured over and peeked into the room, where she found that four rusty dish cabinets had torn from the water-softened walls. Dented and bent, they had bounced off the warped kitchen countertops and landed randomly against one another in the middle of the small floor.

Sighing, Allie went in and tried to stack them.

Jerome waited a moment and followed after her. "Sweetie, I need to know something."

J. Scott Fuqua

"What?" she asked, struggling as she worked.

"This is going to seem to come out of the wild blue yonder, but I'm stuck for time and I gotta hurry. Dear, you would've told me if ever you experienced anything strange, right? I mean personally. Have you noticed anything strange about yourself? Anything inexplicable is what I mean."

Allie shook her head.

"If you had, you would let me know, though?"

Above, the hotel's partially toothless, always worrisome elevator motors pumped to life once more.

"There's nothing. I promise," she told him.

Calmly, Jerome stepped back. "Allie, I think you're about to go visit two dangerous men. So be careful." Jerome moved into the shadows.

A minute or more passed, and down the hallway a pair of elevator doors screeched open, allowing a heavy-footed contingent to step out. The group pounded down the hallway and eventually arrived in front of the apartment. Someone inserted a key into the door, which whipped open so violently that the knob bit a divot out of the wet wall.

5

There stood Oda, lifting a hanky and blowing her nose. As usual, she was decked out in her blue mechanic's jumpsuit. The scowl on her face was akin to a rodent's prickly expression. Slowly, she curled up her powerful fists and rested them on each hip. Licking her teeth, she ambled silently through the threshold, then stood, scowling at Allie.

"Eh, River Rat, this place is a watery mess!" Oda said. "What ya been doing in here?"

"Cleaning, ma'am."

"That so? Well, I don't see no signs of a good faith effort on your lousy part." Behind her, in the hallway, stood four massive men dressed in fancy clothes whom Allie had never seen before. One held a cane and another clutched a closed umbrella. The other two simply stared hatefully, their massive shoulders testing the fabric of their extravagant dress coats. It was as if someone had outfitted professional football players with garments sewn and stitched in the late nineteenth to early twentieth century. Atop all of their heads were tall black top hats of the type worn back in the days of steam engines, textile mills, and coal fires.

Glowering, her mechanic's suit slowly soaking, Oda said, "River Rat, ya mouthy little tramp, a couple folks wants to

see ya straightaway, and these boys are gonna haul ya up ta make a introduction."

As the four behemoths surrounded Allie, she felt lost in a forest of stony columns. They watched her with suspicious eyes as they marched her from the room and down the halls. In the elevator, their mouths hung slightly ajar, and their putrid breath filled the small compartment like a great wet dog with a pungent ear infection.

The man with the cane scratched his wide nose and adjusted his top hat. He flexed his fingers as if he wanted to strangle something. "Boys," he grumbled distantly, "you remember when this place was first built? Was something back then. A first-class flophouse. Lookit now. It's a dump."

"Oh, yeah," one of the enormous men replied, his voice like a rock scraping the exterior of a Gristle Brand bushel of oysters encased in their shells. He laughed aloud. "Hey, but we had some good times here." He lifted a hand to point. "You remember beating Conrad Ritterhouse near to death on the twenty-eighth floor? You recollect that?"

The fellow with the umbrella snorted humorously. "Didn't take that rich bloke more than an hour before he was happy to sign over every penny to Marvin."

The fourth man, who had an ear like a curled slug and hair so gray it reflected light as if it was a solid sheet of steel, grinned nostalgically. "Them was good times."

"Darn right," the guy with the oyster-shell voice said. "Could beat a man senseless and nobody asked any questions."

Nervous, Allie studied her feet.

The man with the umbrella whacked the tip against the elevator floor. "Makes a person wish for simpler times."

"Yeah," said the giant with the cane. "It's all work and no play now."

The guy with the cane said, "Leastways, I'm hoping the bossman'll let us break a few bones in this little tramp."

Allie tried not to tremble, but she desperately wanted out from between the men.

"Yup, let's hope," said the man with the odd voice as the elevator stopped. The doors screeched back like rubber rubbing glass, and they stepped out. Without a moment's hesitation, Allie was directed along the same twisty-turny hallway she'd been led down by Privet and Caskey the day before. And, like the day before, they eventually came to the thick steel door. The men unlocked it, brought Allie through, and quickly came to the dreadfully carved elevator doors. The man with the umbrella punched the service button, and the brightly upholstered interior of the elevator car was exposed.

Nearly senseless with fear, Allie considered running for her life but had no idea where to go. On top of that, what if the men caught her?

J. Scott Fuqua

They entered the elevator car. The elevator rose and stopped, the doors sliding back. The five of them stepped into the massive living room Allie had labored to clean the day before. The men ushered Allie forward, then stopped.

"Hey, stupid," said the behemoth with the cane, "stand up straight."

Allie, who was glancing around, didn't realize the man was talking to her.

"Hey, idiot! You hear me?"

Oblivious, Allie stared out at the balcony, wondering if she could jump—if it was possible to use her dress like a parachute, the way she'd seen cartoon characters do back when she'd still watched Saturday morning cartoons.

The guy cracked her across her head with his cane. "Pay attention when I'm talking to you."

Shocked, Allie nodded. "Sorry, sir."

"Sorry nothing," the guy said. "Now, stand up straight."

She straightened like a soldier at attention.

The slug-eared guy stomped indelicately into the armada of ancient furniture Allie had helped unveil the previous day. He stopped and appeared nervous as he bent down to speak to two men halfway hidden by the wings of the wingback chairs.

A moment passed, and one of the men rose, stretched, and cracked his knuckles before turning about dramatically. He saw Allie and fashioned the most wonderfully soothing grin she'd ever seen. He was a gentleman of about fifty, with a sociable, extremely handsome face and a substantial pelt of salt and pepper hair. He seemed fit, as if he enjoyed polo or fox hunting. On the whole, he resembled a star on a soap opera, which was a type of television show Allie had often seen her mother watch.

The man, like all of the men, was dressed in rich, heavy clothing. He wore a brilliant red tuxedo top with long tails that tastefully brushed at

his calves. He sported a luminous pair of white riding pants and highly polished black leather boots. As he approached, more large men stepped from the shadows and trailed behind him.

A few feet from Allie, the mystery man spread his arms joyfully, stopped, and exclaimed, "Why, Ms. Argos, you look absolutely smashing."

This she immediately recognized as a lie. Her clothes were wet, her hair was stringy and damp, and her shoes were splitting at both toes.

J. Scott Fuqua

She was far from "smashing," though it was possible she looked as if something had smashed her. *Maybe that was what he meant,* she thought.

The man toting the cane shoved her roughly. "Say something back to him," he directed.

Allie tucked her hair behind an ear. "Why, thank you, sir."

"Please," the gentleman replied, "call me Marvin."

She nodded.

The thug with the cane whacked her painfully in the leg. "Don't just nod," he commanded.

"Thank you, Marvin," she said.

Marvin replied, "Yes, yes, my dear. Let me, instead, thank you." He smiled gracefully before his eyes seemed to redden like the coils on an electric stove. He shifted his glare onto the man with the cane. "Ehrlich, she is but a child, the dear child of a dear friend, and I don't want you prodding her that way once more. Do you quite understand?"

Ehrlich appeared horrified by his misstep. He stumbled back and placed a hand the size of a bear paw over his heart, which was likely the size of a toilet lid. "Sorry, sir. I meant no harm."

"Yes . . . of course you didn't," Marvin said menacingly. His glare seemed to cool, and he threw a mesmerizing smile upon Allie, easing her fears. "Ms. Argos, allow me to introduce a friend of mine. Would you like that?"

She wasn't exactly sure but answered, "Yes, sir," figuring it was better to say "yes" than "no."

"Good." Marvin turned. "Herman, I'd like you to meet a darling friend of mine."

For a moment, the person named Herman didn't budge. He sipped some drink from his glass, then brushed something from his knee. Slowly, he rose and pivoted toward Allie. His face was broad and smooth, as if he used gallons of wrinkle cream to eliminate all visual signs of aging, from creases to pores. His nose was narrow and chiseled. His cheeks and forehead looked like the exterior of a shined, hardened rubber ball. He wiped a miniscule coil of lint from the front of his suit, an ensemble in keeping with the men around him. He settled a coal black bowler on his head, rubbed his hands down his slippery cheeks and, eyes like gun muzzles, he lowered his gaze "So, how are you . . . *dear*? Do you know who I am?"

She shook her head. "No, sir."

"How could she?" Marvin asked him.

"Yes, how could she?" The man put a narrow, delicate hand in the pocket of his suit coat. "I am Herman Gristle—the Herman Gristle of Gristle Brand Meat Products." His face grew stern. He was, in fact, the very Herman Gristle for whom the company was named, a man known by poorly compensated employees in two dozen slaughterhouses around the country as the King of Cartilage, the Baron of Carrion, and the Heartless Herman Gristle. "I am also the patriarch of the family. And my child was kidnapped by none other than your woeful parents. Your parents, Allie Argos, kidnapped my boy, for which they are doing life in jail. *Life*."

As Herman Gristle spoke, his breath rumbled out thickly, enveloping Allie like the putrid and tear-inducing discharges from the rear of a hyena. She was pushed back a few paces. Bad as it was, though, it was the power of his words that shook her raggedy form more and more violently, as if huge, bony hands were rattling her from side-to-side. "No," she muttered. "No," she said again, stumbling against a chair.

"Yes," Mr. Gristle replied. "Yes."

Allie couldn't meet his eyes.

Herman smiled. Then he waved his hands as if the tragic details of his son's abduction were irrelevant. "Allie, call me 'Mr. Gristle,' or call me 'sir,' whichever you find preferable."

Nervously, she raised her teary gaze and peeked at him. Guilt washed inside her stomach as if pumped full of dirty ocean water. "Sir . . . sir, I am so, so very sorry they did that. You . . . you must hate us, my whole family. You must. And I've always wanted to apologize to the people they hurt. I've really wanted to apologize for what they did, and now here you are. But . . . but I imagine there's nothing I can say, right now, to keep you from hating me and my family." She stopped.

Her lips trembled. Then, like a jolt, it occurred to her that he was there for no other reason than to seek revenge, to get her back for her parents' crimes.

Herman Gristle's frightening eyes seemed so hot and cruel that she thought they might smolder. "Of course I don't hate you, Allie," said Herman. "At least not for the reasons you think. Besides, I can honestly say it wasn't your fault, dear." He smiled once more, then he wiped a plucked eyebrow. Bending sideways, he picked up a riding crop, used by jockeys to crack the thighs of their horses in an effort to eke out every driblet of speed. Eyeballing Allie, Mr. Gristle pivoted and suddenly slapped the crop down across a side table.

"Allie," he said loudly, "how would you respond if I did that across your face or shoulder? What if I struck you across the knees?"

Marvin opened his mouth and looked at his companion as if he was more than horrified. "You wouldn't?"

Allie, for her part, wondered if she might deserve that sort of treatment.

"I would do it. I might," Herman said. "Now, listen closely, child. I am a busy man. A busy man. I have traveled from Wyoming for this interview, amongst other various and sundry business. Therefore, I cannot waste my time here if there is nothing worth wasting my time on. Do you understand?"

"I do, sir," she said, though she didn't. She was trying to be polite, seeing as her parents hadn't been.

"Tell me, what if, just to be mean, I directed one of my men to break your arms? What would you do?"

She studied him, worried that he might do just that. "I . . . I don't know, sir."

"Would you try to stop him?"

"Sir, I . . . I'd try to run," Allie said, being honest. She studied his cold, smooth face and coughed. His breath was oddly similar, she realized, to Gristle Brand Meat products that had long passed their freshness date.

Herman closed his eyes, blinking imperiously. "If I asked one of my men to bite off your ears, would you, somehow, some way, defend yourself?"

Allie touched an ear.

"No response?"

"It would be so gross, sir."

J. Scott Fuqua

"Without a doubt. Now, I have many pressing issues to attend to," said Herman. "I am an important man, child. I merely came here as a courtesy to Marvin."

"I thank you," replied Marvin Greaser.

Once more, Allie didn't speak.

Herman cracked a large grin. He straightened his white collar and checked his spotlessly filed and pampered fingernails. Looking up, he said, "Marvin, before I depart, I'd like to know your thoughts. Do you think my work sufficient?"

Marvin rubbed his chin. "Jigsaw puzzles," he announced, "are not put together at a glance. The assemblage of little pieces cannot be envisioned as a whole without a certain degree of familiarity and concentration, which is not your strong suit, Herman."

"So true. But there are times when children must die to assure prosperity," Herman said. "You know this."

Allie studied the two men, her guilt momentarily overcome by total fear.

Marvin held up a finger. "But it is for a thoughtful leader to properly costume illegitimate decisions in an air of impeccable legitimacy. Further, one can and should do such things when and if the situation calls for it. Preemption is the response of the fearful."

"Polished lies, Marvin, are the currency of the world you are about to enter, not mine." The Barron of Carrion smiled a gristly smile, picked up his bowler, and placed it on his head. "But I remind you that you yourself have said that death can be a kindness. Some must die so that others can live . . . well," he said, waving a hand casually. "Might that apply to this circumstance?"

Allie desperately wanted to ask what they were talking about, but she stayed silent, having been trained to do so by the chunky knuckles and cruel punishments of the Friendly family.

"That could be so," Marvin said. "But think. Are we not businessmen, you and I? We, more than most, recognize that great risk, if properly managed, is the prelude to great reward."

"A capitalist to the last," Herman said, making a show of doffing his hat. "I will see you at the governor's mansion tonight. You may do with our guest as you deem fit. Now I must slip away." He signaled to his men, two of whom were standing by the glass windows to the balcony while the other was located at a portable bar crowned with large bottles of liquor and partway concealed by a curtain. The contingent stepped forward spryly, their supple movements in contrast with their large bodies. One of them mashed the elevator button with a thumb-pad the size of a quarter. The doors opened and Herman Gristle strode forward into the gaudy interior, followed by his security team. The doors closed, and the lot of them disappeared.

Allie stared at the elevator doors, her heart pumping so hard that the hem of her dress shook. Taking a deep, deep breath, she tried to control her burned and frazzled nerves.

J. Scott Fuqua

6

Marvin waited a beat, then suddenly swept forward and swung an arm around Allie's shoulder. His palms were warm, his body powerful.

"Ignore the conversations of adults, my dear. It could be said, and should be noted, that Herman and I frequently speak to one another in code or metaphor. Do you know what those words mean?"

"Midge told me about metaphor."

"Good ol' Midge," Marvin said, smiling broadly. "My dear friend Herman, sadly, possesses a rather unlikable way about him, but he means well. You shouldn't question that. But he is somewhat blind to the subtleties of power. He sees things in simple terms, while I am aware of all the complexities. Who is to say which one of us is more correct?"

"He hates me, sir. He should."

"No, no. He shouldn't. And he doesn't, not for the reasons you would think. I guarantee that," said Marvin. "Now, let the two of us forget his comments about his boy and the part your parents played. Let us discuss our lives." He paused and tapped a foot up and down humorously. He took a sip from his drink and studied the edges of his glass. "To that end, my love, where would you prefer to locate yourself—outside on the patio or in front of a crackling fire? Your choice."

Allie tried not to flinch, but she was shocked to find that he, too, had the most horrendous breath. Inhaling through her mouth, she answered, "Outside. I really want to sit beneath the sun."

"Of course you do, dear. Why, of course. Now tell me, what if I direct Ehrlich to fetch you a Coke? Would that be to my lady's liking?"

"You mean a real Coca-Cola?"

He smiled. "Yes, my sweet, a real Coca-Cola."

She nearly burst into tears. "I'd really, really like one, sir. I haven't had a Coke in forever."

"Well then, by all means, let us get you a bottle," Marvin shouted, "Ehrlich, a cold Coke right away. And don't dawdle."

J. Scott Fuqua

"Yes, sir," Ehrlich replied, nearly tripping over his own monstrous feet.

Marvin watched him go, and then called over the man with the strange oyster voice. Marvin leaned and whispered into his ear before guiding Allie onto the terraced balcony, where they took a seat at a little ice cream parlor table of twisted metal legs and a wooden top. Allie felt her muscles—muscles which seldom rested—vibrate joyfully for lack of effort. She struggled not to smile like a little girl, but it was hard. Above, a flock of geese, arranged in a V-pattern, beat by as clouds shivered across the horizon.

"This is nice," she said. Her heavy hair didn't respond to the gentle breeze, but parts of her dress blew softly about her pencil-thin arms and legs.

"So," said Marvin, crossing his legs and tucking a hand beneath his chin, "tell me about yourself, Alexandra Argos—everything."

Surprised that he knew her name, and that anyone other than Jerome and Midge wanted to hear of her life, she tried to think of interesting details before giving up. "Sir, there's not so much to tell."

"Oh, Allie, aren't our lives endlessly rich and complex? There must be something."

She felt desperate to find some suitable subject. She really wanted to please him. "No, sir. My life is boring."

"Don't be so modest. Tell me, dear, what is it like to live in my grand hotel? Is it wondrous?"

Allie slumped down. She didn't want to offend Marvin. "Ah . . . maybe a little bit, sir. Sometimes . . . it's scary. Once, see, I was working in an apartment on the fifth floor, and the floor fell away into the room below it. I barely saved myself by grabbing a water pipe."

Marvin's perfect mouth fell open. "How dreadful!"

She tried not to choke on his breath. "Yes, it was."

"Speak no more of such horrors, Alexandra, please. I will have engineers look into the building's physical integrity early next week. Oh what a story. Dreadful, my dear." He sat forward, his face twisting into an expression of eternal optimism. "Tell me something pleasant. For instance, what of your father? For that matter, what of your parents? How are they?"

Allie flinched and studied the table's edge. She traced it, lifted her eyes, and cast them onto the blurry summits of Baltimore's tallest skyscrapers, all of them smaller than The Greaser. Hoping not to offend, she said, "I . . . I would prefer not to talk about them, if you don't mind."

Marvin shook his head. "Is it true? Can there be so many sad subjects in a life so young and a child so beautiful?"

She liked that he'd called her beautiful and said, "Mostly, I just don't like thinking about my parents. Mr. Gristle might not be mad at them, but I am. What they did doesn't make sense."

"Of course it doesn't. How could it after they have caused you so much pain? Alexandra, see, I should admit to you here and now that I was once very close to your father, Gordon, long before he became so despicable."

Allie inched forward in her chair. "You . . . knew my father?"

"Ah, yes. Very well, in fact. I knew him when he was a young man. In those days, he was a crusader for the poor and downtrodden." As if saddened, Marvin lifted his graceful hands off the table and turned them palms-up. "Shortly after that, he changed. Your father became the epitome of selfishness, which I should add is very different from being both good and selfish, as many have categorized me and the considerable charitable donations I make."

Allie nodded, saddened by the description of her father but touched by the fact that Marvin gave to charities. Despite Jerome's warning, she liked the man quite a bit.

"Allie, dear, your father is a bad man. I am sorry to say this."

Momentarily, Ehrlich rushed in with a Coca-Cola bottle balanced on a small tray. He placed the dark drink on the table in front of Allie.

Made dizzy by mounting fondness, Allie glanced distantly at Ehrlich and recoiled at the sight of his face. One of his eyes was swelling shut, as if he'd just been on the losing end of a fight.

"Look at you," said Marvin. "Now what have you done? Walk into a wall?" Marvin waved the man away. "Why do I keep you employed? I don't know myself. Go away. Go hide. I don't want to see your disgusting features around here for a while."

Terrified, Ehrlich scurried into the darkness of Marvin's penthouse.

Marvin paused, sipped at his drink, and said, "Alexandra, isn't life a balance? And balancing, my dear, is both an acquired and instinctive skill. Your father, to be blunt, lost balance."

She thought about his statement as she sipped her wonderful Coke. She wasn't surprised, even if she was saddened to hear the truth.

Marvin stroked the square tip of his jaw. "Dear child, it didn't help that he was so very stupid."

"Was . . . he?" she stammered mournfully, hurt for her flawed father.

"Consider this dilemma, Alexandra. Here is a test that completely flummoxed your father. If you, my beautiful woman, had to lose five individuals in order to save five hundred, including yourself, would you not do it?"

Allie found the question slightly horrifying.

"Would you?" Marvin asked sharply.

She said, "Maybe. I mean . . . I guess."

He grinned. "I guess, too. Isn't that wonderful? Already you comprehend what your father never did—that selfishness can be good for almost everyone." He took a deep, comforting breath. "Now, Alexandra, tell me, how is my loving associate Mrs. Friendly treating you? Well, I expect."

Allie straightened. To this question, she wouldn't have any trouble giving him a direct answer, because she despised Oda more than anyone else she could think of. Further, Marvin seemed not to know that Mrs. Friendly lacked a friendly bone in her whole strapping body—that she ran what amounted to a prison camp and treated Allie, Midge, Arnold, and Rena like slaves and stray dogs. Allie wanted to blurt out all of this, but tried to maintain a guise of thoughtful scrutiny, as if she was a scientist.

"Allie," Marvin said loudly. "You appear furious all of a sudden. Please tell me, dear. What's troubling you?"

"Sir, she . . . she's not so nice to me or anyone, really. She's mean. Very mean. Really. I . . . I have worked every single day since I got here, like a slave. Every day, and that's not an exaggeration. I've gone without food or water for as long as three days, and she thinks nothing of slapping me across the face. Plus, have you seen? Her boys carry guns and threaten us. Sir, if . . . if you saw how she treats me and my friends, you would be furious too. You'd take the hotel away from her." Allie's hands were clenched and each fist was veiled in a delicate, nearly imperceptible mist.

Marvin sat back. "We couldn't be speaking of my friend, Oda Friendly."

"We are."

"Truly, dear Alexandra, we must be discussing two very different souls. The Oda I know is . . . ah . . ." He paused to think. ". . . loving and . . . and all of that sort of stuff. This woman you describe is not the woman I know."

"Look at the terrible clothes she gives me," Allie said, holding up an arm to show him a torn sleeve. "We look gross."

Marvin appraised the sleeve. "Is that not the way all teenagers dress these days?"

"No, sir, it's . . . not. At least I don't think so." She held her small, rough hands in her lap and pleaded with her eyes.

"I will, of course, have words with her," Marvin said. "This will not continue. You should all have the freedom to come and go as you please."

Allie exhaled. "Thank you, sir," she said, and turned her face toward the sun's brightness. It felt hypnotic to sit out beneath the open sky, to be located so close to a man as considerate and helpful as Marvin. She touched the Coke glass and rubbed away the condensation. Her mother, she remembered, had loved Coca-Cola. When Allie was in preschool, they'd walked to the grocery store around the corner from their house, and her mother would buy a Coke for herself and a lollipop for Allie. "Marvin, sir," she said. "What else do you know about my parents? Anything good? I know they're no good, and even in jail, but do you think they might want to see me one day?"

He shook his head. "No, I don't believe either would. Dear, both of your parents are such tragic figures. Your dad is a blithering idiot, while your mother is an untrustworthy charlatan. Doesn't that say everything? Besides, they're in jail and will never be out of jail."

Allie's entire body shook, sickened as she was by the news that her parents would never want to see her again. She had such warm memories of her mother, who'd held her when she was sad, taught her the alphabet, and sung songs to her in the evenings. She recalled being tucked in at night and kissed on the forehead. How could a person like that be a charlatan? What, in fact, was a charlatan?

"What's a charlatan?" Allie croaked, scared to find out.

"A liar, swindler, or con artist, my dear."

Pained, Allie stood up. Her lungs felt injured, as if she'd been lying on the sidewalk far below and gotten struck by a brick dislodged from the very summit of The Greaser Hotel. Laboring to breathe, she walked slowly to the wall of the terrace, where she looked across the city. Turning, she was startled to find Marvin right behind her.

"Alexandra?" he said.

"Ah . . . yes?"

"Is it acceptable for me to change the subject?"

She nodded.

"Good. Good, my dear. So . . . do tell me, has there ever been an indication that you possess any surprising . . . skills?"

Allie wiped at her eyes. "What kind of skills do you mean?"

Marvin adjusted his jacket about him. "Oh, let me see. Your

brainless father had aptitudes like few men." Marvin caressed his handsome chin and raised his gaze toward a police helicopter as it buzzed past. "Primary amongst them, I would say, is a rather unheard of talent for creating and controlling a type of fire."

"He could control fire?"

"Yes, dear, of a sort."

Allie peered down at the city. What a strange, crummy family she'd come from. "I can't do that. I'm just me. If I could control fire, I would've roasted Mrs. Friendly and the boys by now."

He clicked his tongue humorously. "Is that so?"

"Probably."

"And Allie, my beautiful lady, how old are you?"

"Either fourteen or fifteen," said Allie.

"A young woman. Any gifts you possess may still remain hidden."

Allie was confused.

"Oh, Alexandra, that is too bad." Marvin withdrew an ancient silver pocket watch and made a show of calculating the time. "Ah, tsk, tsk. How unfortunate," he said, tucking the watch away. "How dreadfully unfortunate. It pains me deeply, Alexandra, but I have a vital meeting to attend shortly. I hate to appear as fickle as dear Herman, for I am not. I am a loving man. Therefore, it is a great injustice that you and I can't spend more time together at this moment, but we will in the coming days. And, trust me, I will discuss the situation with Oda and force appropriate changes in her behavior."

Allie didn't want him to force changes in Mrs. Friendly's behavior. She wanted him to punch her in the nose—to humiliate the woman, then chase her out of Greasy Blight forever. Disappointed, she mumbled, "Th—thank you, Marvin."

"No, dear, thank *you*."

Together, they entered the penthouse, where Marvin said to the man with the odd voice, "Give Oda a message from me."

"What, boss?"

"Inform her that she needs to treat our dear girl better."

"Will do, boss."

Merely knowing that Marvin was about to leave made Allie lonely for his company. From the intensity of his hopeful and kindly interest in her well-being, she felt dizzy and her head swam. She would miss him even if he had provided her with nothing but unfortunate news. He was a gentle, caring person, of whom there were too few in her world. Worse, she knew, deep in her overworked and underappreciated heart, that Marvin's instructions to her foster mother would not inspire Oda to change.

J. Scott Fuqua

⋇ 7 ⋇

Allie was returned to the room she'd been trying to clean earlier. As before, water spewed down at an amazing rate, and as she stood getting soaked and studying her cleaning cart, she felt as if she'd never sipped Coke in the sun with Marvin—as if it had all been a dream.

Stepping forward, she peered out the window that Scratch had torn the boards from earlier in the day. For a few moments, she imagined herself a bird, swooping breathlessly over the city, circling, and returning to The Greaser Hotel's upper terraces, where she could once more sit across from Marvin and experience his thoughtful and kind company.

Leaving the window, she returned to her cart and located a sponge, which she used half-heartedly to wipe down a brown-streaked wall, which caused the plaster to slide away and plop to the floor like a tilted bowl of cream of wheat.

Snickering sullenly and sick and tired of toil, Allie fetched the dust pan and replayed the slightly fuzzy events of the last few hours over in her head. As she did, the elevator's overworked cogs and sprockets quaked again. Aided by the squeal of metal on metal, Allie listened to the elevator descend and stop at her floor. Far down the hallway, she heard someone tromping closer and immediately feared that Oda Friendly was about to check on her progress.

Frightened, Allie finished scrubbing the white plaster smear off the floor, spun about, and jammed her mop into her cleaning cart. She noticed that the trim around the bathroom door was once again coated in a sandy, plaster grit, and she grabbed a rag and rushed at it. She was polishing wildly when the apartment door flung open.

Allie glanced from the trim and back a few times before locking gazes with Mrs. Friendly.

Straining to smile, Oda stepped ominously into the room, clutching a large Walmart bag. "Beautiful job, Allie Ra—I mean, Allie, dear. Now," she said, giggling unnaturally, "let's the three of us"—with a hand, she indicated Scratch, who'd been guarding the door—"go relax, huh? How 'bout that?"

Allie stared at her, confused. "What?"

"Relax. You know, take it easy? Rest our barking dogs." She held up a foot.

Allie remained confused.

Growing annoyed, Oda said, "I'm talking about taking a rest, ya blockhea—" She caught herself and forced another grim grin before reaching into her Walmart bag and pulling out a box with a cheap doll baby inside. The toy's hair was standing straight up like she'd been scared senseless, then flash-frozen like a vegetable or package of pork chops. "I want ya to take a break, child. Relax. Heck, I even went to the Walmart and, 'cause I likes ya so much, I rustled ya up

J. Scott Fuqua

a doll baby and a flashy sorta teen magazine with all the boy movie stars inside. Come on with me and Scratch, and ya can play and read to your heart's content. And . . . by the by, ya should oughta know this is a deluxe doll baby I'm holding. Nothing cheap for ya," she said. "This baby drinks, then, miracle'a miracles, she starts wee-weeing all over her ownself and ya gotta change her diaper. Ain't that gonna be a real silly kick in the pants?" Oda tried to appear excited. "Well, ain't it?" she said harshly when Allie remained silent.

"Yes, ma'am," Allie replied, suspicious. She tucked away her cleaning rag and reached for the handle of her cart.

"Leave it, ya . . . ya sweet pea. I'll send one'a the boys to fetch it later. Don't want ya pushing that big heavy thing round. Might could end up with a hernia or a strain or something, and wouldn't that be a awful mess for our little princess?"

Allie tentatively followed Mrs. Friendly and Scratch, who was toying with the touchy trigger of his pistol, down the hall and up and away from the miserable apartment.

Allie spent the afternoon seated in a soft living room chair drinking Tab, which sort of tasted like the rubber tires on her cleaning cart, which, being nearly starved

on a daily basis, she'd licked once, wondering if they might be edible. She filled her taut stomach with sticks of spicy beef jerky that rumbled down her gullet like a mouthful of hot pebbles. At least it was food, which she hadn't had with any consistency since arriving at The Greaser. Between sipping and chewing, she paged through a magazine with pictures of cute boys who had somewhat strange expressions on their faces, like they were pouting or upset or had horrible, stomach-churning gas. Regardless, Allie enjoyed looking at them and could hardly even figure out why.

To make Mrs. Friendly happy, she dumped water into the hole that was the doll's mouth, and the little plastic girl urinated wildly through her fake diaper and onto Allie's dress.

J. Scott Fuqua

"Don't that goofy little thing just make ya giddy?" Mrs. Friendly asked, her nostrils twitching like a bull restrained by ropes and harnesses.

Allie nodded, but the doll didn't make her giddy at all. She'd been wet most of the day and was again soaked through. "Yeah."

Oda stood up. Face pinched like Midge's when she'd had a tender tooth, Oda excused herself and left the room, so that Shoat, who was admiring himself in small mirror, was alone with Allie.

After a time, he blew a kiss to himself, placed the mirror down, and strutted over to Allie. As usual, his nose was leaking, so he dabbed at it with the back of a bony hand while making a point of brushing his patchy hair. He pointed at her. "Hey, Rat, sorry 'bout being so mean for the last like—what—nine years?"

Allie put her teen magazine on a table beside piles of beef jerky wrappers. "It was a long time."

"Yeah, well, Momma says your position in the family's changed, and we can't treat ya bad till Marvin's gone." He sat down alongside Allie. Flashing her a smug smile, he said, "Ain't that your good luck, Rat?"

"What?"

"That I can treat ya nice for a few days."

Allie got up and moved over to a large window. During long years of incarceration, Shoat had been one of her nastier jailers. Crossing her arms, she frowned harshly and contained the urge to whack Shoat across his wet nostrils with the spine of her boy magazine.

"Admit it, you like me," he said, straightening the collar of his red silk shirt.

"You're wrong," Allie said.

"Hey now, Rat, ya should ought to be flattered. I ain't exactly stale beefcake."

"Whatever, Shoat."

"Ya gonna let me kiss your cheek now?"

"No," she said, thinking she'd stomp on his foot if he approached her.

Shoat's eyes grew intense and mean. "Well, leastways now, Rat, I know right where the two of us stand! Ain't it the truth, huh? Far as I'm concerned, we're done, except that Momma says ya gotta come eat with us tonight, even though ya just broke my heart."

Allie spun about. "Am I really eating at the table?"

"That's what Momma said, and don't ya know I ain't happy 'bout it. Not now."

"Is . . . is Marvin going to be there?"

"Marvin! What, ya got a crush on the boss or something?"

"No."

"Good, 'cause, naw he ain't."

8

Seated awkwardly at the dining table for the first time, Allie noticed how the buffalo-skulled chandelier flicked reddish light about the walls, giving off an illumination that seemed haunted in its motion, catching the high points of the snarling dog-head design on Marvin Greaser's ancient silver service.

All the while, her stomach turned from too much spicy Gristle Brand beef jerky. Since gorging on the chewy meat product, her throat and chest had seemed ablaze with acid.

Beside her, Privet scratched insanely at his head. "Yow!" he exclaimed, checking his broken fingernails to see if he'd caught something in them. He held up his hand to investigate, then showed it to his mother. "Been scratching all day. You think I got some sorta critter on my head?"

"Don't see nothing," she growled, "'cept dandruff."

Lesion rolled his eyes. "Get that dirty hand outta Momma's face, Privet. Filthy meat hook of yours ain't exactly an appetizing sight."

"Lesion," Privet shot back, "if I wanna ask Momma a question, you ain't gonna stop me."

"That what you think?" Lesion asked, rising.

But Oda, located at the head of the table, made a show of loudly dropping her pistol, a weapon that somewhat resembled a hand-held cannon, alongside her plate, causing her silverware to hop.

All the boys looked at her.

She pointed from Privet to Lesion and back. "Gonna wing the first'a ya who makes for the other. I ain't kidding, neither, not with the mood I'm in, what with having ta be so phony and all that skokum."

Lesion lowered himself back into his seat.

Privet glanced away.

A moment later, Midge carried in two silver platters piled high with roasted muskrat, a Friendly favorite. When she placed them down, her eyes fastened curiously on Allie. "Allie?" she said.

Embarrassed, Allie said, "Midge . . . yeah, hi, I . . . I . . ."

"Midge Fly, ya rickety old party planner, do your job and shut up!" Mrs. Friendly shouted. "Don't dare say a word ta Rat. Not a word, or I'll personally stick the sharp nozzles of my new boots up your butt. Got it?"

J. Scott Fuqua

Midge turned slowly and made her way back to the kitchen.

Allie studied her plate, a sense of injustice rushing through her. At least for a few hours, she could talk back to Mrs. Friendly without immediate punishment, so, with that in mind, she tentatively said, "Mrs. Friendly, you shouldn't be so mean to her. She just wanted to know why I'm sitting here."

Oda's cheeks flushed like two slabs of raw liver. "Well, she ain't gonna get an explanation. That kinda thing ain't none of her beeswax."

"I had to give her one, though," Allie said. She grimaced, scared for Midge. "She's my best friend."

"No she ain't. Not today."

Unsure how to proceed, Allie ran a hand across the ironed white napkin in front of her. "You're only being nice because Marvin's around, so it doesn't matter what I say because I'm going back to join Midge and all soon enough."

Oda laughed cruelly. "Dang, Rat, ya caught me. Course, I didn't try to hide it, did I?"

Allie glanced at the boys, then back at her foster mother. "I'll tell Marvin when I see him. I will."

"No ya won't," Oda hissed, shoving out her chair and stepping from it. "See here, I've nearly had it with ya, Rat. Ya won't tell Marvin nothing, see? I'm warning ya right now. Don't push my better nature."

"I'm not pushing anything. I . . . I just want Midge treated nice this evening."

"Well, that ain't gonna happen, so zip it."

Behind Oda, Midge returned with two gargantuan bowls of cooked pig's brain.

Oda said, "Give 'em all to the Rat. Every last one of 'em. We're gonna treat her extra special till Marvin's gone, ain't we, boys?"

"Yes, Momma," the boys said together.

"I won't eat them," Allie told her.

Midge swallowed, clearly frightened for the child she thought of as her responsibility.

Oda snarled, "Oh, so now you're telling me what ya gonna do and not do, Allie Rat? Ya got the gumption ta do that? Ya must be a comedian. So, joker, grab yourself up a swine brain and eat!"

Nervous, Allie looked at the bowls of steaming gray matter. "I . . . No!"

Oda slammed a fist down, causing plates and glasses to leap and one charred muskrat to roll off a platter and bump into a candlestick. "Allow me ta 'splain something, Rat. I can do whatever I feel like doing whenever I feel like doing it. I done spent a lotta long years treating ya like the rodent ya are, and now the boss tells me I gotta go out and be pleasant with ya. Well, not even Marvin can change me. I'll do what I can do, but I won't do no more. Me, I'm siding with Mr. Herman Gristle. He don't see nothing special in your sorry frazzled self, and I don't neither." She resembled a serpent with a facelift. "And, right now, I am warning ya, don't ya dare say another word, or I will grind ya down till ya ain't nothing but a ghost'a yourself."

Oda straightened her mussed hair and swiped up a haunch of muskrat to gnaw on. "Have I made myself clear?"

Midge touched Allie's shoulder in an obvious effort to make the child see that Oda was very clear.

Allie, for her part, touched Midge's hand gently, then held it tight. She felt a fire inside of herself. It was growing in strength. It helped that her punishment wouldn't be immediate and, if Marvin stepped in, it might never be at all. Allie said, "Mrs. Friendly, if . . . if Marvin knew how you've treated the four of us all these years, he'd fire you on the spot. He might even call the police."

"Oh, really?"

"It's true."

"Is it now, you pucker-faced mutt? Well, all right then!" she spat loudly, her face aglow with resentment. "Let's just mosey upstairs and ask his highness 'bout all that, huh?"

Under her breath, Midge hissed, "Don't go, Allie."

Knees trembling, Allie stood.

Midge tightened her hand on Allie's shoulder. "Do not go visit Marvin Greaser."

Allie pulled away gently. "He'll help us."

"We'll see 'bout that," Oda said. Using a fat finger, she searched the cooked muskrats for one she liked the look of, took it up in her palm, and then strode forward. Snagging Allie by an arm, Oda gave a tug, hauling the child through the dining room and out past the elevator.

Allie tried to hold her ground, to walk beside her foster mother, but the woman's grip was like a vice. Eventually, they came to the familiar steel door, where Mrs. Friendly clutched her muskrat haunch between dirty teeth, jammed a key into the appropriate hole, and aggressively spun the combination dial. The door opened, and they passed beyond it and over to the elevator, which carried them upward.

Stepping into Marvin's penthouse suite, Allie searched the forest of ornate furniture, hoping that Marvin had finished his business and was around to see, firsthand, Oda's reprehensible behavior.

Oda, however, seemed to know something that Allie didn't. The woman gobbled at the tendons and connective tissue of her muskrat, swallowed, and shouted, "Marvin! Hey, Marvin!"

Nothing.

"Well, what do ya know? Looks like Marvy ain't here. I b'lieve he's off with Herman, visiting with the governor, don't ya know."

A few of Marvin's enormous, well-dressed aides emerged from the shadows of the room. One of the guys, a towering troll of a man sporting a lemon-yellow ascot, said, "He's off, Oda. But he guessed you'd be coming up here to complain."

"Well, ain't he a stinking prophet, Leon, 'cause that's what I'm doing. I'm here ta tell him that if he wants me ta do my job, I need ta be my old self again and treat this tramp like the tramp she is."

The big man appeared unconcerned.

"Well, fine," Oda told him. "If 'ins you don't care either way, I think I'll go out ta the patio and shake this brat up a bit. Any of ya boys gonna snitch me out?"

A horrified Allie looked frantically at Marvin's men for help.

Finally, Leon shook his head. "Course not. Have fun."

"Well, goody for me," Oda declared. With a grunt, she hauled Allie, who was pulling back like an untamed horse, across the tile floor and out through the patio doors. Once outside, the big woman tossed the skinny teenager like she were an empty pillowcase.

Allie struck the balcony's low brick wall with a crunch. Behind her, Oda closed the French doors and sauntered forward, stopping a few feet away.

"Ya sorry imp! Ya think you're something important, but ya ain't. Ya ain't got nothing on me."

Frightened, Allie tried to rise, but her legs were trembling too hard.

Mrs. Friendly kicked her.

Allie moaned, more fearful than hurt.

"Eh, now, ya little guttersnipe, ya still think Marvin can protect ya from me?"

"No . . . ma'am," Allie managed. "He can't."

"That's right. He can't." Sneering, Oda hurled her muskrat bones into the air so that they glimmered like metal shards before starting a long descent to the city streets. She pivoted and caught Allie by the front of her dress. She lifted her up close to her face, assaulting her with breath like a septic tank. "'Pologize ta me."

Allie didn't even consider refusing. She coughed and whispered, "I . . . apologize!"

Oda dangled her over the side of the building. "Louder."

Looking down at the distant city street, Allie spotted a bus so far away it resembled an oblong freckle. "P-please, Mrs. Friendly, I apologize."

Oda playfully bulged her eyes out at Allie. "Ya sorry little spore! Ya cheap little Porta-Potty. Next time ya talk back, I'll kick ya about like a can. Here I go and buy ya a nice doll baby and a pricey lil' magazine, and ya still don't treat me right. Here I work my butt off ta make ya feel wanted and happy and ya ain't grateful an iota. Instead, ya wanna tell me what ta do. Well, I don't take orders from ya, Rat. Git it?"

"S-sorry, ma'am."

"Ya should be!" Oda said, whirling about and tossing Allie onto the balcony's hard tiles so that she slammed into the table where only hours before she'd been sipping a soda with Marvin. Sore and dizzy, she scrambled to all fours and searched about for a place to hide. She kept wishing that Jerome would show up and save her, or that she'd magically vanish.

Smiling broadly, Oda clicked her tongue. "Look at ya. Just another sorry bag of bull droppings." Oda unzipped the top few inches of her mechanic's suit, stretched her muscular neck, and approached once more.

Like a fearful animal, Allie scrambled backwards on all fours until she reached the wall.

"What's this?" Oda said in mocking wonderment. "Ya scared of me now, Allie Rat? I can see it in your eyes. S'pose you'll do what I say from now till eternity, huh? Reckon you'll jump when I say *jump* and sit when I say *sit*, huh?" She kneeled down and shook her head. "Did meany weany old Mrs. Friendly learn ya good?"

Allie refused to speak.

J. Scott Fuqua

"I asked ya, did meany weany Mrs. Friendly learn ya good?"

Allie hated the smug smile on Oda's face. She hated the woman's swagger, and she hated her cruel, bloodshot eyes, which resembled two copper bolts holding a water pipe tight. After all the years of abuse, Allie refused to say that Oda had taught her anything. Fearful of the consequences of what she was about to say, she croaked, "No. . . ah. . . not completely."

Oda stood. "Well, well, what a surprise. Arnold Armstrong broke easier than ya, that's for dang sure. A few more good wallops, though, and I believe we can remedy the situation." Oda cocked a booted foot like a soccer player, then, with a quick dip of her axle-like hips, she let it fly.

Instinctually, Allie avoided Oda's foot, which struck the wall with a thud.

Oda gaped down at her toe. "My God," she said in disbelief, her expression darkening, "I b'lieve ya just caused me to mar my new cockroach killers. Now ya've gotten me officially angry, ya rashy little idjot. These beautiful boots cost me a shovelful of cash, and now the one is partway scuffed. Ya see what ya done? Looky." She pointed.

Allie didn't see a scuff mark.

Oda made a show of withdrawing her gargantuan pistol. She leveled its wide barrel directly at Allie. "Girl, I hated ya the moment I laid eyes on ya. So it's funny ya didn't think I could touch ya with Marvy in town. Well, I can. I'll tell 'im ya attacked me, that's all."

Staring up at the barrel, Allie stiffened with a sudden and growing hatred of her own. It rose from the depths of her stomach. It felt like a shivering stack of hot plates pressing against her lungs, her throat, and her hands.

For nine years, Allie had toiled for the woman. She'd done precisely what she'd been ordered to do—cleaned and cooked and washed and served. She'd been beaten. She'd been humiliated. She'd been screamed at. And she'd never wielded a moment of power. Never. Between the two of them, she had earned the right to hate, while Oda hadn't earned a thing. She simply hated because she was hateful. Voice cracking with fear and rage, Allie said, "I hate you worse."

Oda's finger tightened on the trigger, and the gun popped.

J. Scott Fuqua

✣ ❾ ✦

Allie threw out a hand, and in the instant that the bullet passed down the muzzle of the bulky gun, her disdain swelled upward and into the tips of her calloused fingers, erupting outwards and striking Mrs. Friendly like a rising white comet. On impact, the woman's body flexed inverse to the area struck hardest, similar to a squarely hit baseball. Her extremities looked like cotton-stuffed nylons suddenly rising and fluttering in a gale.

Then, in the blink of an eye, Oda was slammed to the balcony's tiled deck, where she was momentarily pinned by a blistering force that quickly dissipated in a flurry of circular movement, like the satellite view of a hurricane or the whirlpool of a flushed toilet.

Oda's breath expelled in painful gasps. She moaned and muttered unintelligibly.

Allie, meanwhile, lay unconscious, bleeding from a shoulder.

Shortly, a huge man came out and grabbed Allie by a foot, made a U-turn, and dragged her inside.

Leon returned and carried Oda through the French doors, dumping her roughly atop a couch with a pattern of ghoulish faces sewn into the upholstery. Crowning the center backrest was a carving of an emaciated, winged bat, and that's what Oda saw as she drew open her charred lids, eyelashes, and brows. "Gawd, that's a disgusting creature." With great effort, Oda sat up and swayed like a clipped bowling pin.

Leon gave her some room, but he appeared furious, his wide face wrinkled like a Shar Pei dog. "Oda, you idiot!" he hissed once she seemed reasonably steady. "You went and shot her! You actually shot her right in the shoulder. If you'd told us you might do that, we wouldn't've let you go out there!"

J. Scott Fuqua

Mrs. Friendly, who was suffering a concussion amongst an array of other abrasions, bruises, and fractures, said, "I had ta, Leon. She attacked me is why. Left me with no choice at all. Ya gotta 'splain that ta Marvin for me."

"She attacked you?" He indicated skinny little Allie.

"She's a animal. She's a wild creature. How else ya think I ended up on the mat?"

"Maybe because your gun backfired," Leon said. He indicated Oda's howitzer-like pistol, which had plainly exploded at the tip, making it resemble a gray flower with four jagged petals and a fat, curved stalk more than a gun.

Oda cast her gaze from her ruined weapon to Allie, who was attempting to rise off the floor. A big man in a bowler hat placed a foot atop the small of her back.

Irritated, Allie struggled against the big man's weight, trembling and forcing herself to rise. He applied more pressure, though, till finally she surrendered and lowered herself to the floor. Humiliated, she closed her eyes and didn't speak, worried she might start crying. Her injured arm throbbed terribly. She tried to flex her fingers but wasn't sure they moved at all.

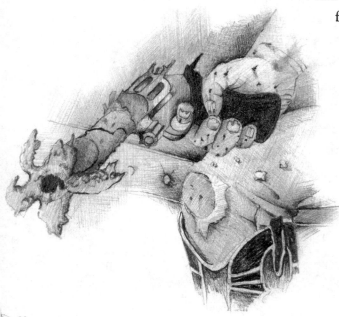

The Secrets of the Greaser Hotel

Mrs. Friendly staggered forward, her face red and chapped as if she'd spent a week in the desert without sunblock or a hat. She took a finger and examined the row of newly loosened teeth in her mouth. She looked over to Leon. "S'pose the gun backfired. I s'pose you're right 'bout that one, yeah. 'Cause there ain't no way this mudlark coulda hurt me."

Leon adjusted his yellow ascot. "Marvin's going to be furious."

Allie smiled, sure that Marvin would fire Oda.

"Leave Marvin ta me," Mrs. Friendly said. She looked at the man standing on Allie's back. "Now move over, Grover, so I can get this mustard weed downstairs and punish her for how she made me ruin my fine-crafted gun."

The guy, whose name wasn't Grover, lifted his foot, and Oda gingerly bent down and grabbed Allie by the collar of her dress. That little effort, however, caused something in the woman's back to crack loudly. Grimacing, she straightened with the help of the man in the bowler hat. Lip quivering, Oda said, "Now, come on, Allie Rat, drag yourself along and follow me downstairs." Oda swayed on her feet and grasped the back of a chair. "Hey, ah, one'a ya big boys wanna cough up a pistol for me ta use? Can't escort this monster 'round unarmed."

Dazed, Allie struggled to her feet without help.

Leon handed his weapon to Oda, and she gave Allie a shove toward the elevator.

Downstairs, they stepped into the hallway and Mrs. Friendly slammed Allie against a wall, jamming the bone of her elbow against the girl's fragile neck.

Allie was too tired to resist, so tired that she didn't even notice the bullet fall from the wound in her shoulder and roll across the carpet.

"Rat, do ya know what ya done out on that patio? Do ya got any notion at all?"

Allie shook her head. She didn't, but in the split second before the pain in her shoulder overwhelmed her, she'd felt wonderful and free from the years of pain and anger, both of which had bound together in a single moment of release.

"Of course ya don't have no idea, do ya? Why would ya, huh? I've had ya here most'a your sorry life. You're completely in the dark, ya moron."

To avoid Oda's putrid exhales, Allie snuck in air through her mouth.

"But *I* know. I know what's going on, Rat."

Allie gave up and said, "What?"

Oda, her face singed and her hair shrunken and frazzled from the heat, paused for a second, straightened, and wiggled a tooth with her tongue, causing it to come free in her mouth. Annoyed, she sucked on it as if it were a watermelon seed, then spat it onto the hallway carpet. "Nothing, Rat. Absolutely nothing. Now get walking a'fore I shoot your other arm."

Within the confines of her sealed room, Allie swayed painfully. She was dog-tired, psychically pained, and sad for reasons she couldn't completely fit together. She turned on the light and lowered herself to the dirty floorboards. She rested flat on her back and gazed distantly at the cracked and sagging ceiling.

She missed Marvin's company. She missed Jerome. She missed

not knowing that her parents were evil. Her memories of her mother and father, despite what they had done to Herman Gristle's little boy, had always provided her a smidgeon of hope in her hopelessness. She'd imagined they'd one day leave jail and come to fetch her. She hadn't realized it till that moment, but her criminal parents had been a glimmer of blue sky visible from behind The Greaser's heavily boarded windows, and now it was gone. Who would be her sky now? she wondered. There was no one.

Allie started to cry, her shoulder throbbing as she whimpered. "Why?" She cried until she started falling asleep. *Why? Why?* she thought, over and over, until she dreamed of crushing Oda with a

J. Scott Fuqua

white light that twisted and constricted around the woman like a monstrous snake.

"Allie?" Jerome said some hours later.

Waking, Allie turned her head to him. "Hey."

He touched a paw to the blood-stained fabric on the shoulder of her dress. "Did . . . did Marvin do something to you?"

She shook her head. "No. But he's going to be upset when he finds out what happened." Allie swallowed and sat up weakly. When she felt steady, she tested her injury by rotating her arm, which hurt her shoulder. "It was Oda. She . . . shot me."

Jerome's throat abruptly rose and fell as if he was swallowing. He focused on her, his eyes pained so deeply that it touched Allie. "My God!" he said. "How are you, dear child?"

"Better," she told him, her eyes welling up once again. Tears zipped down her cheeks. Desperate to feel loved, she scooped Jerome up and pressed him to her.

The big cat gently tucked in his blocky head alongside her neck and beneath her ear, whereupon he began to purr. "You're okay. You're okay, my dear," he rasped. "I'm here." But as he spoke, he shook his head the way a distraught parent might. "Who hurts people this way?" he whispered to himself.

"Oda," Allie replied.

He nuzzled her ear. "I hope you know I care for you beyond words. You're practically my child. For all intents and purposes, I've raised you. At least I've tried."

She laughed. "I'm the daughter of a cat?"

"For the time being," he said.

Smiling and feeling less fragile, she gently placed Jerome down.

At her feet, his purr dissipated. Eyes narrowing sternly, he said, "Allie, I've been waiting for some sort of opening, some moment when everyone's defenses were lowered. That no longer matters. After what has now happened, I have to get you out of here. We've got to take the risk, and Oda had better not get in my way."

Allie winced at the jabbing pain in her shoulder and lifted her injured arm to flex her numb hand. She studied Jerome. "Yesterday, you asked me if something strange had ever happened."

The cat licked his mouth. "I did."

"Well, yesterday something did."

"What?"

Allie leaned forward and spoke in a hush. "I don't know."

Jerome seemed to swell, to grow larger. "Like what?"

She shrugged. "I think I . . . attacked Mrs. Friendly."

Jerome leaned forward. "Attacked?"

"Something happened. Something strange. After she shot me, she looked sunburned and . . . well . . . like she'd been in a fight. She thinks her gun backfired, but the bullet got me. I thought if guns backfire, the bullet goes backwards."

Jerome's gaze grew intense. He sucked at his sharp teeth. "Not all the time. But, it's possible that you have done something."

Allie studied her hands and added, "I felt something in my hands. In my whole body."

"Tell me what."

"Like strength. Like anger going into my hands."

Jerome circled her, then stopped. "How does one determine something that they haven't seen? How does one make a diagnosis? Still, at this point, I am going to make a guess. So, here it is. I suspect you might have come upon your miserable inheritance, my dear. I suspect so. Seems the sins of the ancestors continue to be passed down the line."

She shook her head. "I don't understand."

"Allie, dear, I'm sorry to say, but hatred, greed, and unimaginable narcissism run thick in your blood and deep in your bones."

Confused, Allie rubbed her forehead.

Jerome cleared his throat. "Sadly, at this moment, we don't have the time to discuss all of this. We need to focus our energies on Oda, who is now pondering whether you have what Marvin wants and Herman fears. Therefore, I've been considering how she will proceed given this type of circumstance, and I figure she won't ever accept you as a superior, given the vague and unlikely possibility that this might happen. Therefore, I suspect she's going to try to kill you, and she's gonna say you caused it."

"Kill me?" Allie blinked.

Jerome's voice grew parental with authority. "Allie, you have to make yourself ready to leave this place, because I'm coming back soon, girl. Very soon."

✻ 10 ✻

Allie had attempted to escape from Greasy Blight on three previous occasions. Twice, she'd tried it alone, and once she'd almost flown the coop with Midge. During each effort, the building itself had seemed to come to life and turn against her. Hallways doubled back on themselves. The elevator stopped a few floors above the lobby. Carpeting developed large wrinkles that seemed to trip her intentionally, and antique wall sconces continually bonked her on the head. Most infuriating of all, dozens of doors bolted closed as she passed through them.

During her two solo attempts, all of these things slowed her progress, the first time allowing Mrs. Friendly and a few of the boys to corner her in a stairwell, and in a broom closet the second.

Working together, however, Allie and Midge had navigated these assorted problems to reach the hotel's once grand lobby. It was there, as they rushed from the creaky stairwell, that they'd stumbled upon a pack of enraged Rottweilers.

The bear-sized guard dogs responded to their presence like they'd been starved and tortured for weeks, their teeth snapping, their claws gouging the ancient mahogany floors as they gave chase through The Greaser's entrance hall. It was adorned with a mixed bag of architectural clutter, from decorative gargoyles to a forty-foot marble statue of the first Marvin Greaser, a man who looked remarkably similar to the third Marvin Greaser, dressed as a Roman emperor. Allie and Midge never had a chance. Surveillance cameras were trained on their progress, and more than three dozen booby traps were located around the large room. Midge was sprayed with darts dipped in a powerful sedative, and she collapsed. Allie, on the other hand, ducked the darts but had a heavy iron cage slam down around her. Then, she was unceremoniously blasted with tear gas that made her choke.

Now, Allie scrubbed at a glaze of grime, causing her injured arm to throb. Her jaw, which she was clenching in response to the pain, began to ache, too. Mrs. Friendly's poor condition gave her some satisfaction, though. Her foster mother had missed breakfast.

In an apartment on the twenty-ninth floor, Allie moved to a patch of mold embedded in the linoleum wall above the bathroom sink. She worked her sponge one way, then back, wondering if Jerome's plan included breaking her friends out, too. She couldn't leave if they, and especially Midge, remained trapped. Midge was so different than she'd seemed on television years and years before, back when Allie had watched her homemaking program with her mother. In The Greaser, Midge had been like a mother to Allie whenever they could steal time together. She'd made her laugh just by the expression on her face. She'd made her smile in the small ways she got back at the Friendlys, like soaking ham hocks in various detergents from her cart, from pine floor cleanser to blue toilet bowl goop. And they'd never noticed. Midge had given her hope on hopeless days and nights when life felt as dim as a two-watt bulb.

Allie ran orange, rusty water into the sink and started in around the drain. Far above, the elevator rattled to life, shaking the building and dislodging a few bricks on The Greaser's exterior. She straightened her hair and listened nervously as the lift screeched toward her floor, hoping that Marvin had finally arrived to save her from Oda.

The distant elevator doors whined open and footfalls began rumbling toward her. Then they stopped at her door. There was a brief, muffled conversation followed by the clanking of keys. Allie could hardly keep from hopping up and down with joy. She stepped from the bathroom, and in that instant the door crashed open. Oda, seated in a wheelchair, rolled in, took quick aim, and sprayed a line of fat bullets in Allie's direction.

A portion of the doorframe Allie had been peeking around exploded in a shower of splinters as she ducked back into the bathroom, striking a knee painfully against one of the sink's corroded chrome legs.

"Damn if I didn't miss," Oda shouted, sounding surprised. "Must be this new pea shooter."

One of the boys said, "I'll go grab her up for ya, Momma."

"Naw ya won't," Oda told him. "Not unless ya want her ta do ta ya what she done ta me. We gotta initiate Plan B." She twisted about in her wheelchair and shouted, "Hey, Shoat!"

"Yeah, Momma?"

"Haul little ol' Hammerhead in here, why don't ya?"

Allie silently crawled forward on her stomach.

In a playful voice, Oda hollered, "*Allie Rat!* Oh, my stinky, blinky Allie Rat! Hustle your carcass on out here."

Allie peeked around the doorframe. Mrs. Friendly was holding a gun to Rena's shoulder while Shoat, Lesion, and Privet approached the bathroom, their silver pistols drawn from their tooled, leather holsters. Allie pulled back.

"Hey now, did I just catch sight'a ya there, Allie Rat? Did ya just now see that Hammerhead's in a heap of trouble?"

Allie slumped to the loose floor tiles. "Mrs. Friendly, why are you doing this?"

"On account'a Herman gave me tha big go-ahead."

Allie wiped her palms down her dress and stood nervously. "Why'd you bring Rena?" she called.

"Broughts along Hammerhead ta keep ya in check. I figured that if ya actually do give a hoot 'bout your old pokey mates, then ya ain't gonna allow me ta hurt this dunce."

"If I come out, are . . . are you going to kill me?"

"Either gonna be ya or ya and Hammerhead together. Take your pick."

Allie felt faint and struggled to breathe properly. She searched the small bathroom for a weapon of some sort and picked up the brush she'd used to scrub the blackened toilet bowl. She swung it back and forth like a club. It was so light that it wouldn't put a dent in Oda's or the boys' hard noggins. Still, she told herself to try. She figured that maybe if she came out swinging, her foster mother would remove the gun from Rena and try to pick her off instead. If that occurred, Allie hoped Rena would run for cover.

She grabbed the can of Bon Ami powder and decided that she could heave it like a weapon, too.

"Come out, come out, ya raggleworm, or I'm gonna count ta ten and shoot li'l Hammerhead's yapper off!"

Allie straightened her worn dress. Tears started down her flush face. She was so sick of crying that she slapped at her cheeks, then felt sort of crazy for doing so.

"One," Oda started counting, "two, three, four, fi—"

Allie rushed into the living room. A cloudburst of bullets struck the grubby walls and floors around her. She screamed but didn't slow. Shoat reached for her, and she shoved the toilet brush's spiky bristles against his pasty-looking nose, causing him to shoot two holes in a set of skewed wall switches.

With her bad arm, Allie lobbed the can of Bon Ami at Privet, spreading a large

J. Scott Fuqua

white cloud that wafted into his pale eyes, making him wince and rub at them wildly.

One of Mrs. Friendly's bullets whizzed by Allie's neck, curling the hairs on her nape. Directly in front of her, Lesion leveled his large handgun, grinned, and attempted to squeeze the trigger. It didn't budge.

Her life having flashed before her eyes, Allie's entire body went rubbery and weak, causing her to stumble and fall forward, slamming into one of Lesion's knobby legs so that it gave way with a loud snap, causing him to collapse to the floor.

At the door, Oda pitched forward in her wheelchair and screamed, "Evr'body check the safeties on their pistolaros! Take tha safety off, ya hear me, ya idgits? Take it off!" She let fly two shots that just missed Allie's hip and arm.

Allie leapt behind her cleaning cart. Bullets whistled across the room, punching holes through bright plastic bottles of detergent, which sprang leaks in every direction.

"What'cha gonna do?" Oda called. "Stay behind that cart for the next month, Rat?"

Allie said, "Maybe, ma'am."

"Okay then." Mrs. Friendly's wheelchair squeaked as if she was adjusting her position. She got up from it, a tad shaky but still strong. "Let's get your little friend talking. Hammerhead, say something ta Allie Rat. Speak, girl!"

"A-Allie," Rena said, her voice trembling like an old jumpy recording. "She's pointing a gun at me again, and I . . . I don't wanna die. Please. Please, Allie."

Allie slumped against the cleaning cart. She had no answers for the tight spot she was in.

"Privet and Shoat're coming round ta hogtie ya," Oda said, "and ain't nothing ya can do, not unless ya wants ta say 'Bye bye Birdie' ta Hammerhead."

Allie, her clothes drenched in detergent, closed her eyes. Once more her sorry life commenced to running through her head like a slideshow. Oda, who'd gotten the better of her for years, would beat her one final time. And who would care? In all the world, she thought, only Jerome and Midge and . . . maybe Marvin would be sad if they ever found out what had occurred.

J. Scott Fuqua

Directly, Privet and Shoat leapt around the cleaning cart like members of a commando team. They snagged Allie's arms, causing her to scream from the pain in her shoulder, and dragged her into the middle of the room.

"Oh, gross, Momma," Privet said, a distasteful expression on his face. "She's all slimy—blood and cleaners."

"Ignore it."

"But I got some on my jacket cuff. See?"

"Shut up."

Privet touched the area and looked over toward Rena. "Hey, Hammerhead, can you wash this sort of thing out?"

A gun against her, she answered, "I . . . I . . . guess. I . . . mean . . . maybe. They're just . . . cleaners."

Oda smiled imperiously at Allie and released Rena. "Well, well, we're at the end of the road, huh, Argos? Must not sit too well with ya that you're gonna die, and ya won't even know why." Oda laughed and staggered forward. "It really was just a Podunk life ya had, now, wasn't it?"

Behind her, in the doorway to the hall, something moved.

Shoat's eyes grew wide. "What the hell! Momma!" he yelled. "Watch out!"

☼ 11 ☼

From the darkened corridor, a nightmarish creature came down on Oda.

Instinctively, Oda raised an arm to shield her face. The animal's rapier-like claws took a quick swipe, ripping through Oda's muscular elbow and tossing her to the floor.

Landing, the massive beast bounded toward Privet in a single motion, striking him in the center of his chest so hard that his legs whipped out from beneath him as if somebody had yanked a carpet from beneath his feet.

Twirling about, the animal brutally lacerated Shoat's hand, forcing his gun from his dirty fingertips so hard that it slammed against a wall.

"Jump on my back," the creature instructed Allie.

As if in a trance, Allie recognized Jerome's voice. Somehow, he'd grown huge and dangerous-looking.

"Now!" he roared.

Wobbly, Allie slid onto his broad shoulders and wrapped her hands tightly in his fur.

With one powerful leap, Jerome crossed the room and bounded out

J. Scott Fuqua

into the hall. Like a nimble stallion with an off-kilter gait, he bolted down the passageway and crashed at an angle against a wooden doorway, breaking it wide open. Without a moment's hesitation, he entered a tumbledown stairwell that ran all of the way from Marvin's penthouse suite to the building's disgusting basement.

Ahead of them were twenty-eight flights of disintegrating wooden stair treads that traced the wall in a descending square. Worse, in the center of the stairwell was a broad shaft that, from the looks of it, ended in the basement. Jerome, seemingly unconcerned, sprang

down the first flight without a thought, alighting on a dusty landing that cracked and popped beneath the shock of his load.

Holding tight to her friend, Allie worried she might faint. "Everything feels blurry," she mumbled.

"I bet it does." Jerome leapt the next ancient flight, landing by the doorway to the twenty-seventh floor. He continued descending that way, in huge leaps and gentle landings until one of his front paws, the size of a gravy boat, went through dry rotting boards and caught on a thatch of thick, rusty nails. Grunting, Jerome struggled to yank himself free. He pulled and pulled and finally, with a loud tear, retrieved his paw.

"Great," he mumbled, bending back toward Allie. "Can't let you ride anymore, sweetie, not with this injury. I cut it to the bone and tore the pad."

Allie slid off his back.

"You mind ripping a part of your dress and wrapping the shredded area closed?"

Silent, Allie tore along her hemline and created a filthy floral bandage.

"Thanks, Allie."

The two of them started down again, one flight at a time, frequently stopping to listen for pursuers or to avoid a series of disintegrating stair steps. On the eighteenth floor, they heard voices whispering from below.

Somebody said, "Now, what did Oda say we're trying to kill?"

"That little gnat of a girl and a giant tiger of a thing," said a familiar voice. "Hey, don't you look at me that way. I didn't make it up. That's what she said."

"Ehrlich, that lady's on drugs or something. There isn't a tiger anywhere round here."

"I'm just telling ya what she told me."

They stopped speaking for a few minutes, their progress marked by the cracks and moans of ancient boards and beams. Then Ehrlich said, "Winchell?"

"What?"

"You ever wonder what cat tastes like?"

"Raw or cooked?"

"Cooked."

Softly, Jerome told Allie, "We taste like chicken."

Allie stared at his huge, misshapen form, unable to respond.

"I'm joking," he assured her, as faint footfalls and voices began echoing down from above. "Looks like we're going to get squeezed between hunting parties."

Allie scratched the spot where a bullet had grazed her cheek. "What're we going to do?"

"Gotta go down, dear." He lowered himself against the steps and crept tight against the wall as if he was commencing to hunt through tall grass. He froze.

Allie did the same.

A large man emerged from below, and Jerome didn't dawdle an instant. He sprang at him from across the wide gap between the stairs.

Twisting about, the guy managed to land a glancing blow against Jerome's airborne form, but it wasn't enough. Jerome raked the man's thick arm, knocking him backwards past Ehrlich.

A few flights above, Allie and Jerome's pursuers picked up speed.

Ehrlich easily dodged Winchell's tumbling bulk with a sidestep. He tugged at his cane, exposing a long, dangerous blade. Gripping it in one hand, he threw down its casing and charged the cat savagely, lunging and thrusting, driving and hacking so that the gleaming metal bit into the century-old banister, the withered looking plaster walls, and stair treads that sagged like cheap book shelving.

Jerome ducked and jabbed, unable to parry Ehrlich's sword.

On the landing below, Winchell hollered, "Move over, Ehrlich, and I'll put some buckshot into that tabby's butt!"

But Ehrlich was in a brawl he couldn't back out of.

Jerome slipped beneath Ehrlich's guard and slashed open one of his powerful thighs.

"Ahh!" Ehrlich bellowed.

"I can take him out!" the other guy insisted.

"Will you shut up?" Ehrlich yelled back as he cut through a series of railing spindles.

Jerome rose on his hind legs and nearly tore off Ehrlich's shoulder.

Ehrlich cried out, lurching forward, attempting to spear the enormous cat's head with a straight thrust. He missed, the tip of his sword digging deep into a surprisingly solid stair tread.

Jerome rammed Ehrlich in the midsection, shoving him through the shaky banister.

Pinwheeling his arms, Ehrlich fell and was swallowed by the darkness.

Two roaring gunshots peppered the wall beside Jerome, removing four of his thick whiskers, which fluttered to the steps like broom bristles. He cocked his head in the direction of the approaching lynch mob as it descended from above. Calmly, he smiled, as much as a cat can smile. "I've been in loads of worse situations," he promised Allie, and sprang across the wide void once more. Like a deflected bullet, he rebounded against the far wall, then came down atop Winchell's back, slamming him mercilessly to the floor so that his head actually dented a stair tread.

Allie and Jerome continued their harrowing descent, their pursuers hot on their heels and gaining. Three flights down, they came upon Ehrlich, dangling one-handed from a landing.

Passing by, Jerome said, "I thought you were gone."

J. Scott Fuqua

Ehrlich spat at him, his black eye shining in the glare cast by a single antique light bulb.

Allie said, "I should stomp your fingers loose."

Jerome advised, "He's not worth it."

"I am too worth it!" Ehrlich shouted.

Allie and Jerome made it to the eleventh floor before concluding they were about to be overtaken from behind. Thus, Jerome slammed against a locked hallway door, eventually breaking the framing around it. Rushing through, they were halfway down a poorly lit corridor when Allie's forehead connected painfully with a wall sconce. Bleary eyed, she fell to her knees, blinked a few times, and struggled to her feet. She looked at the lamp she'd somehow hit and found that it was mounted far above her head. Under the circumstances, she had no time to consider how her skull had connected with it and instead continued after her friend, who was waiting for her at a hallway intersection.

Behind them, their pursuers burst from the stairwell and broke into a thunderous dash.

Somewhere ahead, Allie heard the screechy Greaser elevator slowly descending. She ducked a second wall sconce that seemed to droop magically downward and followed Jerome around yet another corner, arriving in the small elevator lobby just as the conveyance's steel doors squealed open.

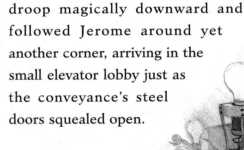

12

Oda, her injured elbow wrapped in cloth and her square butt planted tightly in her wheelchair once more, spotted Allie and didn't hesitate. Gritting her teeth, she let loose with a long round from a Tommy gun.

Precisely at that moment, Allie tripped over a large carpet wrinkle and fell forward onto her hands and knees. Above her, the bullets transformed a dingy wall into an avalanche of swirling, brown horsehair plaster.

Dusted like a cinnamon donut, Allie rolled and clambered to all fours just as the posse of pursuers rumbled into the small space. However, due to swirling dust, visibility was so poor that one of the big men actually stumbled over Allie as she attempted to slither away.

Driven nearly senseless by hatred, Oda shouted, *"Where is that gutter snipe?"*

"You tell me!" someone hollered back at her.

Crazed, Oda didn't see the need to reply. As a substitute for cordialities, which she wasn't good at anyway, she swept her Tommy gun about the lobby, firing upwards and downwards and sideways. Dust swirled so thick that visibility diminished to inches.

J. Scott Fuqua

She ignored the howls of pain rising from the mouths of her associates in crime until she shot out the room's only light, blanketing everything in darkness.

Like a forest on a foggy night, silence overtook the space.

"Oda!" one of the big men finally said.

"Is she gone? Did I pop her?"

An injured person moaned.

"That her?" odoriferous Oda Friendly demanded to know.

"Let the dust clear and we'll find out," one of the big men said. "And watch out you don't shoot us up anymore."

"Lump it," Oda snarled. "Rat was here. Saw her with my own two peepers." She paused. "Hey, feel round on the floor! Stomp the floor and see if ya can find her body!"

In the darkness of the room, Allie curled up like a potato bug, imagined herself tiny, and tried not to breathe.

Then, what remained of Jerome's whiskers brushed against her cheek and the cat placed his dry nose to her ear. "Hold on to my tail and follow along," he whispered.

While the big men stomped back and forth across the obscured floor, Allie and Jerome slithered right past Oda's wheelchair and up to the elevator doors. Jerome soundlessly mashed at the call button, and the elevator entrance pulled loudly open, illuminating the roiling clouds that filled the lobby.

"Is someone there, or did that thing just open?" a big man asked.

"Sometimes it's ding-y," Oda said, "but I don't trust nothing and ya shouldn't neither." She circled about and kept her gun at the ready.

Hidden behind a veil of dust, Allie trailed Jerome between the elevator's smudgy metal doors, where, once inside, the cat turned and slipped a paw beneath Oda's wheelchair. At the very moment

The Secrets of the Greaser Hotel

Allie hit the button for the lobby, Jerome flipped the woman over backwards.

The doors shut and the elevator started to descend.

From above, Oda shouted, "They're in the elevator! They're using the elevator, for crummy sake!" Furious, she shot up something (or someone) else.

Inside the elevator, Allie and Jerome took the opportunity to catch their breath. Jerome, his paw oozing profusely, rested flat on his great side, like a tiger sunning in a windowsill. Allie, in turn, leaned against a shaking, scratched, and marred wall. Both of them kept an eye on the clock-like dial above the door so as to keep track of the floors they were passing. Bending his head back toward Allie, Jerome wrinkled his nose.

Between the fifth and sixth floors, the elevator banged to a hard stop and bobbed on its fraying cables.

"Now what?" Allie asked.

Jerome rose and gimped about the small elevator car. "They turned off the motors, which is what I suspected they'd do. I was hoping we'd make it to the third floor. I believe I can survive a jump from there, though. Course, I've lost a lot of blood, and I can feel it. My batteries are running low, so you might have to leave me behind."

"I won't," said Allie.

"Look, it's not something I'd enjoy, but you might have to. Them's the breaks." Jerome rubbed a cheek against a tiny hatch beneath the elevator's buttons. "Open this," he said.

At their feet, a soft hiss commenced, like air seeping from a spray can.

"Hurry up," Jerome told her. "They're trying to gas us."

Allie yanked open the panel and found an S-shaped hook.

"Hold your breath," Jerome instructed. "That thing you're holding is a handle, a crank, okay? Place the bumpy end of it into this hole beside the elevator doors and start turning it counterclockwise."

Allie did as she was told and, with great effort, the elevator doors slowly opened—at first just an inch, then a few inches, and then she exposed the top half of the fifth floor and bottom half of the sixth floor, as well as the hefty steel joists between them.

"The car's nearly filled with gas," Jerome said. "Don't breathe, girl. Don't breathe till we're outta here."

When the crack was wide enough, Jerome extended his claws and wedged them into the gap between the second set of elevator doors— the safety doors—leading to the fifth-floor lobby. Slowly, he separated them and leapt down. Limping, he said, "Now you."

Allie, whose lungs were burning, snapped a quick sip of air, leaned forward, and felt her body go limp. Like a rubbery sack of blood pudding, she tumbled forward, her muscles indifferent to her commands. A graceless bird, she landed smack on her injured shoulder.

Standing over her, Jerome said, "Don't you worry. It's nothing. You breathed in some gas, that's all. Just take long, slow breaths. Long, slow breaths. Ah . . . isn't real air nice?"

Shortly, Allie felt her arms and legs respond to rudimentary instructions. She sat up, her healed bullet-wound aching madly.

Jerome pursed his black cat lips. "Good. Good. Now, my dear girl, you and I are going to vamoose." He glided over to the edge of the lobby and gazed down a long corridor.

Allie said, "Jerome, I'm . . . I'm just . . . maybe a little fuzzy."

"It's the gas wearing off. It induces temporary paralysis."

She nodded.

"Lean on me," he said.

Allie did, and together they made their way along the shadowy passages, past shabby, dilapidated, and garishly colored apartment doors that led to places Allie believed she had cleaned at least once, if not twice, in the previous few months. "You . . . you think they're still chasing us?"

"Oh, yeah. Tell me, dear, would it surprise you if I said Oda really, really wants you dead?"

For some reason, Jerome's question made her snicker. "How could it be?"

"How could it it be?" Jerome repeated humorously.

Together, they searched for the last few flights of The Greaser's rickety fire escape and stairwell, which seemed to have changed locations. It was nowhere to be found. After nearly half an hour, Allie said, "Jerome, somewhere around here there's an apartment with a hole in the floor. I know because I was in it when it collapsed. I've cleaned it twice since. We could maybe jump down to the fourth floor from there."

"You remember the apartment's number?"

Normally, she did, but her mind was scrambled by the day's events, making details of any sort seem completely unattainable. "I forget. My head's a big mess."

"Then we still have to find the stairs. Can you run yet?"

"I think."

"We need to," he told her, and he started loping painfully in that way that's unique to cats with injured paws.

Feeling clumsy, Allie followed behind.

The two navigated a labyrinth of ugly halls, randomly taking corners and picking likely and unlikely directions out of desperation. Beside Allie, Jerome suddenly slowed. He seemed to hear something she couldn't and adjusted the furry points of his ears as if they were sensitive antennas searching for reception. Allie focused intently on his cautious movements, curious at the way his shoulder bones seemed to rise behind his neck. He tiptoed along—if an animal with paws can tiptoe—his chin nearly touching the threadbare carpeting.

All at once, a wall sconce inexplicably swung loose and struck Allie hard in the nose. "Ouch!" she said.

Before Jerome could hush her, two huge men stormed from the shadows of a broom closet and slammed against him, wrapping their bulky arms about his torso and chest and pounding at his muscular body with fists, elbows, knees, and an expensive looking umbrella, which one of the men waved about like a harpoon.

Allie staggered backwards, desperately wondering what to do.

✻ 13 ✻

Allie blinked. The men, like all of the other individuals whose arrival had coincided with Marvin and Herman's, were dressed in fine, old-timey outfits, a stylistic statement that seemed incongruous with the way they brawled. No matter. Allie staggered forward and slapped as hard as she could at one man's snazzy checkered pants.

Without looking, the guy twisted his rock-hard shoulders and struck Allie with the back of his hand.

Off balance, she tottered away, holding her jaw.

"Run!" Jerome gasped as the man with the umbrella slugged at his underside while the other, the one who'd hit Allie, scrabbled and toiled his way atop the handsome cat-monster's wide back. So situated, he pretzeled a muscular arm beneath Jerome's front legs, at which point he began applying pressure so that the cat's head bent toward the floor in painful, agonizing submission.

"Run," Jerome groaned, his eyes bulging against his lids and his injury-weakened body trembling with effort.

Allie wasn't about to leave him. He was one of her best and most loyal friends in the world, and she would never forget that.

J. Scott Fuqua

With a terrific shout, the man atop Jerome rose and wrestled the massive cat in both arms. On cue, the other fellow nimbly tumbled away and rose off the hallway floor. In a single motion, he checked the tip of his umbrella, which squirted some sort of medication or poison, and cocked back his arm to strike the big tabby's exposed belly.

Allie yelled, "Don't you dare!" And her voice, as if amplified, shook the floor while a flash of piercing white light illuminated the dark, dank, and slightly off-kilter passage. Instantly, a thick dark shadow slammed the umbrella man into the wall with such force that the unconventional weapon's thin metal framework snapped in three while its black fabric shredded as if torn into strips of confetti. All of it landed atop the man's unconscious, injured form.

A heartbeat later, Allie's energy changed direction like a flying carpet knitted of translucent filament. It came down hard against the man holding Jerome at bay. As if struck by a long-haul rig, the guy

was launched backwards, his pocket watch popping from his vest and his bowler hat somersaulting from his head. Allie didn't stop. She was furious and wanted to inflict the same pain and mortification the man had exacted upon her friend. Twitching her fingers, she snatched the guy up and slammed him effortlessly against the ceiling, where he stayed, his clothes starting to smoke and his skin turning an uncomfortable, worrisome red. Glowering at him, she pressed the air from his lungs.

Jerome got up with a heave, his tongue dangling from his sharp, toothy mouth, his fur disheveled. "Dear," he said softly, "that's enough. Don't kill the fool. You are not that way. It runs contrary to your nature."

But he had no idea what her nature was. Until that moment, it seemed that she herself had never known, either.

"Allie," Jerome said, "please."

Above, the man's face appeared perilously purple, like someone choking to death on a wad of meat.

"You aren't this way. I know!"

"But I am!" she said.

"You're a good person," Jerome told her forcefully. "You are a good and kind young girl."

Allie considered this. She didn't feel like a good person. In fact, the idea that she had been *good* made her feel somewhat unpleasant, almost nauseated. In retrospect, she disliked her old self and the way

J. Scott Fuqua

she'd allowed people to kick her around. Moreover, she never wanted to be that way again.

As if she was leaning into a tornado-like wind, Allie's grimy hair slapped back against her thin face and neck in response to the awesome power discharging from her. It was a curious sensation, but one she enjoyed. And for her, enjoyment had been most rare. Over the last nine years, she'd hardly enjoyed anything aside from Jerome and Midge's company.

Her anger wavered. If not for a few caring individuals, she would hardly have experienced any pleasure at all. She thought of Midge, Arnold (in his better days), and Rena, whom she hardly knew but felt great pity for. She thought of her mother and father's long-ago touch. And always there was Jerome. He'd watched over her for years. He'd told her jokes and explained weekly events transpiring in the outside world, like wars, presidents, and popular movies. Allie trusted him more than anyone else.

She dropped the man to the floor. "Okay," she said.

The guy looked as if he'd spent far too many hours on a tanning bed.

Allie stood above him and, as her anger diminished, so did her energy, which seemed to have materialized from, and was retreating back into, a series of tiny trapdoors located somewhere beneath her chipped nails. When the power was gone, it felt, once more, as if it had never existed. It felt, Allie realized, completely alien to her—a mystery, if not an invention of her stressed brain.

She pointed. "I . . . I did this to him?"

"Yes."

She looked at the cat.

"You're a complicated person," Jerome said. "But aren't we all? Except I'm a cat." He indicated the unconscious umbrella-man.

"When you threw the twerp, his body punched a nice peephole through the plaster. Did you see what's inside?"

Hesitant, Allie took a look and smiled. "It's the room I told you about. The floor's missing."

"Collapsed. We found it." Jerome slammed against the apartment's door, eventually caving it inward. The two dashed through, and Allie clambered onto Jerome's shoulders and rode him down through the chasm to the fourth floor, where he landed with a pained grunt, mumbling profanities beneath his breath. When Allie climbed off, he proceeded to limp around the small dining room, his paw clearly bothering him. Every step Jerome took, no matter how light, seemed to leave a large red print in its wake. Out in the hallway, the posse ran past.

"They're everywhere," Jerome whispered to Allie, shaking his head. "Those creeps are all over the place."

Unable to supply any sort of hopeful response, Allie gnawed at her lip.

"So we have no choice but to exit the building from here."

"Here?" Allie said. "You told me you could maybe jump from the third floor, not the fourth."

"Yup, that's what I said." Jerome limped over to a boarded window and worked a claw beneath a seam of water-stained plyboard. Pulling at it, he ripped the panel loose on an edge, allowing a triangular prism of light to illuminate the room and create a long yellow streak across black and white linoleum tiles so dirty they appeared brown. Using his mouth, he pried off the rest of the board, which popped and splintered.

Allie, trying not to be heard, placed the board softly against a chalky wall. Jerome boosted his front paws onto the rotten sill and looked down at the grimy Baltimore streets, garbage twirling in a coil of wind that followed the passage of a long, rectangular city bus.

J. Scott Fuqua

"Is it far?"

"Oh, yeah."

"Can we make it?"

"I guess."

Distant footsteps reverberated down through the large hole above, and both Allie and Jerome realized that someone was about to find the two men Allie had worked over.

"Follow me out," said Jerome. He moaned as he passed through the half-boarded window and padded inelegantly onto a narrow stone ledge. Years before, until neglect and Baltimore's fearsome elements had removed large sections, it had encircled the monstrous building.

Allie looked out the window and down at the distant pavement. Something in her head commenced to spinning. She ignored it, took a deep breath, and pulled herself through the window onto the brownstone ledge. Pressing hard against Greasy Blight's brick exterior, she followed a few feet behind Jerome, passing large indentures that housed other boarded windows and former public housing apartments and chemical storage units. At the distant corner of the building, looming as if it presented a deadly threat, was a grouping of enormous stone gargoyles. Each seemed to beckon them closer, as if they were looking for a meal to augment the various bones, one of which was a human skull on which they eternally gnawed.

Behind Allie, someone said, "Hello, Rat."

Allie steadied herself by grabbing a decorative coursing of brick. She looked back, and there was Scratch Friendly, poking his lopsided head through the window only moments before she'd stepped out of. The man was, unfortunately, smiling at her. His poor dental care, characterized by the broad brown stains encircling his incisors and the spongy white plaque piled up about the edge of his gums, always reminded Allie of the mouths of three gator-sized catfish she'd once boiled the boys and Oda for dinner.

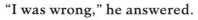

"Allie, ignore him," said Jerome. "You need to climb on my back so we can depart."

But she didn't move. "You . . . you can't make it from here," she said.

"I was wrong," he answered. "Now, slip on over and scamper aboard."

Scratch took out his big pistol and carefully screwed a long, skinny piece onto the end. "This here's a silencer, Rat. It's so if I gotta shoot ya two dead, nobody will hear nothing." He scrambled onto the ledge, tucked his large gun in the stretchy waistband of his purple designer leisure suit, and started along the ledge toward her.

"Get on my back, dear," said Jerome.

Allie stared at the pool of blood collecting about his injured paw. "You're so hurt, though."

"I'm hurt, but I'm not so hurt. It won't kill me. Now, please."

Somebody began tearing the boarded barrier from a window separating Allie and Jerome, while Scratch tottered ever closer, his lazy eye doing lazy things and his pig nose wet around the nostrils. The combination was all the motivation Allie required. She rushed across the ledge and slipped over the cat's rump, then scooted onto his shoulders. Beneath his fur, she could feel his entire body trembling. "You okay?"

"Yup," he said, waiting for something.

J. Scott Fuqua

She pressed herself against him and didn't glance down.

"Allie, hold tight to me and don't let go."

Somebody peeled the boarded apartment window beside them inward, and Lesion looked out. "Well, well, well, Rat. Looks like I done caught ya," he said. "Bet if I pinched your rear, ya wouldn't dare say nothin' mean ta me right now, not in the circumstance I got ya backed into."

She didn't answer.

"She's mine. Leave her ta me," said Scratch. Snickering, he raised his pistol.

Jerome leapt.

Off balance, Scratch let fly a few rounds, striking the sidewalk and a long-dead tree, its branches cluttered with plastic grocery bags far, far below.

❈ 14 ❈

Falling away and gaining velocity, Allie and Jerome appeared small and helpless as they whistled past the gargantuan, ramshackle exterior of the ancient hotel. On reaching the pavement below, they'd doubtless shatter like porcelain striking tile. In fact, they'd hit the pavement so hard that even experts in anatomy and physiology would be incapable of distinguishing between the various parts—like arms from legs, or heads from tail.

115

J. Scott Fuqua

Jerome, all herky-jerky and spastic, swept his uninjured paw sidewards, claws out. "Hold tight," he hissed to Allie, catching the plastic casing of an electrical wire that arched from a pole to The Greaser. His effort redirected their deadly course toward an oncoming transit bus.

Allie knew that they were about to die. She knew and winced even as she held tight.

Jerome closed his eyes and braced himself.

The air seemed to grow thin and cold about them.

First there was a sickening crunch. Immediate and painful deceleration followed, as if one of the Friendly boys had driven Allie and Jerome spear-like into a cement pillar. The bus's metal rooftop plunged inward as if struck by a comet soaring in from the outer

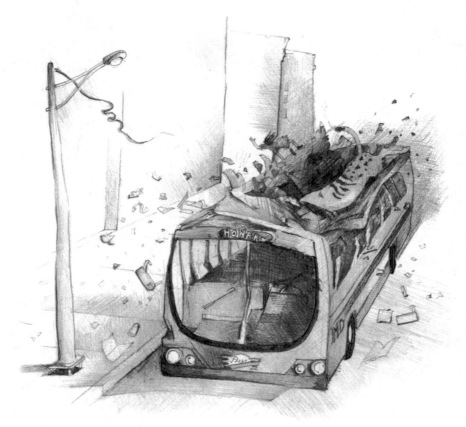

reaches of the solar system. In yielding that way, however, the terrible impact was significantly diminished, and Jerome found himself shoulder-deep in wreckage, his injured paw wonderfully numb.

Allie, meanwhile, bounced and skidded across the bus's slick roof. Spinning over the side, she reached back and barely caught a seam in the shiny metal with a single index finger. Dangling, she let go and fell to the pavement, just as a large Cadillac Eldorado screeched up alongside her. The car window rolled down and an old man poked his head out. "Allie," he said, "get in, child. Get in or they'll be on us."

She wobbled to a crouch.

Fur a mess, ears adjusted in odd directions, Jerome pounced down from the bus roof and dove toward the car's front window. In

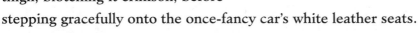

flight, his enormous body appeared to fold, to crease and bend and crease some more, until he was smaller than normal cat-size. That way, he passed right through the window and landed softly on the man's far thigh, blotching it crimson, before stepping gracefully onto the once-fancy car's white leather seats.

To Allie, he again commanded, "Get in!"

Allie yanked open the car door and fell into the backseat. At once, the old man behind the wheel of the Cadillac stomped the gas pedal, and they accelerated so fast Allie's door slammed shut on its own. She rose, her head aching terribly, and looked back to see an army of what appeared to be homeless people from both sides of the street tossing off blankets and giving chase.

J. Scott Fuqua

Jerome, who had unfolded back to his regular-cat dimensions, laughed. "Allie," he hooted, "we're out!" He rose and locked eyes with her. "We're out, baby!"

She felt numb and was hardly able to recollect the journey she'd just taken. She looked at her hands, then back at her friend. She blinked and coughed. "But how?"

"We jumped. You were there."

Jerome watched Greasy Blight vanish behind an ancient department store husk before he appeared to relax. Calmly, he pointed at the driver with his bloody paw. "This fine fellow, by the way, is Zachary Brion, professor emeritus at Johns Hopkins University, a silver medalist in the bow and arrow during the 1972 Olympics, an avid runner, a culinary genius, and a voracious reader of history. He is seventy-three, friendly, and quite funny, when he tries. His special interest is business history and ethics, which is important to know. And he is a very good friend of mine."

"Hello," the old man said, tossing her a grin.

Allie nodded but couldn't manage to formulate a greeting. She didn't even smile politely at the man. Instead, she leaned back. She was free of Oda Friendly, her repellent boys, and The Greaser Hotel's confining, crusty walls for the first time in nine years, and she hardly knew what to think except that her life and her identity were as much a mystery as how they'd broken free.

Meanwhile, Zachary Brion drove like a man unfamiliar with traffic laws, the big whitewall tires of his Eldorado tearing up Baltimore's rutted roadways. He took corners with the grace of a hippo, clipping curbs, roaring through pedestrian crossings, and running stop signs. After quite a few minutes, during which endless stone, brick, and glass buildings in varied states of repair and disrepair zoomed by, Zachary yanked the steering wheel hard to the right, and the car fishtailed into a filthy alley, where he hit the brakes like he was stopping a runaway train.

Allie, unfamiliar with riding in cars, was slammed into the back of the passenger seat, her meditation abruptly concluded.

Climbing out, Zachary said to her, "Sorry." He jogged to the trunk, where he located a battery-powered screw gun and proceeded to remove the car's license plates and install a set of new ones. Getting back into the car, he grinned at Allie once more, his neck shaped somewhat like one of the vulture sculptures on a chair in the corner of The Greaser dining room. It was the only slack part of the old man's amazingly fit body. "Can't be too careful when it comes to the Organization," he explained.

"What . . . organization?" Allie asked, adrenaline slurring her words.

"The Greaser Gristle Group."

Allie leaned forward. "Do . . . do you know Marvin?"

Zachary glanced at Jerome, whose injured paw seemed to be hurting again. He placed an arm on the back of the seat and looked

J. Scott Fuqua

deeply into Allie's eyes. "Yes, Malevolent Marvin. He is, my dear, the most unusual president and CEO of Greaser Consolidated Enterprises, and easily the most feared and vicious takeover artist and racketeer in this country's sad history of worker abuse, corporate greed, and outright corruption." Zachary removed his arm, turned about, and stomped on the gas. In response, the Eldorado accelerated through the alley as if fired from a cannon.

"I just met him the other day," said Allie.

"He's a mysterious fellow," Zachary commented.

They swerved back onto a primary road and, thrown off balance, Jerome nearly toppled. "Allie, see that strap on the seat beside you? It's called a seat belt," he said. "It's for holding you in place if we crash. Please wrap it about your waist and slide the flat part into that slit in the boxy part located on the seat beside you so that good old Zachary doesn't kill you unintentionally."

Allie remembered precisely what a seatbelt did and instantly put it to use.

They traveled north now, amongst myriad other vehicles. On both sides of the street were beautifully maintained brownstone townhouses occupied at street level by elegant shops of every conceivable sort and catering exclusively to Baltimore's wealthier citizens.

They hit a rough patch in the road, and the townhouses dropped away behind them. The car seemed to gather speed, bounding across a bumpy bridge located high above a six-lane highway that, in the golden glow of late afternoon, resembled a meandering lava flow. Off to the side, Allie caught sight of an impressive, low-slung building with a clock above its front entrance.

"Penn Station," Zachary said, pointing. "It's where the trains come in."

"Trains," she said, envisioning engines and freight cars from her youth. "I like trains."

The bridge disappeared, and ranks of pitched and cockeyed red-brick row houses claustrophobically close to the roadway took its place. These were the sort of dilapidated city residences that made Baltimore a well-known test tube for social scientists and urban planners studying once functional communities imploded by drugs, crime, and piles of garbage so prevalent that they resembled a new and assertive variety of tumbleweed.

City parks and vacant lots emerged and disappeared. Narrow alleyways exposed the grizzled backsides of rows that had been, during their one hundred years of difficult existence, retrofitted, rehabbed, and rebuilt by unskilled craftsmen, landlords, and homeowners with such a wide variety of proper, improper, and absurd products that to Allie they resembled, more than anything, distinct heaps of debris woven together below the bottom edge of a quilted blue sky.

Turning, Allie searched behind her. Broken glass, like jewels, twinkled in the street's concrete gutters, while the Eldorado's exhaust and loose tailpipe left the thinnest blue streak stretching out behind the car like a ghostly rope. She lifted her gaze to the crumbling, once-attractive rooflines, which she momentarily studied before noticing a frightening rectangular

smudge of a building looming over all of downtown. For some reason, dark birds appeared to be circling it—perhaps buzzards sizing up road kill. Fascinated and repulsed, Allie gazed at the disturbing structure as it drifted in and out from behind trees before she realized that that place had been her home and prison.

Turning back around, Allie saw that they were now cruising through a well-kept neighborhood of three-story row houses of every shape and color. She stared out the car windows at the spacious front porches and hordes of dog-walkers, commuters, and pedestrians making their way in the late afternoon light. Then they departed the community and ripped past a large hospital compound. Veering left, they zoomed along a broad thoroughfare with wide lawns and tall, beautiful apartment towers of the sort that made Allie's former residence look like an ill-conceived stack of brick and stone. To her left, she could feel Greasy Blight's enormous presence following them like a full moon. She tried to ignore it.

They passed behind an expanse of woods and mansions, made a right turn, and entered into a gracious little neighborhood of colonial townhouses. They drifted along slowly before turning down a potholed, narrow alley that felt more like a trail. Then Zachary slowed the car to a crawl and gently tucked it into the open mouth of a small garage and parked.

Zachary yanked the key from the Cadillac's ignition, pressed a plastic box clipped to the driver's-side sun visor, and the garage door slowly closed behind them. Climbing from the car, he said, "Allie, on the other side of this is my home, where I want you to make yourself comfortable. There's Coca-Cola and food in the refrigerator, wine in the cabinet beside the stove, and a bed on the third floor with your own private bathroom and fresh towels. Also, my dear, per Jerome's instructions, I purchased you some new clothes."

"Zachary, where have you been for the last seventy years?" said Jerome. "She can't have wine. She's just a kid."

"Oh, sorry. Allie, don't drink the wine, please."

"Okay . . ." she answered. She hesitantly got out of the car. "Sir, can I ask you something?"

"Of course." Zachary moved forward and opened a door located near the front bumper. He started briskly across a nice little yard toward the rear entry of his house.

Allie chased after him. "Where are we, and who are you again?"

"I told you, dear," said Jerome, limping at Allie's heels, "he's Zachary Brion, a professor emeritus in Johns Hopkins University's business department, and a friend." Zachary stopped. He turned around. He had two large purple numbers on the front of his shirt, a pair of khaki pants belted to his slim waist, and new jogging shoes covering small feet. "Surely you have more questions than that," he said. "Am I correct?"

"Yeah, I guess, sir."

"And I really do want to take the time to answer as many as I can. In fact, I believe that I might be able to furnish you with quite a few

J. Scott Fuqua

helpful details about your life—even as many of my responses will, sadly, generate more and greater mysteries. Perhaps Jerome can further enlighten us on those subjects; I don't know. But first, Allie, I suspect that you'd like a shower and a change of clothes before we begin any discussions."

Not wanting to contradict him, she shrugged. The truth was, however, that she was willing to put off bathing in order to get a few answers. She'd already put it off for nine years or so. "Well, can you at least tell me where we are?"

Zachary rubbed his chin and put his hands in the pockets of his wrinkled trousers. "We are in Roland Park, just off of University Parkway."

"There now," Jerome said, "that should explain everything, sweetheart."

Zachary briskly started up the backdoor steps and stopped. He rubbed his chin and pointed at her. "While you wash up, Allie, I'll make us a bite to eat. Would you like that?"

"Ah . . . I guess," she told him, her stomach achy and hollow. She was terribly unfamiliar with being treated with any consideration at all, much less being served a home-cooked meal. "Thanks, sir."

"Zachary," he said. "Call me Zachary."

After her shower, Allie sat drowsily atop a checkered blanket on a tall, four-poster bed. She looked through a window and down onto a number of backyards, where flowers were in bloom and elegant stretches of grass seemed an impossible shade of green. Shrubs of all sorts decorated the ground, while variegated ivy embraced the thick trunk of tall pine trees and even covered the sides of a few of the white, wooden garages situated behind each home, the nearest of which housed and hid Zachary Brion's Cadillac Eldorado getaway car.

Turning and studying the items on the dresser in front of her, she found herself bewildered. There was a plastic item called "Secret Deodorant," a little tin of something labeled "lip balm" (like the explosive, she figured), as well as a tube of "hair gel," which sounded to Allie like a type of food the Friendlys would eat for dinner or dessert. Allie even tasted a little bit of it but found it a disgusting flavor.

After placing her filthy dress and boots in a corner, she slid into an old-fashioned pair of white, polyester slacks, some brown leather shoes that stayed put without laces, and a wide-collared shirt of the type that matrons might wear to work in a garden. To her, they felt wonderful, as did her hair, which, after nine years of neglect, was satisfyingly clean and partway untangled. She'd scrubbed it with soap three separate times before experimenting with shampoo, which she hadn't seen in years. The soaps reminded her of a detergent she'd used on The Greaser's worn hallway carpets. The shampoo had done the job, though. Her hair shined and smelled like flowers. It even curled delicately around her shoulders, so that when she looked in the mirror, she felt, for the first time, like she might actually be attractive. That was nice.

Once more, she looked outside at the yards and tall trees. She smiled and allowed her feet to dangle off the edge of the bed as the window darkened. She felt so peaceful that she actually jumped when there was a knock at her door.

"Yes?"

"It's Zachary. Are you decent? Might I come in?"

Nervous, Allie stood up to appear alert. "Yes, sir."

The door opened, and there was the old man. Short with white hair, he gave her a wide, kindly smile, like a grandparent looking at a granddaughter. He hesitated before saying, "My . . . Allie, you are indeed a lovely young woman. Jerome was absolutely right."

She blushed. "Ah . . . thank you, sir." Nervous, she clasped her hands together so that the muscles in her forearms, made sinewy by perpetual labor, tightened and loosened dramatically. "Um, did I do something wrong, sir? Is that why you're here?"

"No, of course not. Unless you burn the house down, back up the plumbing, or, God forbid, contact Marvin Greaser or Herman Gristle, you are a wonderful guest."

She found it strange that he thought of her as the type who might burn down a house or mess up the plumbing.

Zachary scratched his nose and indicated the room. "Is everything in here suitable to your needs? May I get you anything?"

She glanced around politely. "No . . . it's all wonderful, sir."

He nodded. "Don't call me *sir*, please. My name's Zachary."

"Okay."

"Good."

"Ah . . . Zachary?"

"Yes?"

"Where's Jerome?"

"Downstairs. He's in a good deal of pain. A good deal. Later tonight, I believe I am going to have to take him to the twenty-four-hour pet hospital on Falls Road. He tore up his paw pretty badly."

"Yeah." Allie looked down again and wondered at something he had said. "So . . . ah . . . I have another question. Because you're taking him to the pet hospital, is he your pet? Did you send him to me a long time ago?"

"Jerome? No, of course not. He went and found you," said Zachary. "Jerome is his own man, even as a cat, and far too smart to be anyone's pet. The problem is, he's a cat. He needs a pet hospital despite the fact that, technically, he is not a pet."

Allie smiled. She'd never thought of him as a pet, either.

"Hungry?" Zachary asked.

Together, they descended the stairs, and Allie found the mere act of walking magnificent. She was used to the oily, thin fabric of her unwashed dress brushing against her knees and legs, her ankles chafing and blistering in her pointy work boots, and her steamy mat of hair plopped against her neck and shoulders like the wedge of a wet cloth. Now she felt unencumbered and free to move about wherever she wanted. The polyester of her pants even stretched.

J. Scott Fuqua

Downstairs, Jerome rested alongside an empty flower vase in a wooden box atop the polished dining room table. Beside him was a bowl containing something that resembled fish, as well as a saucer of milk. The paw he'd slashed open during their escape continued to bleed, though it had already improved considerably thanks to Zachary's care. Spotting Allie, Jerome raised his large cat-head.

"You feel okay?" she asked.

Jerome scrunched up his nose, shaped like a miniature police badge. "Well, no . . . not really. Paw hurts. Slashing up Oda's boys probably gave me an infection or something."

"Quit with the whining, cat," Zachary said, dismissing Jerome with a wave of the hand. He turned to Allie and winked at her. "He'll be all right, dear. He's got a large serving of smoked sockeye salmon, a dish of heavy cream, and a bit of catnip from the garden to douse the pain. He'll survive. We'll have him bandaged and sewn up properly tonight and, I expect, he'll be good as new in no time."

Jerome stuck his tongue out at him.

Zachary clapped his hands together. "Allie, tell me, what do you prefer: dry-cured beef marinated and grilled in a pepper sauce, with roasted garlic potatoes and marinated asparagus, or a simple selection of Mexican?"

Allie brushed her bouncy hair from a shoulder, an act that felt so wonderful she decided to do it again. Grinning sheepishly, she asked,

"What's Mexican?"

"Well, in fact, I cook Tex-Mex, not quite Mexican. Either way, it is a type of ethnic food noted for being spicy and flavorful, frequently combining the clean taste of peppers with the acidic tang of tomatoes and the smooth, elegant texture and flavor of cheddar cheese and sour cream. Oftentimes, it comes encased in a soft flour wrap or a hardened corn shell." He smiled. "Any preferences?"

"Well," she answered nervously, "I don't really like to see or touch meat so much. So . . ."

❦

For the first time in years, Allie's hunger was completely satisfied. She couldn't ever remember eating Mexican before that night, but she decided it was her favorite type of food (far better than oatmeal), and that she would eat it as often as possible. Of course, while Zachary was happy to encourage her to try all the different sauces and dishes he'd cooked, he also made her eat slowly and moderately so as to try and avoid making her sick. As he explained, a lot of spicy, rich food on an empty, unprepared, and generally malnourished stomach can sometimes be a recipe for gastric disaster.

She sipped a third glass of water and watched Zachary remove the dishes from the table and replace them with dusty canyons and plateaus of books and research materials that he had gathered together since his retirement nine years prior. He began paging through his antiquated books about business and businesses and Greaser Consolidated Enterprises, which had apparently been called Greaser Industries seventy years before. The old man turned a large book toward her and pointed at a black and white image amidst a field of ancient text. "Allie, do you recognize this man?"

She leaned forward, her eyes growing wide with surprise. "It looks like Marvin."

"Doesn't it?"

She touched the caption beneath the image. "It's Marvin Greaser the First, huh?"

"Looks a lot like Marvin the Third, though, doesn't it?" Zachary lowered the book. "Allie, I met Jerome eight years ago, shortly after your parents were tossed into jail for trying to kidnap Herman Gristle's boy, Godfrey. In an attempt at full disclosure, it was Jerome who brought the subject of Greaser Consolidated Enterprises to my attention. Without him, I wouldn't have thought to investigate the company, which is amazing, since it seems they've had their mitts in every successful and unsuccessful venture in this country's recent history."

He paused and sat back. "Now, let me start by asking *you* a question, Allie."

"Okay," said Allie.

"Do you find it strange that, of all the people in all the world, your parents had it in for little Godfrey Gristle, the firstborn child of Herman Gristle?"

She stared at him. "I guess they were just trying to kidnap a rich kid."

"Well then, why not pick someone a little more convenient? There are bankers and businessmen and millionaires and billionaires all over the East Coast. Why go all the way to Wyoming cattle country to nab a Gristle?"

Allie shrugged. "Maybe you should ask them."

Zachary snickered. "Did you know that Herman Gristle the Third, of Gristle Brand Meat Products, is Marvin Greaser the First's second son, making Godfrey his grandson?"

Allie tried to wrap her head around his comments. "I'm confused."

"Aren't we all?" blurted Jerome, who'd been hitting the catnip a little too hard.

"Therefore," said Zachary, raising his brows, "it seems somewhat coincidental that you were trapped and abused in The Greaser Hotel for nine years, considering that the grandfather of the child your father kidnapped owns the building."

"But I met Marvin, and he didn't seem mad about anything," said Allie. "He didn't even seem to care about what had happened to Godfrey."

"Didn't seem," Zachary said. "*Seem.*"

Allie sighed.

"Allie, the Gristles and The Greasers have worked hard to hide their familial relationship. What helps obscure the situation is that Herman and Marvin don't appear to the outside world to be related in any way."

"Why does it matter if they are?" she asked. "They're just two men."

"It's complicated. I'm telling you all of this because we'll come back to it shortly. Keep it in your head, though." He tapped a finger on the edge of the table. "Did you know that both men—Marvin and Herman—claim to be fifty years of age. A father and son the same age? How can that be?"

Allie recalled their features, and it was true—they did look the same age. It was sort of weird. Except maybe Marvin was so rich he used special skin products to look younger.

"They are strange, the father and his son," Zachary said. "Marvin is exceptionally—make that unbelievably—well-preserved. Then again, I was directed to investigate the two by, of all impossible things, a talking cat."

Allie blinked and waited a moment. "It's not normal for a cat to talk?"

"Not at all. He's the only talking cat I've ever known."

"I guess I used to wonder, but I stopped after a while. I haven't seen too many other cats in nine years."

"And you were so young and terribly in need of a friend." One of Zachary's hands grazed the stubble on his chin. "Do you even know why you were there?"

She sat forward. "Mostly, I . . . I thought it might have something to do with what my parents did. I thought I was sent there because they were so bad."

Zachary shook his head. "Why would anyone punish a person who had absolutely nothing to do with said atrocity? It's not lawful."

Allie answered, "Maybe the crime was that bad?"

"The punishments one receives for being bad are not, at least in this country, handed down generation to generation," Zachary stated.

Allie sat quietly for a minute before speaking. "I tried to escape, you know, Mr. Zachary. It seemed unfair that I was treated like that."

Zachary smiled kindly. He squinched his lips so that he looked as if he was going to spit into the air. He didn't. Instead, his mouth returned to normal, and he leveled his eyes on Allie. "There is a pile of circumstantial evidence that, to me, says there is something strange, if not very irregular, about Mr. Greaser and Mr. Gristle, their business empires, and their behavior over the past few decades."

Allie wasn't sure that it was all that strange, but, to be polite, she considered his words anyway.

Zachary, for his part, searched around the table before locating an ancient, leather-bound book recording the birth of newborns at the King James Hospital, an English-speaking healthcare facility in Hong Kong. On the book's broad spine, Allie read "1910 to 1915."

Zachary opened the volume to a page he'd marked, ran his finger down a column, and found, "'April 1911. Herman Gristle Greaser. Nine pounds, seven ounces. Nationality: American. Parents: Marvin and Escapel Greaser.'"

Then Zachary closed the book and picked up a folder. "Allie, please assay this photocopy of a newspaper clipping from *The Colonialist*, Hong Kong's largest English-language newspaper of the time." He held it up for Allie to see the headline: "Billionaire Industrialist Marvin Greaser and his Pregnant Wife, Escapel, Travel to East Asia for Business Prospects." Below was an image of Marvin and an expecting Escapel.

Zachary said, "Clearly, in 1911, Escapel and Marvin were expecting a baby, and apparently that baby was born in April," said Zachary. "He was named Herman Gristle Greaser."

Zachary placed the image back into its folder and retrieved a manila envelope from between two large tomes. He pulled out a series of pages. "I found this four years ago in Chicago's Office of Public Records and Name Changes." He pointed out that the year was 1931, then ran down a list of name changes, until he arrived at "Herman Gristle Greaser." The document said, *"Name changed to:* Herman Grouser Gristle the First. *Age:* 20. *Born:* Hong Kong. *Parents:* Marvin and Escapel."

Zachary smiled. He touched his long nose and pointed at Allie. "Now do you see? The man changed his last name from Greaser to Gristle in order to hide his relationship with Marvin."

Uncertain and overwhelmed, Allie didn't reply.

"I bet you're wondering what's going on here," Zachary said.

"Sort of." She looked at Jerome and realized he was asleep.

"Allie, I believe that Marvin and Herman are clearly working together—that both companies are feeding off the other," said Zachary. "I don't believe that they are the sons and grandsons of the founders of their businesses, either. Not at all. I have concluded, through research and extrapolation, that they are the very men who established their companies. In Marvin's case, that makes him 137 years old, while Herman, his son, is 102."

Allie blinked. "Sir, Marvin and Herman aren't that old. I just saw them."

"I grant you they don't look it. But I believe they are," said Zachary. "Of that, I am convinced, even if they both appear to be the same age."

★ 16 ★

"*Allie, think.* Why did you get incarcerated in that old hotel?."

Allie stared. "I told you. 'Cause of my parents."

Zachary put up a finger, indicating that she should consider his argument. "Allie, you have to ask yourself why. Why? And why Marvin Greaser's hotel? And why his employees? Why?" asked Zachary. "I'm not saying that I know, Allie. I don't. But that's not to say I don't partly understand why he incarcerated everyone else in the building. But why did he incarcerate you?"

"Incarcerated means locked up, right?" said Allie.

"Yes."

"Mr. Zachary, he wouldn't do it. He seemed . . . really nice. He actually gave me a soda to drink." She toyed with a clean lock of her hair. "I . . . I mean, maybe Mr. Gristle could have. Maybe he's still mad about Godfrey, even if he doesn't seem it."

Zachary stared at her. "It is indisputable that Mr. Greaser locked up Midge, Arnold, and Rena for reasons of business and probably pleasure. That much is perfectly clear. That was Marvin's work. See, Arnold Armstrong and Midge Darlington were once powerful people running powerful business empires.

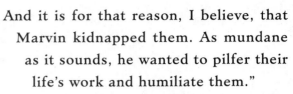

And it is for that reason, I believe, that Marvin kidnapped them. As mundane as it sounds, he wanted to pilfer their life's work and humiliate them."

Allie stared at the old man. "Why do you think that?"

"Allow me to explain. Before disappearing, Midge Darlington gave Marvin control of the entire Midge Media line—her homemaking magazines, books, radio shows, cosmetics, and television programming. All of it was swallowed up by Greaser Consolidated Enterprises for almost nothing. As it turns out, Midge didn't embezzle from Midge Media and run away, as everyone thought. No, she was secreted away to The Greaser Hotel. In a different, less personal manner, just before Arnold Armstrong vanished, his enormous frozen food empire was consumed by Gristle United Industries. And recently, Rena Duchamp's parents' grandly successful Du It! Software and Internet Systems! was purchased at pennies on the dollar by a subsidiary company of Greaser Consolidated Enterprises."

Zachary paused and rubbed his chin. "So, the fact that important businesspeople or their kin were taken off the street does make sense, though I have often wondered about the manner in which it was done. What you need to consider is your place in all of this. I mean, your mother and father were social workers."

Allie didn't hear his question. She was thinking about Midge, Arnold, and Rena, and worrying if they were okay. Maybe they were now being punished for her escape. She especially worried about Rena. What if, God forbid, Rena had been shot because of her?

The Secrets of the Greaser Hotel

She stopped short. She couldn't think that way. It was too terrible. "I don't think Marvin did that stuff."

"Kidnapped folks? No. He didn't personally do it," said Zachary. "He gave the orders, but the acts were carried out by his men—the very men you dealt with when escaping The Greaser. They do his bidding and dirty work. And they, too, have been given the gift of longevity. I've studied multitudes of images of Marvin in the late 1800s all of the way till now, and I've noticed that most of his bodyguards, including Oda and her boys, never change. They've never aged. So, I will give you that Marvin the Third might simply resemble Marvin the First, but it seems odd that everyone he's hired precisely resembles their parents, doesn't it?"

Allie recalled her elevator ride with Marvin's men. "I . . . I heard some guys talking about how The Greaser Hotel looked when it was first built."

As if stung on the butt by a hornet, Zachary straightened in his chair. "You actually overheard them reference their age?"

"They said The Greaser had been a first-class hotel way back when, and that they'd had good times in it."

"Really?" Zachary tilted forward and placed both veiny hands on the table. "Allie, my dear, what is going on here? Do you have any idea?"

"I don't. Until today, nobody told me anything."

Zachary pushed the research materials to the center of the table. He stood, smiled, and gently lifted the sleeping Jerome into his arms. "How about us taking this fine fellow to the vet?"

"I think we should," Allie said, yawning.

"I think it best that we avoid flaunting the Eldorado, at least for the next few days. We'll drive my wife's car," he said, scratching Jerome's head. He pointed toward the front of the house. "It's parked along the sidewalk." He picked his key chain out of a shallow bowl in the kitchen, and they wandered through the front door.

At the street, Zachary opened the passenger door to an old Plymouth Valiant and flipped the seat forward. He laid Jerome out across an ancient, vinyl bench seat and allowed Allie to ride up front.

"So, I guess you're married," Allie said.

"I was, yes. I was married for forty-three years. Just so happens, five years ago my wife died of cancer. It's just me now. Me and sometimes Jerome, depending on how long he stays."

"Sorry."

"Me too," Zachary said, starting the car, its engine reminding Allie of The Greaser's vibrating elevators.

"What was your wife's name?"

He revved the motor. "Stella," he said, punching a button on the dashboard that sent the auto surging forward into the street. Apparently, Zachary Brion always drove as if he was being chased.

✺ 17 ✺

Allie slept until nine the next morning, which she had never done before in all of her fifteen years of life. She woke not to someone pounding at the door, or a loud insult delivered by one of the filthy-mouthed Friendly boys, but to the idyllic cooing of doves from somewhere atop the mossy slate roof. A breeze fluttered lacy white curtains at her window like the hem of an elegant gown, and she gently pushed herself up and sat in the center of the four-poster bed, her back slightly sore from all the softness. Tucking her knees to her chin, she tried to come to terms with her sudden relocation from a dirty room and lobster-print curtain-sheets to a private space on the third floor of Zachary Brion's picturesque row house in Roland Park. In her gut, it felt wrong.

She climbed down from the tall bed and found herself facing a mirror above the dresser. Curious, she stepped closer. Raising a hand, she touched her cheeks. She ran a finger down her nose and across her lips and smooth jaw line. She was starved-looking, as well as sickeningly pale, but that would be alleviated with time and better care; soon there would be a healthy girl in the mirror. She inspected

her arms and found lean, stringy muscle from years of scrubbing toilets and clearing vermin droppings. Despite the malnutrition and physical abuse, she had strength, inside and out.

She wandered into the bathroom and brushed her teeth twice before starting a shower in which she washed her hair four times with shampoo and repeatedly scoured her body with a hard yellow bar of deodorant soap. Shortly thereafter, she dressed in a pair of plaid slacks, a pink polo shirt, and the same shoes as the night before. In the mirror, before going downstairs, she practiced flipping her hair over a shoulder.

On the first floor, Allie followed familiar voices to the front porch, where she found Jerome seated on a wide wooden rail, and Zachary with his back to her. The cat winked at Allie.

Zachary twisted about. "Good morning, Allie," he said.

"Good morning, sir . . . ah . . . Zachary."

"Call him Zach, sweetie," Jerome said, snickering. "Oh, he loves that."

"I think you're joking," said Allie.

"I am." Jerome actually smiled, which was strange. His incandescent eyes were like shimmering kerosene lantern wicks. They had a human cleverness to them.

Zachary scrunched his ribbon-thin lips and took a sip of his coffee. "Allie, what would you enjoy for breakfast this morning? Please allow me to make you something you've been craving—something nice for your first day of freedom."

Unfamiliar with such requests, it took her a while to say, "You know, I . . . I remember that I used to like how pancakes tasted."

"Why, of course. I will clean up from my run and rustle you up a combination of thick and thin pancakes. In the meantime, if you'd like, grab some coffee and shoot the breeze with this good-for-nothing friend of ours." Zachary stood and, laughing to himself, stepped inside.

Out on the roadway, a racy car rumbled past like a prowling gator. Allie watched it and whispered, "Should I be out here? You think Mrs. Friendly is looking for me?"

"Oh, without a doubt she is. But I think you're safe," said Jerome. "You're a needle in a haystack. How do you feel today?"

She thought for a second. "Better . . . even my shot arm. Better, but . . . wrong."

"I know. That feeling will probably linger. Sadly, I wish I could say I was feeling well—not that *I* was shot in the arm, or that *I* even have an arm for that matter. Just a wounded wheel."

She sat down in a chair and looked off toward the red brick houses and tall maple trees across the street. "So what do we do now, Jerome? Do you have a plan?"

Jerome studied her for a moment. Uncomfortable, he adjusted his sore paw beneath him. "This is something we have to decide. Personally, I'm in the dark. I fear our options are limited and our direction is set." He licked his cat lips. "I worry that Marvin has decided that you are a threat to him."

Allie scoffed.

"Allie, dear, you are powerful—powerful and volatile. You proved that yesterday during your escape."

She wiped a hand through her bouncy hair. "What's volatile mean?"

His few remaining eyebrow whiskers rose. "It suggests you've got a mean streak inside you," said Jerome. "For the most part, that's okay with him. Herman Gristle's surely got one, too—he's crueler than a hangman. In fact, he's the prototype of an executioner's executioner. But Herman is loyal to his own sloth, he's street-smart, and he's terrified of his father. Marvin knows these things and controls him with this knowledge."

Allie crossed her arms.

Jerome stood. He wavered and peered from the porch flooring of terracotta tiles to Allie and back. Finally, he said, "I'm embarrassed to ask for your help, dear. Heck, I'm mortified, but can you lift me down from here?"

Allie lifted him gently and placed him on the porch deck. Studying him, she said, "Are you magic?"

He turned. "What do you think? Of course I am. Cats don't talk, and most can't do what I did yesterday."

"Get big, you mean?"

He nodded. "Yup. And small. Now, do you mind opening this for me?" When Allie pulled the door back, he slinked in, stopped, and turned. "Allie, what we do next is a big question. We need to figure it out. We need to think hard. Do we run? What is best for

J. Scott Fuqua

you? You should start asking yourself what you're looking for in this life."

"Okay," she said, but in truth she didn't even know how to start doing something so large and directionless. It was like walking The Greaser's hallways in the dark without a flashlight. It seemed nearly impossible.

☙❧

After breakfast, Zachary put on some bifocals, quickly broke out more books, and began paging through a few as he spoke. Eyes down, head tilted, he appeared bookish and academic, though Allie didn't know either of those words. She said, "Were you really a famous bow and arrow person?"

Zachary said, "You mean, was I an archer? Did I take part in archery competitions?"

"I remember Jerome said you won an award for it."

"I won numerous medals, the biggest and most rewarding coming in the 1972 Olympics."

Allie gazed into the middle distance. It was strange to her that people had such complex lives, that a bookworm could also be an athlete. There was a richness to people that, during her imprisonment at The Greaser Hotel, she'd never known.

Zachary breathed deeply so that his chest swelled with air. "So, we ended the night asking ourselves who these people are, Allie," he said. "The unconstructive answer is, I don't know. Maybe Jerome will honor us with some information, but in all of these years, he's hardly been forthcoming."

"Mostly because I don't have anything helpful to provide," Jerome said.

The old man peeked over the frame of his reading glasses so that one part of his pupils looked the size of a pea, the other the size of a quarter. "No matter. I've been working diligently for half a decade to ascertain precisely what Marvin and Herman are trying to accomplish. Unfortunately, I see no pattern aside from devastation, greed, and power. Their many businesses are about creating enormous wealth for Marvin and Herman, even as they oppress families and ruin people's lives."

Jerome, seated on the table, said, "Wealth is often an end in itself, isn't it, Zachary?"

The professor emeritus rubbed his stubbly chin. "Yes, it's a powerful motivation. Most people equate the acquisition of wealth, no matter how it is accomplished, with comfort and happiness, hence the unethical nature of some, though not all, wealthy people. Many seek perpetual luxury, pleasure, and extreme power, which can feel like an opiate for them. I should add, though, that seldom, if ever, does money provide these two things. In most circumstances, it merely augments a contented individual. That loads of money confers a great blessing is a myth."

Allie struggled to stay attentive. Luxury and pleasure were subjects she could hardly imagine. In her own life, she'd never experienced luxury, while she'd lived good portions of it totally devoid of pleasure. Taking a deep breath, she looked from Jerome to Zachary. She rubbed her forehead, which she'd abraded on a hallway sconce while exiting The Greaser the day before. Now the spot was nearly invisible.

J. Scott Fuqua

Allie tapped her finger on the table, bit her bottom lip, and said, "Hey, you think, even though we're talking here, I might be able to get a soda?"

Zachary rested a large, open book on the table. He took off his glasses and placed them in the seam. "Thankfully, my dear, I have supplied the house with cola for your very arrival," he said.

Zachary hurried into the kitchen. Then, after a bit of rummaging, he returned, soda in hand. He indicated the books and photos on the table in front of Allie. "I know you've been away for a while, Allie, so I think I'd better explain a few things. Though people don't like to admit it, business and industry run the world. Both control enormous wealth. They create middle classes. They lift people from poverty. A decent company supports its employees with an income, and that income is spent by the employees on life's necessities, like houses, cars, and other such items, some of which might actually support the very industry they work for.

"If the employees have extra money, they will probably spend it on luxury goods, like electronics, music, and art. Then, maybe the musicians whose music the employees have purchased turn around and buy drills that our employees' business manufactures. Business is a symbiotic relationship requiring the accumulation of wealth by multiple parties. Do you see? Ours—the American system of commerce—is based on need, desire, and aspiration. It is called capitalism.

"In fact, it could be said that desire is the framework on which a capitalist economy like ours is based. Thankfully, that desire often translates into a common good. The entrepreneurship that

The Secrets of the Greaser Hotel

launches a company, which employs individuals, produces a ripple effect, which is a rise in the standard of living," said Zachary. "However, Greaser Consolidated and Gristle United do not seem to give back. They produce and sell goods, but they don't disperse their wealth. They are monetary black holes. Their capital stays in their coffers. Theirs is a parasitic capitalistic relationship that feeds off the working poor, the plight of other companies that they might have worked to destabilize, and a vast accumulation of capital that simply seems to vanish. Sure, they live well, but everything they use is loaned to them by the company and built for them by their underpaid, abused employees."

Allie nodded, her thoughts wandering.

"Both Greaser Consolidated and Gristle United treat their employees wretchedly," he said. "The companies always purchase thriving businesses at give-away prices because their founders or presidents suddenly disappear or die, and Greaser and Gristle then break up those companies for the worst reasons. They absorb their assets and tear out their souls, leaving shattered, useless shells. They are ungodly rich, unmercifully cruel, and astoundingly unethical— three very destabilizing traits."

Allie, who was only barely following, looked down at her drink, which was fizzing and popping like a chemistry project. She made a face. "Ah. . . Zachary, this soda is really weird."

"Cola is weird, yes. It is carbonated to create small bubbles that rise to the surface."

She nodded. "But this one is . . . well, stale or something. I don't know." She felt ashamed of the ungracious nature of her comment.

Zachary shrugged. "Hmm. Well, to be honest, it is a generic brand, which I assumed to be the equivalent of Coke."

Jerome, who'd been silent longer than Allie believed possible, exclaimed, "Generic? Zach! Come on, the girl's been away for years and you're going cheap?"

"I don't drink soda," the professor emeritus explained, shooting Jerome a knowing, annoyed look for using the nickname.

Jerome waved his injured paw. "Please. I don't either. But I can figure certain things out. I mean, is there a difference between salmon steaks and salted herring?"

Zachary smiled. "I see your point."

"I don't care," Allie said. "Really. This is good enough for me."

"My dear," Jerome said, "you put up with nothing but oatmeal for years. This isn't about what you can tolerate. In providing you with soda, we're not trying to sustain you, because sodas don't do that. We're trying to provide you with something that will help you relax and feel comfortable even as we explore the history of two very sorry companies. And that swill clearly isn't doing the trick."

Zachary said, "I can go out and get some of the real thing. I don't mind."

Jerome yawned, his black gums gleaming beneath his rows of shiny white teeth. He rubbed his good front paw across his brow like a person trying to massage away a headache. "Hmm. I got a wild idea. How 'bout you two wander up to the Pick-&-Grab and see if you can find something palatable there?"

"Is the Pick-&-Grab a store?" Allie asked.

"In the loosest sense of the word," Zachary replied.

Allie's eyes lit up. She hadn't been inside a store in nine years.

Zachary frowned. "Jerome, you do remember that she's being hunted?"

"She needs to get out, see the world. She needs to interact."

"At the Pick-&-Grab?" Zachary said.

"It'll be good for her . . . Besides, we can take precautions. We can disguise her."

Zachary stood up and walked to a window overlooking the backyard. "Seems an unnecessary risk to me."

"So was going to the vet for my paw, but we survived."

❧❧❧

A half hour later, Allie was wearing one of the late Stella Brion's powdery-white wigs, curls bouncing like springs atop her head. Grinning, Allie wove her left arm into Zachary's right arm and carefully descended the steps at the front of his rowhouse.

"Are you sure you're okay with this, Allie?" Zachary asked.

"I'm really sure," Allie replied, giddy and smiling with excitement.

Side by side, the two slowly made their way up the tree-lined street. Every few steps, Allie wobbled atop Stella's high-heel shoes, as if wearing them was substantially more difficult than riding a unicycle or walking on stilts. In fact, she couldn't understand why anyone would intentionally put high-heels on. It seemed like the sort of thing Mrs. Friendly would force someone to do in order to drive them to the edge of sanity.

A brushed aluminum cane, complete with four prongs at the bottom, afforded Allie some stability. However, she had to withdraw her free arm from Zachary's in order to poke nervously at her zirconia-studded

J. Scott Fuqua

cat-glasses or adjust the waistband of her polyester stretch pants (which were straining to contain a couch pillow), all of which gave her a frantic, off-kilter appearance. To top it all off, before leaving, Allie and Zachary had patted on an entire bottle of Stella Brion's old makeup. Therefore, Allie's cheeks appeared pasty, as if her features had been sculpted with putty. All in all, Allie looked to be a decrepit, overweight senior citizen suffering a unique combination of facial psoriasis and old-age vertigo.

It was a beautiful Baltimore day. There was nary a foul odor in the breeze, nor even a hint of diesel fuel or incinerated trash, both of which were oddly common in Baltimore. For Allie, being outside, walking, felt surprisingly complicated, like a huge gift and a gnawing curse. Her eyes, made up like an ode to raccoons, absorbed the inviting sunlight, which reflected brilliantly against row house windows and the shiny paint jobs on a couple of cars. At her feet, the interlaced shadows of tree branches vibrated across the skeletal remnants of fallen leaves. It was, to say the least, both amazing and guilt-inspiring.

Also, it was frightening. What if the wrong person saw through her disguise?

They passed across a busy street, exiting the calm of Zachary's community and entering its rough-and-tumble neighbor, where the Pick-&-Grab waited in the distance, tucked beneath a housing complex for the elderly that seemed to be leaning forward, like a pudgy man over a messy desk.

Noting the dilapidation, much like most of The Greaser Hotel, Allie thought of Midge, Arnold, and Rena once more. A wave of sadness, like a relentless sled dog, pulled her forward. She remembered Midge placing a blistered finger beneath Allie's chin and promising her that she would one day leave The Greaser—that she would one day know what the outside world felt like. God, how she missed Midge, the way she'd attempt to make Allie smile by spontaneously twirling like a dancer. The way she knew how to tap dance and sometimes did so when the boys weren't around. In the briefest of moments, the aging domesticity queen had extended her so much kindness. Once, Allie had found a note written atop the Formica of a crumbling kitchen counter. It read: "Somebody loves you, Allie, and that somebody is Midge!"

Somebody loves you.

"You know," Zachary said, at which point she realized he'd been talking to her in a harsh whisper for some time. "They certainly didn't kidnap you for money. No, they knew you were special. I believe they knew you could be a major threat or a powerful collaborator." He stepped around. "And so we've come full circle to the very place we ended last night and started this morning: Who are they, and who are you, Allie?"

Allie stumbled and caught herself with the rubber tips of her pronged cane. She peered upward at the leaning old folks home. She lowered her eyes and they landed on her dried and calloused knuckles. One thought occupied her mind: Midge, Arnold, and Rena would never know freedom unless someone gave it to them. They had to be saved.

Zachary stopped a few feet from the front door of the Pick-&-Grab. Unbeknownst to him, he stood in a semi-circle of cigarette butts. The number nineteen on the front of his shirt, which was actually a football jersey, flickered in the sunlight. "Allie," he said, "when we first met years ago, Jerome predicted that you would be gifted, and Marvin must believe that now. Jerome said that your father, whom I have never met, was also exceptional. So, if we acknowledge that you possess some sort of unseen gift and that Jerome possesses supernatural qualities, we are tangentially

acknowledging that there is a type of magic in the world.

"I believe Marvin and Herman's longevity and manipulative power to be impossible by almost any means other than sorcery." He leaned forward, causing Allie to stumble backwards. "I suggest to you that we are dealing with paranormal matters—that we, and most especially you, are mixed up in something greater than criminality and corporate corruption."

Allie could hardly reply, mostly because she really hadn't understood a majority of what he'd said. Confused, she croaked, "My toes feel jammed into the tips of these shoes."

Zachary smiled.

"This thing is also scratchy," Allie informed him, pushing her fingers beneath the edge of the wig and scratching her temple.

"Then let's hurry in and buy your soda so we can promptly get you home."

They pushed into the withered store and down the busy aisles, past all sorts of products, including, if Allie had looked closely,

Gristle Brand corned beef hash, as well as cans of the company's well-known spiced wieners, secretly made from horse meat and rat droppings. There was even a bag of Gristle Brand extra salty, "extra greasy" pork rinds of the type that put innocent snackers at great risk for a sudden coronary.

Allie, despite aching for her friends, was amazed by the quantity of food and drinks that the Pick-&-Grab sold. There were more food groups than she remembered or even imagined. What was a slushee, and what were Cheetos, pickles, and peanuts? Also, apparently, Mrs. Friendly had lied when she'd told Allie that oatmeal was the favorite food of the general populace, because Allie didn't see any of it on the shelves.

Zachary found a stack of dusty plastic bottles of Coke and grabbed two by their skinny necks. "I believe this is all we'll need," he said.

They passed back through the store, past the candies and electrical tapes and bottles of pills for upset stomachs. Allie's pronged cane squeaked with each unsteady step.

Then the door they'd entered swung open and a very large man walked in. He stopped and looked around. His expression—disdain mixed with hate—froze Allie. She was sure it was one of the men from The Greaser.

Zachary grasped Allie by the elbow and forced her forward. "Stay calm," he rasped into her ear.

The big man, his wide shoulders swaying, walked to the back of the store and fetched himself a black package of Greaser Brand Shredded Meat Jerky, a product so unhealthy

J. Scott Fuqua

that even the Friendlys refused to eat it.

Standing at the checkout counter, Zachary whispered to Allie, "Calm. Calm, child."

But Allie felt as if her heart was about to come out of her mouth. Her neck throbbed so hard that it felt as if her back teeth were moving.

Clearing his throat, Zachary straightened and smiled at the cashier, who didn't smile back or even make eye contact. Attempting to be polite, Zachary said, "How are you today?" as he handed her a ten-dollar bill.

The cashier jammed the bill into the register. Then she slowly counted out Zachary's change, as if each coin weighed somewhere in the neighborhood of thirty pounds.

"Ah, thanks," said Zachary, but the woman returned to watching a soap opera on a little television located beneath the cash register.

Allie glanced back at the large man as she passed through the door to the sidewalk. Outside, she started across the street alongside Zachary, who, upon reaching the far sidewalk, said, "Allie, he was just a big guy. Not all big guys work for Mr. Greaser or Gristle." He smiled oddly.

Zachary straightened and took a deep breath. "Allie, you know what I think?"

"No," she said, trying to calm her nerves.

Zachary tousled her wig, which caused it to shift on her head. "Allie, I think that you, Marvin, and Herman are magic. The three of you are . . . different, is what I'm saying."

Allie, stumbling, cane in hand, stared straight ahead, her mind a blank.

Zachary said, "Allie, I started my research with the hope of exposing corporate corruption of the type that, if left unaddressed, might cause people to lose faith in our economic system—capitalism—

and our government. I had hoped to see Marvin and Herman jailed. But if they are . . . *special people* . . . what then? And if we destroy their companies, will we cripple America's economy with a triumvirate of corporate scandal, job loss, and public withdrawal of money from the private sector?"

Zachary tightened his grip on the bag of Coca-Colas he was carrying. "No matter. Something must be done, because, as things now stand, they are bleeding this country and its economic engine dry. They gain power and influence daily. Therefore, we must try to understand how everything fits together."

Allie didn't want to say it, but she was tired of thinking about Mr. Greaser and Mr. Gristle.

"You, Allie Argos, are special," said Zachary. "And it is, for that reason, why Jerome believes, and I concur, that they seek to kill you or turn you to their cause. It will be one or the other—death or the devil."

18

That afternoon, cleaned up and dressed more appropriately for her age, Allie wandered into the backyard and sat in a wooden lawn chair with dark green paint flaking off the armrests. Seagulls and buzzards circled lazily above. She felt oddly uncomfortable, as if she was suffering some sort of low-grade anxiety from all of her new, unnatural freedom.

At the same time, it felt good not doing anything.

She walked to the edge of the yard and peeked around the garage, where the Eldorado, with its fake license plates, was hidden. She touched the side of the building and felt the rough texture of the small cement blocks used to build it. For some reason, it made her curious—curious to see and touch the outside world, to stroll beneath the huge trees once again, to walk past little kids playing games or the women pushing their infants in strollers.

She stepped over a partly collapsed chain-link fence and out into the alley which had evolved into a stretch of cracked and bumpy asphalt.

She walked down the alley and out into the neighborhood, with its tall and welcoming row homes. She smiled when she saw a handful of kids' toys in a backyard. She wondered how old someone had to be to give up riding in a toy car with a plastic roof.

Up and around the lane, she walked, onto a larger road sprayed with pebbles that led to a narrow, grassy park where, at the far end, babies sat in swings pushed rhythmically by their mothers or nannies. She watched them for a time and felt both sad and happy. She was sad because she missed her parents, but she was happy to see children just a few years younger than Rena enjoying themselves, smiling and running about without fear or something pressing to do.

She crossed a larger road, where cars burned past. Nervous, she looked for an opening and rushed to the far side of the street, forcing an ancient station wagon to stomp on its brakes to avoid flattening her.

Breathing hard, Allie walked down a trail past a church. She studied a handful of homes clustered on a low ridge to her left. They looked so traditional, so nice, that she imagined how she might live in one when she was older. Maybe she'd have a husband and kids and normalness, whatever that was.

She passed some steps and into a neighborhood canopied by towering, broad trees with black and gray bark of various textures. She touched a few and smiled. She didn't even know why. It just felt good to be outside and not wearing a weird costume, to walk freely beneath the thrilling blue sky, beneath the gulls and vultures forever circling.

She suddenly remembered how to skip. She had learned to do it in front of her old house. She gave it a shot but, somehow, her hips were too tight. She had to loosen them by swaying side to side for a few minutes before she started again, and then her skips looked normal. She skipped along a street, and an elderly lady planting flowers waved to her.

Allie waved back.

The woman, her neck saggy, squawked, "Guess what? I got that exact shirt in a closet somewheres."

J. Scott Fuqua

"I like it too!" Allie called and kept going.

She stopped somewhere deep in the neighborhood and gawked, amazed at a yard decorated with yellow flowers whose names she didn't know, and which she couldn't imagine even had names. The only flower name she knew was the red rose, because her father had once given her mother one for some event ages and lifetimes ago. She stared at the flowers and decided that she'd decorate her home with similar plants one day. She smiled and put her hands on her hips, which felt good for some reason, as if she was in charge of herself.

Above, the sun passed behind a dark gray cloud shaped like an anvil, throwing a shadow across the neighborhood with its older homes made of wood and brick, with its flagstone sidewalks and broad front porches and cats asleep on brightly colored furniture.

She waited for the shadow to pass, but it seemed to take forever. Worse, the darkness slowly and eerily altered everything. The area wasn't friendly anymore. There wasn't a single noise to be heard. The kids she'd noticed chattering in the distance were gone. In an instant, the dirty underside of gutters showed, the curling-off paint on the front of homes became obvious, and every home's yard appeared hard-packed and as solid as the brushed barrel of a pistol.

Then a crow dropped dead from the sky, landing beside her with a soft thud.

Allie studied it. She looked up, through a network of barricade-like branches so thick she could hardly see the seagulls and vultures, so that the cloud covering the sun was broken into tiny jagged fragments, as if she was looking through bars. By some means, she knew that Oda or one of the Friendly boys had thrown the bird at her. She'd been found.

She glanced from side to side and spotted something moving

behind a hedge, possibly someone taking aim at her with one of the old-fashioned hunting rifles she'd seen piled up in a small room beside the kitchen at The Greaser.

Nearly panicked, Allie exploded into a wild run. Swerving back and forth to make herself a difficult target, she angled away from the road and cut through a yard. Above her, a door slammed loudly, and she wondered if someone was rushing through the house to meet her in the backyard.

Changing her direction, she hurtled across the front lawn of the nearby home, leaping shrubs and jumping headlong over a birdbath. She tripped in a shallow hole and slammed to the ground. She got up and kept going.

A few feet ahead, a lair of birds exploded upwards in front of her, as if they somehow knew she was approaching or been scattered by a bullet. Ducking them, she raced between homes and through a backyard. She leapt a low fence and landed in an alleyway, where she slid on rocks and tumbled to the asphalt, scraping her elbow and tearing the knee of her pants.

As she ran, she told herself, over and over: "I'm not going to let them drag me back." She wouldn't wait on them again—wouldn't carry platters of fried, sautéed, boiled, broiled, raw, barbecued, salted, cured, grilled, smoked, or baked meat. She couldn't do it again—ever.

She ran past a crowd of young boys throwing a baseball. She zipped by women jogging. She outran an angry pit bull, his teeth snapping for her hip. Glancing back, she saw something or someone falling away behind her.

Rocks seemed to spring up, as if scattered by poorly aimed blasts.

So as not to lead anyone back to Zachary's house, she slid down into a ravine, ran across it, and clambered up the muddy bank on the far shore. She rushed through some woods and came out at a car-filled parking lot. She crouched, sprinted behind the cars, and circled a large building that housed students from a nearby college before she doubled back and dashed across the busy road she'd crossed earlier.

Time passed.

It was unsettling. The birds she was so familiar with, the ones that had always occupied the skies whenever she peered out, were gone. Out of breath and aching from effort, she ducked behind a wall of honeysuckles and between a fence, where she tried to calm herself. She wouldn't go back, she thought. She wouldn't go back. She could still see the place—could still imagine herself hauling a whopping horse shank onto a chopping block. For a moment, she felt dizzy. Her friends had never left. They couldn't run for their lives because their lives were ruled absolutely, without regard to joy or sorrow or even senility.

"You okay?"

Allie jerked about.

"Wow! You're edgy, huh?"

"Jerome," she said, locating the cat between the greenery. "I . . . I think they found me."

He nodded.

"They've been chasing me for like two miles."

He nodded again and sat.

"How . . . how did you find me?"

"I can find kung pao chicken in a dumpster from three miles away. I can certainly find a loved one who's wandered a few blocks, cause, even though you think you tramped a pawful of miles, you didn't. Also, to be honest, I followed you."

"You did?"

"Yeah. And . . . sweetie, there weren't any Friendlys anywhere. I'm not saying that you don't have a legitimate concern, but you made that stuff up in your head. They weren't there."

"They shot at me, though. I saw it."

He came forward and put his front paws, the bandage having fallen off the injured one, on one of her thighs. He got closer and

J. Scott Fuqua

looked her deep in the eyes. "It's called post-traumatic stress disorder, Allie. Survivors of horrible things experience it. Your mind made it up. What you lived through in The Greaser—it's no wonder you feel hunted. And, it's okay. You'll be okay. We can eventually get you some help. I promise."

"But . . . a crow fell dead beside me."

"That's happening more and more," said Jerome. "They're dropping like flies from something called the West Nile virus. It's carried by mosquitoes. Or maybe that bird had a simple heart attack. Who knows? But it wasn't the Friendlys, or I would've been busy." He showed her his claws, which, at his current size, weren't all that scary.

Jerome turned and studied a bumblebee flying from honeysuckle blossom to honeysuckle blossom. "I'm sorry," he said. He popped his head back around. "But the good news is, you're okay. And you seemed aglow walking about the neighborhood. You seemed happy and excited to be out and about. Warmed my heart to watch you. I'm telling you, it was good for this cat to see."

"It . . . it was nice . . . till I thought I was being chased." She frowned. "Now . . . I'm scared to leave."

"Don't be. There was a crowd of mothers, right over by the seesaw. They've been watching you run for your life and duck in here. Don't think you even saw them, but they saw you. What I mean is, you aren't really hiding from anyone when seven people know exactly where you went."

For some reason, she smiled. "I feel stupid now."

"You *feel*?" Jerome said.

☀ 19 ☀

Cook meat. Clean. Cook meat. Sleep. That had been Allie's world, and it would always be, it had seemed. Amidst its bleak rhythms, small relief had come in the form of secret conversations with Jerome and Midge and Arnold, before he'd lost his mind.

Could she actually be a happy person? If she was allowed to do anything she wanted, what would she do? Might she get a job other than cleaning? Might she make more friends? And what about her parents? They were locked up somewhere in the city.

Allie leaned forward and rested her head against a hand. She felt the sun warm her scalp and shoulders. She tried to imagine herself a mother, a secretary, a car-repair person, or a factory worker who made things. Would those jobs make her more cheerful than she had been in The Greaser? Other than clean, what did people do in life?

She searched across the lush yard and the beds of flowers that swayed at its boundaries. "Nothing will be okay," she whispered, "if my friends remain trapped with Oda and the boys."

J. Scott Fuqua

Allie stood. She studied the back of Zachary's row house. It was busy with wires and mortar and whitewood trim. Off in the distance, she heard the wail of a siren. Sometimes, while cleaning apartments on the lower floors of Greaser's Blight, she'd heard such sirens. Way back then, Jerome had told her that they were either fire engines or police cars trying to save people.

Police and fire fighters had meaningful jobs. She liked that about them. Maybe, she thought, she could get hired someday to be one of them. It seemed like a good way to spend her life.

That's how a sudden, perfect idea came to her. What would happen, she wondered, if she went inside and called the police on Oda and the boys? Police were paid to stop criminals. Maybe if she told them about Midge, Arnold, and Rena, they would storm Greaser's Blight and free them. It was their job.

Tears of relief filled Allie's eyes. She smiled and even laughed giddily. Why hadn't Jerome and Zachary thought of such a simple thing? She'd have to ask.

Excited, she scampered up the yard, took the steps two at a time, and threw open the back door. "Jerome! Zachary!" she called.

Zachary and Jerome both answered her from the dining room: "In here."

She rushed in, grinning at them. "I've got a good idea."

There was an awkward silence, then Jerome said, "What?" He sounded unconvinced.

She gave him a mischievous look. "Okay, smart cat, listen. Why don't we just call the police to go get Midge, Arnold, and Rena? They'll help, right? They have to. It's their job. Why didn't we think of that earlier? Huh?"

Jerome and Zachary's expressions turned slightly pained. Slowly, the cat rose and walked around a series of thick folders. He stopped and played with the edge of a piece of paper. "What a brilliant idea," he finally said. "Really, it's simple and brilliant. Unfortunately, we already thought of it about seven years ago."

Shocked, Allie dropped her hands to her side as if the muscles in her arms were suddenly clipped at the tendons.

"Sorry, but it's true. To put it bluntly, we can't phone the cops, dear. It'd be the surest way to get your friends killed, short of doing it yourself. As soon as you are off the phone, all evidence of Midge Darlington, Arnold Armstrong, and Rena Duchamp will be wiped from the face of the earth, including The Greaser Hotel. Marvin and Herman have quite a bit of influence with the municipal police, the FBI, the CIA, the IRS, and the Justice Department. It has been their habit to collect damaging information on public officials, to threaten their families, and to bribe, bribe, and bribe all the rest. They've done their work well."

Allie felt her stomach swell to the point of explosion. For years, she'd believed that the world outside of her crumbling prison operated on unbreakable rules and laws. Apparently, that wasn't the case. Apparently, laws and rules were as porous as the sponges she'd used to clean bathrooms and countertops. "We. . . we can't call anyone then?"

Jerome shook his head. "No, dear."

Allie leaned against the doorjamb between the kitchen and the dining room. She lowered her head, causing her shiny brown hair to bounce down around her cheeks. After a moment, she said, "What can we do then?"

"Keep you safe," Jerome said. "We need to keep you safe and away from danger so that you can come to terms with what happened over the last nine years and figure yourself out. That's my opinion."

"We think you should leave Baltimore, dear," said Zachary.

Slightly off balance, Allie looked at the floor. "I want to leave. I want to be safe. But I won't feel happy. I can't feel happy with the way Midge and Rena and Arnold are being treated. Midge—she is like my mother."

"But you had a mother," Jerome said.

"Midge and Arnold and Rena, they have to be free, too. I'm not running away without them. I'm not leaving. I'm going to save them."

"You can't," said Jerome.

"I'm gonna try, Jerome. I'm gonna try to get them free. You can watch me try, 'cause I will."

"Allie," he said patiently, "we almost didn't get out of there a few days ago. Remember? We dove off a fourth-floor ledge and landed on the roof of a bus. We certainly aren't going back—unless, of course, they're giving away tubs of precooked Gristle Brand Sunny Day Sausage. I got a weak spot for that, though, come to think of it, it made me sick last time I had it. So, I take it back. Nothing can make me go back to that hellacious hole in the sky."

She turned about. "But I have to. They're my friends. *Friends*. And I don't have any others but you and . . . " she indicated Zachary, ". . . I think Zachary."

Appearing hurt, Zachary declared, "Of course I'm your friend, Allie."

The big tabby was clearly speechless.

Allie didn't blink.

Finally, Jerome said, "You should know, they're not Marvin's only hostages. He's got a miserable, beaten-down collection of half-starved, half-crazy entrepreneurs and millionaire business-types stashed away in places all around the country. In this area alone, there are five rather famous and very secret patients up at the Sorrows State Psychiatric Hospital in Baltimore County. The place has been closed to patients for thirty years, but occupied for a portion of that time by Dr. Erasmus Blood and his miscreant, halitosis-stricken staff. Your friends aren't the only ones being detained and mistreated, and you can't save them all."

"I can't," Allie said, thrown by the news of more victims. "But . . . I can save my friends. I can try to."

Jerome winced. Taking a deep breath, he thought for a few long minutes before saying, "Allie, I'm not well enough to try anything now. You know that. It'll be a week or two before I am. Give me that amount of time to dissuade you, and if, in the end, you still want to die in the dirty bowels of The Greaser Hotel, well, then, we'll have at it."

She nodded.

"A week or two," he restated gruffly.

"Okay," she said.

Zachary made his feelings known by scoffing loudly.

20

For the next few days, Allie, Jerome, and Zachary spent their mornings relaxing, playing board games, watching television, or perusing online (an activity that absolutely amazed Allie). Sometimes they did all three at once. During the afternoons, they discussed Marvin Greaser, Herman Gristle, and their two monstrously mean and unfathomably huge conglomerates.

Thoughtfully, Zachary explained to Allie how each business deal Greaser Consolidated Enterprises and Gristle United Industries swung strengthened their collective power over industries of every type and function—from natural gas to pickled pig's knuckles, from heat-seeking missiles to porcelain toilets—until it became impossible not to concede that, combined, they commanded whole market segments, could make or break any and all state or national politicians, and dictated a majority of large business transactions conducted within the United States. Their control was frightening.

"Um . . . Zachary?" Allie finally said.

"Yes?" He was scratching at a hard-to-reach spot on his back.

"If they're so strong and so large, how come nobody but you figured it out? Can't other people do this type of stuff, too?"

"Not like our Zachary," Jerome said. "The guy worked at Johns Hopkins, only one of the best schools in the country. When it comes to the history and ethics of business, he's a genius."

Rubbing his shoulder against the back of a chair, Zachary blushed. "Please, Jerome, don't embarrass me," he said. "In fact, Allie, two years ago, a reporter for the *New York Times* newspaper pieced together the disparate relationships and events surrounding Greaser Consolidated and Gristle United. He had uncovered quite a paper trail of murder, coercion, blackmail, racketeering, and kidnapping, and he desired my historic perspective. The reporter and I spoke briefly, and it was his plan to publish a series of stories exposing collusion between the two powerhouses. Unfortunately, while he was finishing his exposé, he died."

"Died?" Allie asked.

"Dead as a doornail," Jerome said.

"Conveniently, the man choked to death in a hotel room," said Zachary. "Seems he'd gone out and purchased a frozen package of Gristle Brand Barbecued Chicken Wings to snack upon. Of course, he had nothing to cook the chicken with, what with being in a hotel room. A further misfortune is that, while three frozen wings effectively blocked his windpipe and killed him, his house in New Jersey was burned to the ground, along with all of his records and notes."

"They killed him?" Allie asked, horrified.

"Of course. And I can only guess that there have been others," Zachary said.

"Sure there have been," Jerome continued. "Why, just last fall, the business editor at *The Chicago Tribune* died at home as a result of slipping—*slipping*, I say—on a misplaced chunk of Gristle Brand Scrapple. I'd bet ten dollars he was working on a story about Marvin or Herman. Come on! Who in the world misplaces a slab of scrapple on their kitchen floor?"

"Yes, who?" Zachary said ruefully. "Simply stated, Allie, I delicately and quietly go about my research. I try not to tell anyone what I'm doing, because I don't want to get noticed. I have no desire to perish as a result of a Gristle Brand meat product."

Even though the idea was frightening, Allie smiled. "Me neither."

As the day progressed, Zachary spoke and Jerome listened, adding opinions and anecdotes like salt and pepper over a main dish. Meanwhile, Allie absentmindedly searched folders filled with all of the ancient photographs that Zachary had worked so long to collect.

It was on her third afternoon of discussions and explanations that she came across an ancient image of Oda Friendly herding cows at a Greaser Meat Works plant in Kansas City. Date: 1893.

Allie intently studied the glass daguerreotype photograph. "She really does look exactly the same."

Zachary wandered over and examined the ancient image. He touched it with a pinky. "Strange, isn't it? Herman's and Marvin's inner circle doesn't age. They simply don't."

Allie went through a few more pictures of Oda before coming across a handful of images of Herman Gristle, who appeared to be the same age as he was on the day she met him. She flipped past some of them (Herman giving a speech, Herman ushering in the Pinkerton security firm to break a strike, Herman screaming at a

The Secrets of the Greaser Hotel

woman) before recoiling at the sight of a man with his arm draped over one of Herman's shoulders.

Allie lifted the image almost to her nose and clearly saw that the man standing beside the Baron of Carrion was a slightly older fellow, notable for the acne scars across his jaw line. The tall guy grinned maliciously, providing balance to Herman's equally malicious frown. She turned the ancient black and white photo toward Jerome and Zachary and pointed at the man.

"This is my dad," she said, her voice quavering. "I remember. This . . . is him."

Zachary stepped forward. "Your father? But Gordon Argos was a social worker." He squatted down and looked at the fellow in the photograph. Snatching up a magnifying glass, he placed it to an eye and searched the picture intensely. "I . . ." he said. "I've . . . ah, seen this man quite often in a few older pictures, but I've never figured out who he is. You . . . you say this is Gordon? Your father, Allie? You're sure?"

"Yes."

Zachary straightened. He put the magnifying glass on the table and rubbed at his chin. "Well, doesn't that confuse everything? So who is your father, then?"

"Maybe he innocently worked for Herman?" said Jerome, staring down at the picture.

"Maybe," Zachary said. "But Gordon Argos clearly hasn't aged much either, has he, Allie?"

"No," Allie said softly. Her mind seemed to wander, then she added, "Marvin said he knew my dad once." Allie rubbed a hand through her soft hair, stopped, and yanked at it. She felt tears run down her face and, embarrassed, got up and walked out of the room, down the back steps, and across the lawn. She stopped beside the little garage and sat down hard in the grass.

J. Scott Fuqua

Dabbing at her eyes, she began to pound her heels into the ground. She wanted to have a regular life as a regular person. On television, she noticed that normal girls mostly spent their time dressing nicely, discussing their boyfriends, and shopping. Their lives were very different than hers. In commercials, people smiled while they mopped, fixed automobiles, and scrubbed tubs. They smiled when they did practically everything except have diarrhea, colds, or a fungus beneath their toenails. Seeing the way they went about their days actually made her jealous, because everyone seemed so happy but her.

Gazing off, she slammed the ground with her small fists. The grass around her knuckles withered and darkened as if scorched by burning gasoline. She didn't even notice.

A little while later, the back door to Zachary's house swung open and the professor called out, "Allie, you okay?"

She didn't look back at him.

Zachary seemed to take her lack of response as an invitation. He descended the stairs and walked down the center of the long yard. As he squatted alongside Allie, one of his knees crackled like a branch breaking. He massaged the area around his kneecap and said, "Oh, I just love it out here. I suppose you do, too?"

"It's nice."

"Stella used to call it our sanctuary. We'd have cocktails in the yard every Sunday evening, no matter the season, as long as it wasn't raining."

"Sounds nice."

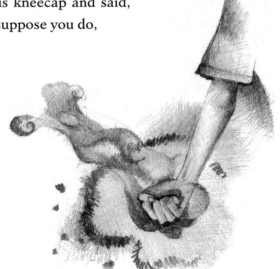

The Secrets of the Greaser Hotel

"I loved doing it, of course. Years ago, we'd haul a television out and watch Colts football games. More recently, we cheered on the Ravens."

Allie sniffled and wiped her eyes once more.

"You probably didn't hear me, but just a moment ago, I asked if you were doing okay. Are you?"

She shrugged. "Yeah . . . . Mostly I'm just confused and feeling stupid and hating everything." She didn't look over toward him. "I mean, I'm glad I'm free and living here with you and Jerome, but it's hard because I don't understand anything. I don't. I just know that seeing my father in that old picture means something awful. I know it." Allie slumped forward. "Mysteries are terrible."

The old man chuckled. "But real life is filled with them. It's full of vagueness and macro and micro decisions. Full. But you will get used to it all, Allie. Soon enough, if somebody doesn't give you options, you will wonder why."

Absently, she picked at the burned grass with her small fingers, lifted a few withered blades, and blew them beyond her shoes. "Are you against me saving my friends?"

Zachary sighed. "Yes, I suppose I am. Not because I don't think they deserve their freedom. It's just—I would hate for something to happen to either you or Jerome. It would devastate me."

He paused. "Then again, I understand. Take my wife, Stella, for instance. She was diagnosed with a brain tumor in May of 2000. It was inoperable, and it spread. By September, cancer had metastasized to her neck, her lungs, and almost every other organ, until it became clear that she would soon die. At that point, I never left the hospice unit she was in. I didn't want her to pass alone. And I've never been sad for a minute that I stayed. Sure, it was uncomfortable and depressing and, at one point, I even developed walking pneumonia, but I really had no choice. I needed to be with her, just as you, right now, need to go to your friends. Allie," he said, "I suppose you've got no choice in the matter, do you?"

"I do have a choice, though," she said.

"No. You need to endeavor to save your friends if you ever hope to be at peace with yourself," said Zachary.

"I don't understand what you mean sometimes."

"I know."

21

That night, Jerome instructed Allie to look through a clothing catalogue on the dining room table.

"Why?" she asked from the living room couch, where she was staring at a newspaper cartoon about a talking cat, which made her nervous since Zachary had said he'd never heard of such a thing until the day he'd met Jerome.

"Because you don't look normal," said Jerome. "You look like a teenager wearing out-of-date granny clothes. You need to blend into the environment just a little better than you currently do, okay?"

Zachary looked up from the glossy pages of his *Gourmet* magazine.

"Now, Allie," Jerome said, "would you choose some clothes? Zachary will be happy to pay for it all, right, Zachary?"

"Oh, yes. I can't wait. Now I know why cats—rather conveniently, I might add—don't possess pockets."

"Ingenious animals, are we not?"

Zachary fluffed his magazine and pointed at Allie. "Get whatever he thinks you need, dear. He knows the styles. But," he said, raising an admonishing finger, "don't allow him to buy a single item for himself."

"Nothing for him," Allie said, smiling.

"Great," said Jerome, "and I was dying for a thousand-pound bag of clumping cat litter."

"I bet," Zachary replied as he perused a recipe.

A few minutes later, Allie followed Jerome into the dining room, where she lifted him onto the table. Together, they went a few times through a clothing catalogue chockful of unsatisfied-looking girls and boys before, at last, Allie picked out a dress with a nice flower pattern on it.

"This is good," she said.

"That's it?" Jerome gave her a disapproving look.

"Yes."

"Allie, I want you to pick a *wardrobe*," said Jerome. "That means clothes for a week, not a day. Believe me, out in the real world, no person ever considers wearing the same dress for five days straight, much less nine years." He touched the magazine with his injured paw. "Love, please mark the items I tell you to."

She nodded, and found herself circling shirts, pants, skirts, shoes, a pair of laced boots, some socks, a heavy-duty belt, a baseball cap and, for no apparent reason, a cowboy scarf. When they were done, Allie said, "I can't wear all of that ever. It'd take years."

"It'll take a week," said Jerome.

Allie said, "Did you notice that one pair of pants I circled is already ripped around the knee?"

"Yes, sweetheart. Torn pants are cool, chic, hip, with-it, all the rage, phat, and fly. That's why I want you to get them."

Jerome gave Zachary their list, and the professor made a scene of trudging to the computer, filling in a few questions, and ordering the clothes. He chose "express mail" and closed his computer down. Turning, he said, "Your order, Allie, should arrive the day after tomorrow."

"Great," Jerome said.

That night, the bone-white moon illuminated the innumerable city row houses from South Baltimore to Pigtown, from downtown to Canton, and all of the way north to Loch Raven Village in Baltimore County. Meanwhile, Allie dreamed of her father, Gordon Argos.

In her dream, he wore a tee-shirt and carried an overlarge, fat-barreled pistol, as if he was Oda's brother or uncle. Inside the hostile hallways of The Greaser Hotel, he leveled his gun, like a small cannon, at her. Allie ran, and he madly chased after her, down the crumbling halls and stairwells.

Allie ran for nearly an hour. At last, she turned and yelled, "Why are you doing this?"

"Because I'm an evil man."

"But I'm your daughter!" she hollered, leaping over a growing wrinkle in the hallway carpet.

J. Scott Fuqua

He caught a toe on the wrinkle and stumbled, slowed, and stopped. "You are?"

At the intersection of two hallways, Allie faced him. "Yeah. And I haven't ever done anything to you, and I don't want anything from you. Nothing."

A look of confusion on his face, he lowered the pistol. "Dear, I'm sorry."

She bit her lip, hesitant to accept his apology.

Her father approached cautiously. Behind him, the brown walls seemed to dribble like water-soluble paints in a driving rainstorm. "I won't hurt you," he said breathily. "I'll never hurt you."

She didn't say a word.

"I won't. I didn't realize it was you, Allie. You've gotten older."

She put a hand to her mouth and felt her face warm with joy. "You're not really evil, are you?"

He laughed. "Whoever told you that?"

She wavered. "Well . . . you did, Dad. You did just a minute ago."

"Oh, well, in that case . . ." He raised his massive pistol. "Yeah, I am," he said, and shot her in the shoulder.

With a cry, Allie awoke. Beside her bed, the hallway door creaked open, and in bounded Jerome, limping only slightly. With a single sweeping glance, he searched the room. Satisfied Allie wasn't under attack, he peered over at her. "Ah . . . dear, why're you sleeping on the floor?"

She tucked the blanket around her pale feet. "Because the bed seemed too soft."

"Too soft?"

"I'm used to sleeping in hard places."

"Old habits," Jerome said darkly. "So, let me guess: You had a bad dream?"

"About my father," Allie said. "He was evil. Really evil." She sat and felt the floor press against her hip.

Jerome took a deep breath, came over, and sat atop her toes, which were hidden beneath the blanket. His tail bobbed like a molting snake behind him, and he cleared his throat. "You know, I've really got to ask you something that's been weighing on my mind."

"What?" she asked.

His demeanor appeared very stern. "It's about my breath. Is it bad? Unlike dog breath, you never hear people talking about cat breath, but I've got a wicked diet. I eat a lot of fish—some of it rotten—as well as the occasional bird and, well, sometimes garbage and mice. None of it will ever be mistaken for an after-dinner mint. So does my breath offend you as badly as the Friendlys' assorted mouth stenches offended us?"

Allie gently scooted her back to the wall. "I never noticed it was bad before."

"Good. Whew." He waited a second. A breeze fluttered the trees outside and slipped like invisible waves across the lacy bedroom curtains. Insects chirped loudly and a helicopter whined in the distance. "Your father would never hurt you. I know that. I've met him, and he has told me how much he loves you."

She scooted forward. "You've met my dad?"

"Yeah, I have."

Her hands trembled, so she stuck them under her arms. "Like, when . . . exactly?"

He studied the sloped ceiling and appeared to be counting. "Once, seven years ago, and I've spoken to him three other times since. I knew . . . I knew he was in some of those pictures."

179

J. Scott Fuqua

Jerome cleared his throat and raised his sinewy, fur-covered shoulders. "What I think about, when I think about him, Allie, is how much he loves you. He partway died for you once, and he'd do it again. He would.

"Of course, like all men, he's not simple. He's complex. And he struggles within himself, as we all do. Even us cats. But he's not a bad person. If that's him in that photo of Zach's, then there's a legitimate reason why he's there. Legitimate."

"He partway died for me?" she said, having missed the rest of his statement. She was under the impression that people never partway died.

"He needs to be the one to explain that to you."

"But I might never see him," Allie said, chewing on a fingernail. "He might never tell me."

"He will. Have faith."

She stared at the tabby. "Jerome?"

"Yeah?"

"Why didn't you tell me about the pictures?"

"Because you needed to see them for yourself."

"That's a weird answer," she said, unsure. "Also, Jerome, I have another question."

"Yeah?"

"Were you . . . ah . . . guarding my door?"

"I suppose so. Maybe."

"But I thought I was safe here."

"Just being cautious," the cat said.

"Cautious about what?"

"The things that people are cautious about. Closed doors, empty hallways, nighttime. People, not cats, are always scared of that sort of thing."

☀ 22 ☀

By the middle of the following week, Allie no longer dressed like an upstanding member of the Junior League; Jerome had gotten his stitches removed and was walking without a limp; and Zachary had pulled out a significant number of ancient photographs showing Gordon Argos, wearing fine clothes, glowering after a series of brutal industrial accidents, and seated at various dinners beside Malicious Marvin Greaser.

Studying them intently, Allie wondered about her father's place in Marvin Greaser's empire. Drawn to him, she slipped a tiny photograph of him into a pocket so she could secretly study his face in her room. But questions about him continued to absorb major portions of her waking thoughts. Was he a criminal, too? Was he actually as bad as Herman and Marvin? Had he ever really loved her, or anyone, for that matter?

J. Scott Fuqua

The bulk of her remaining brain space was taken up by two other issues, the first being her mother. Zachary had gone through his entire collection of images twice and hadn't located one of Melinda Argos in the entire lot.

The second matter of great concern to Allie was the fate of her friends. She fretted about their health, and worried they were being punished for her escape. Worse, she feared that Rena was dead. That fear was growing daily, too—that Rena, on the day of Allie's escape, had been shot to death.

It was dark out. It was late, somewhere a little past midnight. Behind her door, Allie could hear Zachary breathing regularly. While Jerome was off running what he'd referred to as "important errands," Zach was guarding Allie.

"What kind of 'important errands' do cats traditionally run?" Zachary had asked.

"Hmm. Let me see," said Jerome. "I'll probably survey the dumpsters outside the Broad Street Fish Market, check the Cloverleaf Dairy for spilled milk, search the waterfront for unsuspecting seagulls, or maybe I'll just go spy on the comings and goings at The Greaser Hotel."

"Oh." Zach took a sip of wine. "That last one does seem rather pressing." Before eight the night before, Jerome had exited the back door of Zachary's home and vanished into the shadows, where he tumbled across the lineup of fenced yards. Hours had passed and Allie sat awake. Nervous, she focused solely on the sounds of the house. There was a sudden crack, like something very solid had struck the hallway floor. She figured it was Zachary putting something down. So she listened to the distant call of police sirens, the honk of geese heading southward, and the phony laughter of a television sitcom blaring out of someone's open window. The noises seemed innocent and oddly pleasant to Allie. It was difficult for her to believe that, at that moment, she was likely being hunted.

Growing anxious, she got up from the floor and removed the picture of her father from between the bed's mattress and box springs. She gazed at it for a while before putting it down and wandering to the window that overlooked the flowerbeds and garages. She studied the silhouettes of willowy treetops as they moved like green static, the blinking lights of passenger jets roving across the velvet sky one after the other, and all the stars (there weren't many) visible in the well-lit night.

She had experienced hundreds of restless evenings at The Greaser during which she'd longed for someone to talk to. Now, having left that crumbling prison and former public housing project, she still yearned for company. Leaning against the windowsill, she peered into its dusty corners. She tested the strength of a small cobweb and watched a tiny spider adjust its position, as if she'd annoyed it.

"Hi, little lady," Allie said, but it didn't appear to hear her. She looked beyond the window screen and wondered where Jerome might be. She hoped he was safe. The environment outside The Greaser was much more welcoming than the world inside, but it was also unpredictable. Cars, trucks, and bikes zoomed past without warning. People slammed windows shut without checking them for occupants; others slammed car doors, lit grills, and threw rocks. She figured that getting crunched between two hard objects, or kicked viciously were dangers that always existed for pet-sized animals, but none of them approached the brutality Jerome would experience if the Friendlys got their hands on him.

Upset, she spun around and stared at the door to the hallway and stairs. She crossed the floor, twisted the knob, and stepped out.

Zachary was sound asleep in a chair. A rusty shotgun had fallen from his lap to the floor of the landing. The barrel pointed at one of his shoed feet. His mouth was open and his dry, pink tongue draped like loose carpeting across the unorganized icebergs of his yellowing teeth.

Allie carefully surveyed the hallway. The walls threw knife-sharp shadows across the floorboards. The windows appeared accented with reflected light. She peered hard into the dusky, violet front yard, where she knew hedges with reddish leaves partially blocked the view from the road.

She searched the darkness.

Downstairs, something popped loudly, as if someone had attempted a soft step on a creaky floor. She stood up straight. She waited, her ears straining, searching the silence for one more secretive footfall. And it came, slightly louder, more obvious.

"Zachary," she hissed. "Zachary?" She shook his shoulder.

He opened his eyes slowly and cleared his throat. He wiggled to an upright position in his chair. "Allie?" he said.

She put a finger to her mouth.

Confused, he mouthed, "What?"

She pointed to the steps. "Someone," she hissed, "is looking around."

He lifted his gun. "It doesn't shoot," he said quietly. He stood stock-still and listened.

"Did you hear that?" Allie asked.

"No."

"There's someone in your home," she said quietly. She had a sense of familiarity, and knew it was the Friendlys, as if she had the ability to perceive their proximity after so many years in their horrendous company. Possibly it was their breath, wafting on air currents before them, polluting every space they entered.

"Allie?" Zachary said, puzzled.

She stiffened. This time she wasn't going to run, not like the other day, when they'd chased her from the neighborhood. Not so many days back, but a lifetime ago, she had held her own against them with nothing but a canister of Bon Ami cleanser. Before that, she had, somehow, made Oda pay for shooting her. If she maintained her composure, she could be formidable. This time, she wasn't going to disintegrate like wet plaster because they menaced her. They weren't unstoppable.

They weren't even in The Greaser anymore. They didn't have the hotel to help them.

She glanced at Zachary, smiled, and slipped down the steps. Near the bottom, she missed a tread and pinwheeled into the living room, mashing her knees and elbows. Standing, she scanned the darkness, furious at the Friendlys, irate at the world. She waded forward.

"Where are you?" she hissed. Then, louder: "Where are you, because I'm right here! I'm right here!" she screamed, a light suddenly emanating from her hands, illuminating corners and animalistic furniture that recalled the *National Geographic* magazines she had fallen in love with that afternoon. A sofa like a sleeping hoofed animal. Tables approximating gazelles. A footstool not unlike a tortoise. A bear of a bookshelf and chairs similar to coiled sea lions resting atop chimney andirons. The creatures flickered in the wavering light.

Sensing someone behind her, Allie peeked over her shoulder.

"Privet?" she said. "Is that you?" She smiled. "Scratch? Are . . . are you scared?" she asked. "You should be."

She moved into the dining room. The glow followed her. She passed into the dark kitchen, and the light filled the impeccably kept space.

"Allie?"

She swept about violently, lunging for the person who'd spoken.

J. Scott Fuqua

Her narrow, malnourished wrist struck metal—annealed steel, which easily bent. "Oda!" she shouted, nearly psychotic with rage.

Zachary fell back, tumbling into the legs of a chair tucked beneath the dining table. On the floor, his unloaded shotgun curved sharply at the precise point Allie's wrist had made contact. He filled his lungs, coughed, and said, "Dear . . . Oda is in The Greaser Hotel."

"Liar."

Zachary calmly indicated something around her midsection. "Your hands are glowing."

Allie lifted them, curious. Her palms resembled the orange-yellow of a fiery log. The tips of her fingers were the bright blue hue of a burner flame. Startled, she staggered forward and propped herself against the doorframe, her palms darkening the white paint. "Oda?" she slurred.

"Zachary. It's Zachary."

She blinked. "You're not Mrs. Friendly?"

"Hope not."

"Where're the boys?"

"They weren't ever here, sweetie. We're alone—me and you."

"But there was something down here."

"I believe," he said, "it was your imagination."

"It was nothing?"

"No," said Zachary. "It was something, Allie. It was the after-effects of trauma."

A half an hour later, back upstairs, Zachary calmly lifted the rifle and looked down the very bent, dark barrel. Curious, he blew into it, causing a storm of red and black dust to swirl up and stick to his gray whiskers. Coughing, he waved a hand in the air and said, "Don't worry about Jerome. He always goes off on 'errands.' Sometimes he doesn't return for weeks. I've learned not to worry."

"Yeah, but he was just hurt."

"Even hurt, Jerome is rather formidable."

Allie nodded and sat on the top step. Pivoting on her butt, she leaned her back to the wall. "Do you mind if we sit and talk?"

"Ah . . . no."

"It's because, when I couldn't sleep at The Greaser, I always wanted to talk to somebody. Also, it's because I seem like I need someone to watch me. I . . . I sort of feel like a mess."

"For good reason," Zachary said softly. He rested his ruined shotgun in the crook of an arm.

They spoke for nearly half an hour, until Allie yawned and said, "I'm tired now."

"Yes, then go to sleep. Go to sleep, my dear. I'm watching."

J. Scott Fuqua

Allie didn't get up and go back to bed, though. Instead, she closed her eyes right there and slept until Jerome said, "Meow, baby," at five in the morning.

Allie woke up and said, "Hello." It seemed as if she'd been snoozing for all of a minute.

"I'm back," Jerome said.

Allie frowned at him, reached out, and touched an ear. "Are you real?"

"Real as dirt," he assured her. He stepped about. "Boy, it's a good thing I left you in Zachary's watchful hands."

Allie glanced at the old college professor, who was snoring softly, his useless shotgun leaning against his leg. "That gun of his won't work," Allie said.

"Looks like he found it in a sunken ship. Besides, the barrel's bent funny."

"The gun's just to scare people," she said. "Also, I bent the barrel last night. By mistake."

Jerome studied her, shooting his eyes to the side to imply how strange her comment about the gun was. Then he huffed and yelled, "Hey, Dr. Brion, wake up!"

Zachary nearly fell out of his chair. Wiping his eyes, he gazed sternly at Jerome, reached into a pocket, and found a Lifesaver, which he popped like an aspirin. "Now, cat, what if, because of your rather rude wake-up call, I had just now suffered a serious heart attack? What would you do and how would you feel about that?"

"I'd feel horrible."

"I bet. How did your scouting mission go?"

"Well and not well," said Jerome. "I got inside the old hotel. That's easy enough for me to do. Then I—"

"Did you check on Midge or anyone?" said Allie.

Jerome shook his head. "Sorry, dear. No time. Didn't even see them." He licked around his mouth. "So I've returned with okay and not-so-okay news. The okay news, the news that might save our lives, is that Marvin is not there. He's probably off crushing the downtrodden or blackmailing the competition. Still, it's hard to figure why your escape wouldn't draw his attention. You are important to him."

Jerome said, "The bad news, Allie, is that Herman is currently managing the search for you."

"Herman," Zachary grumbled distastefully.

"He's a slash-and-burn guy," Jerome explained. "He'll do whatever he needs to do to find you. I worry about anyone in his way. I carefully searched the living spaces for a hint at what he's doing. I got nothing till I cased the Friendlys' dining room table. That's where I found a list pilfered or purchased from the Motor Vehicle Administration. On it was a registry of Cadillac Eldorado owners in Maryland."

Zachary sat forward.

"It had the address and phone number of each and every owner. A few of them were crossed out. I suspect they've already paid those folks a visit."

Zachary's watery eyes were hard with anger. "Clearly, we have to leave the house," he said.

"We do?" Allie asked, not clear as to why, not realizing that a Cadillac Eldorado was the type of car in which she and Jerome had made their grand escape.

Jerome said, "Allie, Zachary's name was on the list."

"I should've stolen a getaway car," said Zachary. "I considered it, actually."

"Either way, it's too late now."

"I just last night thought someone was in the house," Allie said.

The old man stood. "No one was here. I promise you, child."

"But . . . I heard. And I felt . . ."

"It's normal. It's okay," said Jerome.

Zachary said, "Jerome, is there anything else we should know?"

"Herman has brought in his Rendering Team," said Jerome. "They aren't quite as rational as Marvin's posse of hoodlums. The Friendlys are driving teams around the city, searching every neighborhood. They've gone so far as to post 'missing child' flyers with Allie's picture on streetlamps and message boards. Luckily, the image of our Allie looks like a juvenile convict, with her stringy hair and gaunt face and that crummy thread-worn dress. She's much better looking now. But there's still a chance that someone will recognize her."

Feeling distant, Allie peered off.

"Zachary, got any ideas about where we should go?" Jerome asked.

"In the short-term, I'd say my office at Hopkins. It's a small room in the basement. It doesn't even have a phone yet."

"Any idea after that?"

"Some ideas, yes. It depends on what you and Allie choose to do."

"Either way, we've got to get out of here this morning," said Jerome. "Allie, sweetie, what I want you to do is grab your clothes and bring them downstairs."

"Can . . . I take deodorant, too?"

"Of course."

"How about that little thing of lip gloss?"

Jerome raised his eyebrows. "Haven't we become a girly girl this week?"

She didn't smile. "It's just that, on television, most girls my age wear makeup. I don't have any except lip gloss."

The cat tilted his large, square head. "Tell you what. If the three of us survive the next two weeks, Zachary will buy you a basketful of cosmetics."

ⓒ⤳↩ⓞ

Forty minutes later, following a breakfast of bagels and smoked salmon (Jerome's favorite, minus the bagel), they carefully packed Stella's old car with food, water, and loads of other items Allie could only guess at. After Zachary locked up the house and set the alarm, he calmly went downstairs, rummaged through a box, and pulled out his archery silver medal from the 1972 Olympics. Then he picked up a picture album and a large case. He said to Allie, "My best compound bow is in here. Feel like I should take it with me." Then, like people fleeing in the face of a coming storm, they passed down the front walk, at the end of which Zachary paused, stepped about, and gazed sadly at the front of his home.

Allie asked, "You think something's going to happen?"

"Can't imagine what," he said.

Nevertheless, Zachary appeared reluctant to leave. Expressionless, he deposited his gear and luggage in the trunk, unlocking the passenger side of Stella's car and holding it open so Allie and Jerome could scramble in. Then, jangling his keys, he went around and got in behind the steering wheel. After rubbing his nose, he started the engine, froze, and cut it off, all in the same motion. Turning toward Jerome, he said, "We can't take this vehicle."

"Why?"

"It doesn't have a Johns Hopkins parking sticker. It'll get towed."

Jerome rolled his greenish-yellow eyeballs. "A sticker! You

humans and your obsession with details. Okay . . . okay, then, let's at least park the car away from here. That way we can return to it if we need to."

Once more, Zachary started the engine. He punched the vehicle's push-button transmission and crushed the gas pedal. The dull blue Valiant screeched loudly, leaving two tire marks on the gray roadway.

Five or six blocks from home, Zachary swerved into a parallel parking space, striking the curb with an audible *whop*. A wave of small brown and yellow pebbles swamped the sidewalk alongside them. Turning off the engine, Zachary patted the steering wheel as if it was a puppy. Getting out, he went to the trunk, unlocked it, and counted out six boxes of research material. While he organized them, Allie put on her baseball cap and a pair of Stella's gaudy old sunglasses. Looking bizarre but sufficiently disguised, she hefted up two grocery bags full of her new clothes before reaching to grab another.

"I'll get those, Allie," Zachary told her.

"They're light," Allie said.

Zachary studied the items in the trunk and withdrew the case containing his compound bow, the other four boxes, and slammed the trunk shut. Weighed down, he started on foot for Johns Hopkins University with Allie and Jerome behind him.

Within five minutes, they crossed the wide lanes of University Parkway and stepped onto the large and growing campus. They turned onto a picturesque pedestrian lane that ran in front of the school's large lacrosse stadium, where they walked amongst plantings of gray beech trees with trunks that appeared camouflaged and mottled.

Around them, college students stumbled by, the proximity of fall midterms apparently heavy on most of their hearts, because no one smiled or laughed. To Allie, they all seemed a little sad.

The same morose scene, though, apparently thrilled Zachary. His steps grew lighter, his conversation more jovial. Without a doubt, teaching and the campus had been elixirs for him. He stopped in front of the student union building, placed his notes on a bench, and purchased a copy of *The Baltimore Sun*. Tossing it on top of his load, he said to Jerome, "On the off-chance the Ravens complete a blockbuster trade, or make a major free-agent acquisition, I very much want to know about it."

"Whatever, boss," the cat replied, vigilantly scanning the area.

A few minutes later, Allie, Jerome, and Zachary entered the business school's northern wing. They scuffed down an extended corridor of large, pale wooden doors and shiny flooring comprised of beige linoleum tiles that reflected the fluorescent lighting above. Arriving in the main lobby, they took an elevator down to the poorly illuminated basement, where Allie removed her hat and glasses. They shambled past the janitor's closet and a series of assistant professors' offices, until they stopped at a door opposite the boiler room.

Tired, Zachary put his load on the floor, fished for his keys, and said, "My new office."

Jerome took in the cave-like hallway. "Hate to say it, Zach, but I think I liked your old place better. This one, well . . . it sucks."

"Sucks?" He smiled. "You're right. I guess it does. My old one was taking up too much vital space in the business school, so I was unceremoniously moved."

"What's 'suck' mean?" asked Allie.

Jerome sat down. "It means *no good*."

Zachary hit the light switch and they entered. He moved his boxes inside the door and hung up his windbreaker. Swiping the folded newspaper, he tossed it atop his desk and took a seat in his office chair, which was black and chrome with leather pads and shiny, silver wheels.

Not exactly sure what to do, Allie sat on a black leather couch. Feeling slightly uncomfortable and confined, she noticed a tiny basement window high above, located just below the ceiling. A small seam of diffused light fought its way through.

"You don't like my office, do you, Allie?" said Zachary.

"Not so much."

"Yes, it's rather unattractive."

"There . . . there should be more light, like at your house," she said. "This feels a little like The Greaser."

"That's why I've avoided the place. I prefer to work almost anywhere else."

The Secrets of the Greaser Hotel

A feeling of depression gripped Allie, and she shivered. "I . . . I guess there's nowhere to take showers or clean up in here, huh?"

Zachary pursed his old, narrow lips. "Well, certainly, there are bathrooms where one can wash one's hands and face if necessary."

Allie got up. Slowly, she circled the tiny office, troubled by rattled nerves and a pounding heart. Feeling faint, she asked, "So now what do we do? I . . . I kind of don't think I can stay here very long."

"We aren't staying," Jerome said. "All we need to do is decide our next move. After that, we can scram."

The room felt like it was shrinking. "*Our next move?*" Allie asked. Sweating, she lurched over to the couch and sat down, closing her eyes.

Jerome bounded softly onto Zachary's broad desktop and silently proceeded to the corner nearest Allie. "You're looking sort of pale, dear. You okay?"

Zachary swiveled around. He clamped his jaw tight, then loosened it.

"What's next then?" Allie asked, her heart beating twice its normal speed. She lolled her head back against the seat in an effort to make the dizziness go away.

Zachary stood, went to the back corner of his office, and found a cold bottle of water inside a miniature refrigerator that was humming softly. "Drink this and count slowly to ten a few times. It might help." He unscrewed the top and handed it to her.

Eyes clamped shut, Allie slowly filled her mouth. Instantly, the crisp coolness began soothing her sensitive nerves. Counting, she took a few more sips and breathed easier. "For a few minutes, it felt like the walls were closing in on me."

"We will get you out of here very soon," said Jerome, walking back and forth across the desktop, his head down, as if he was trying to figure something out. He turned, stopped cold, and stared down at Zachary's newspaper. "It's no wonder Marvin's not around," he said. "Have either of you checked today's headline?"

"Ah . . . no," Zachary answered. His chair squeaked as he came around. "Oh my God."

Allie rolled back her lids and asked, "What?"

Zachary lifted the front page for her to see.

Bracketed by *The Baltimore Sun*'s splashy masthead and a striking full-color picture of Marvin Greaser was the headline, "Controversial Billionaire Businessman Making Bid for Presidency."

23

"What's that mean?" said Allie.

The cat wrinkled his triangular nose. "It means, dear, that our friend Marvin Greaser is trying to become president of the United States."

"It's an insult to the public's intelligence," Zachary said, scanning the article.

"It's worse than your average bad dream, that's for sure," said Jerome.

Zachary stabbed the front page with a bony finger. "Oh, you've got to hear this. At his press conference yesterday, Marvin said, and I quote: 'Sure, my employees generally disdain me; I would have it no other way. I make the hard decisions necessary to run businesses efficiently. Every decision I make is intended to make my business stronger. A chief executive officer should only hire individuals whom he can dismiss based on performance. I am the no-nonsense leader this country has needed for many—'"

Zachary slammed a fist down on his desk. "Please! He's a criminal, a murderer. And he calls himself the 'no-nonsense leader we've needed'?"

"Marvin wants to be president of the country?" Allie said, confused.

Zachary kicked back in his office chair and faced the ceiling. "Why is Marvin doing this?"

"Because he has an insatiable appetite for power," Jerome stated.

"But running for president will surely bring unparalleled scrutiny to his life," Zachary said. "He will be under the media microscope, and he knows that."

"Do you doubt he can handle it?" Jerome asked.

"No, I don't. I'll simply console myself with the fact that he can't possibly win."

Jerome snickered. "I wouldn't console myself with that, because I'm not sure he can't. My question is, what value does his campaign now put on your investigative research and our good friend here, Allie Argos?"

Zachary leaned over his desk and massaged the skin on his forehead, which, in the light, resembled translucent paper. "Right now," he said, as he swiveled and waved a finger, "Allie and my work might be the two most valuable commodities on the face of the earth."

"The most valuable and most endangered," Jerome said starkly. He lowered his most intense gaze upon Allie, who was still very pale. "Please, dear, this is it. I need to know. Do we take you back to The Greaser like a gift-wrapped present, or do we leave Baltimore and plot our return at a more opportune time?"

Allie took a long swig of water and studied her toes, all ten of which had broken and jagged nails extending beyond the tips of her pretty sandals. She didn't know that most girls worked to keep their feet clean and presentable, an effort that would have surprised her because feet were hidden a majority of the time. "Jerome," she said almost inaudibly, "I'm sorry. I'm real sorry, because you almost died for me when we escaped the first time. But I need to get my friends. I want to rescue my friends, then leave town."

Like a shark, Jerome circled Zachary's desk before stopping. "We need to make a phone call."

"Right now?" said Zachary.

"Well . . . soon."

"We can sneak into a conference room after the secretary leaves at five."

☙❧

In an empty conference room, Zachary dialed a phone number Jerome, who had been in a chilly mood all day, had memorized. He gently placed the phone on the conference table so that the cat could hear and stepped back.

Someone answered and Jerome said, "Yes," in a phony, stylish voice. "Yes, of course, my good man. I am a Mr., ah . . . Perry Mason, attorney at law. I am calling from Johns Hopkins University, the wonderful college where I frequently lecture on criminal justice and . . . ah . . . procedural rubbish. No matter. I have a pressing issue to discuss with one of my clients, a Gordon Argos, whom you will find in cell block 5186."

At the sound of her father's name, Allie recoiled physically against a large whiteboard. That her dad was going to be on the other end of the phone terrified her.

"Yes," Jerome said haughtily. "I need to speak to him now. Are you denying my client his right to counsel?"

Allie's legs felt weak and rubbery.

"Thank you," Jerome said. "Yes, I'll hold."

While the cat waited, Allie gripped the whiteboard's ledge for equilibrium. "I . . . I don't want to talk to him, understand? I don't."

"You need to," Jerome replied coldly.

J. Scott Fuqua

Zachary walked to the window and cracked open a pair of plastic blinds. He looked outside for a few seconds, then let the pieces pop back into place.

Jerome bent down to the receiver. "Gordon?"

The cat listened to a response and replied, "Yeah, we have her. She's finally out of that hole . . . but now we have a problem. Allie wants to go back in." He waited. "She wants to save her friends—three other people Marvin is detaining at the . . . She's worried something will happen to them." The cat waited once more. "She's here, Gordon. Right here." Jerome listened for a moment, lifted his head, and said, "Allie, this is a conversation you have to have."

"Why?" she snapped.

"Because it's necessary. Now take the phone. He only has a few minutes."

Feeling ill, Allie carefully lifted the receiver to her ear. The room around her seemed to blur and fade as she absorbed the line's soft static for a moment before saying, "Daddy?"

A deep, sickly voice replied, "Allie, dear, is that you?"

Tears instantaneously ran the length of her narrow cheeks. "Yeah, it's me."

"Oh, my lovely child, you sound so mature."

"Yeah, maybe, sir."

"No sirs. Please, for my sake, call me Daddy. I like that."

"Okay."

"Allie, I've waited so . . ." He started hacking, and it took him a great deal of effort to regain control of his shaky lungs.

"Sorry, dear," he said, "it's just that I've waited so long for this conversation. For nine years, you and your mother are all that I've focused on—getting you both away and safe. You are my worl—" He started coughing again. "You two are my world. And Marvin—he took you both away from me."

Allie adjusted the phone to her ear and cupped the mouthpiece harder. "I'm confused," she said. "I'm so confused. Who are you, Daddy? Who are we? Somebody has to tell me, because it seems like you aren't all that nice a person. I've seen pictures of you with Herman."

Gordon Argos waited a moment before answering. "Once, I wasn't so nice. But . . . but the thing is that I'm not that way anymore. People can change by force of will and the helping hand of others. No matter. You and your mother—you've always been good people, Allie. You need to know that, even when being good seems weak or difficult. You and your mother are honorable, innocent people. Now, dear, I want you to quickly explain to me why, after finally breaking free, you would return, intentionally, to The Greaser Hotel?"

Thoughts and images of her friends whisked by like newspapers blowing in the center of a street. "It's for my friends who took care of me. I can't leave them. They'd try to save me if they could." Allie listened to her father struggle to breathe. A lengthy gap of silence passed, during which she glanced at Jerome and Zachary.

Then, finally, Gordon Argos spoke. "Do you remember, about ten years ago, when you saw a squirrel fall out of a tree on our front walk? You saw it and held it and decided it had to go back to its mother. And I told you to leave it on the ground. Do you remember this?"

Allie smiled. "I remember. When you weren't looking, I climbed the tree."

J. Scott Fuqua

"Do you remember how I came out and found you halfway up it?"

Allie thought back to that afternoon, which seemed to hold the memories of another girl: the tree, the overcast summer sky, blue grocery bags stuck on limbs and crackling in a hot breeze, nicely kept row houses on both sides of the street, and the squirrel tucked in the roll of her sleeveless tee-shirt as she went from branch to branch. "I do."

"Do your remember how you didn't listen to me admonishing you to come down. You kept climbing."

"I heard you, Daddy," she said, smiling and crying simultaneously. "I just ignored you."

"And you fell on the way down and broke your forearm. Do you remember that?"

Wiping her nose, Allie said, "No. I mean, I remember falling and hurting my arm, but I don't remember wearing a cast."

"Because you never needed to wear one. Argoses heal very quickly, okay?"

Allie nodded.

"What I'm trying to say—and I'm not doing a good job of it—is that I'm warning you now, begging you now, not to go. I'm telling you to stop. Okay? I want you to listen this time, too. You might incur an injury from which healing is impossible."

Whispering, Allie answered back, "But I can't stop. I know them better than I know you."

Gordon Argos waited before saying, "So you think."

"So I think?" Allie said.

Again, silence, then Gordon Argos, a man whom she hadn't seen in years, said, "You saved the baby squirrel. You paid a price for doing it, but you saved the thing."

"I remember," Allie said softly.

"So," said Gordon. "How can I argue? How? Isn't it the same thing, except they're people? So . . . get them out," he said. "Tell Jerome that if you insist, I support you. But promise me, if you succeed, you'll leave the city. You'll need to run and hide, dear, and never look back. You'll need to forget about your life in Baltimore. Your mother and I . . . we need to become merely a pleasant memory. You—" His words choked, and he labored to clear his throat.

Tears, as if a pipe was seeping, welled up in Allie's eyes and rushed down her face. "Daddy, I can't go away. How can I forget you now that I know you're good?"

"You will . . ." He stopped, swallowed, and started again. "There's a guard coming to get me. I'll have to hang up at any moment. But don't forget, your mother and I love you. That's an unshakeable, unassailable fact."

Allie cried so hard she worried she couldn't speak. "Daddy, are you sick? Are you okay?"

In the background, a guard grumbled, "Hang that phone up now!"

Gordon shot back, "Allow me a couple more seconds!"

"Hang it up now!" the guard hollered.

Ignoring him, Gordon said to Allie, "Been feeling ill for eight years. It's okay, dear. I knew I would."

Suddenly, Allie heard her father grunt. Then it was obvious he was wrestling for control of the phone with someone.

A moment passed, and the receiver was pulled from Gordon Argos' weak hands. As he was hauled away, he shouted, "And trust Jerome! Trust that feline, Allie!"

✻ 24 ✻

The following morning, after a mournful sleep that left Allie more tired than rested, she looked around the small, tightly-packed office and directed herself to stay calm. She scooted against a wall, put her elbows on her knees, and thought.

A few feet away, Zachary was snoring. Jerome, Allie knew, was out in the hallway guarding the door once more. Alone, Allie reviewed the conversation she'd had with her father until, an hour later, Zachary snorted so loudly he woke himself up.

Following a breakfast scrounged from the business school's vending machines, the three sat beneath the buzzing fluorescent lights of Zachary's subterranean office devising numerous plans to save Midge, Arnold, and Rena that, due to the task's impossible nature, were fraught with problems and flaws.

They couldn't blast their way in with firearms and hand grenades because they were outnumbered and couldn't acquire such weaponry anyway.

They couldn't afford to rent a helicopter in order to land on the roof for a stealth operation because they lacked cash and currency.

And they couldn't climb the building's sheer exterior for fear that the upper coursings and windowsills they'd need to rely on would break away as if made from degraded and fragile porcelain pieces.

Jerome decided that he'd have to somehow spirit Allie into Baltimore's great, blackened, stained, and disintegrating monument to self-adoration and asphyxiating urban blight, a haunted hotel that had been booby trapped, bolted, locked, guarded, monitored, and armed to the teeth with a combination of giant, smarmy men and one vicious woman, all of whom enjoyed committing horrendous acts of torment and violence. It was, without a doubt, a hopeless operation. Yet it was the solitary obstacle that stood between Allie's future and her past.

Jerome started laughing quietly.

"What?" Zachary wanted to know.

"We've been poring over ideas for hours, and this is what we've come up with." The tabby appeared almost rabid as he pressed a paw to the papers onto which they'd been jotting their notes.

Zachary smiled. "At least we know how you're getting out . . . Well, maybe."

"If we can get that far."

"I have not a doubt in my mind that you will," Zachary said. He tapped his pen against the table. "My friends," he said, "I am sorry to say it, but in order to make this plan work, we will need to retrieve a few of the items I stowed in the trunk of the Valiant."

Jerome unhappily bunched up his mouth. Behind him, the desk light shone through the perfect, round bullet-hole in his ear. "Easy enough," Jerome said, his peripheral vision still fixed on Allie.

Hours passed, and the afternoon, barely visible through the tiny basement window, faded to dusk. All the while, the three revisited how they might break into the old hotel, tweaking their plans in small, useless ways. There were simply too many unknown variables to calculate what they would deal with or where problems might arise.

Around nine in the evening, Allie, Jerome, and Zachary (who was carrying the case that contained his compound bow), rode the elevator up to the business school's lobby. The doors opened and Jerome was nearly flattened by a horde of sorority girls heading upstairs for a study session.

"Look at the cat," one of them said, backing away to let him by.

"He's a nitwit. Walks with me everywhere," Zachary said as he followed Jerome to the front of the building, where he held the two sets of doors open for the tabby and for Allie, once again disguised in her baseball cap.

Watchful for Herman's scouts and assassins, they headed back across campus, strolling over lawns and commons and around academic buildings and dorms, ultimately arriving at University Parkway's six broad lanes. They hiked along a sidewalk parallel to the roadway, turned right, and entered Roland Park's southern boundaries. Zigzagging a few blocks, they came to Stella's old jalopy, parked exactly where they'd left it.

Without a moment's indecision, Zachary unlocked the trunk and began loading items into the compound bow's case. He dropped in two flashlights, a ball of string, a dark sweater, a knife, a compass, and a first aid kit. Then he picked out a small nylon bag of clanking metal objects that he opened and checked. Evidently concerned by what he found, he called over to Jerome. "We've got a bit of a problem."

"What?" said Jerome, who was standing guard.

"I don't have my bow sight."

"So?"

"So, do you expect me to hit a window from three hundred yards away without one? I'm old, and that's a long, long way to calculate drift, velocity, and arch on my own."

Jerome considered the question. "Can we buy one somewhere?"

"Not around here. Not one I'm comfortable using."

"What's a bow sight?" Allie asked.

Zachary said, "It's what aging archers, like myself, use to place an arrow where we want it to go."

Allie said, "You're shooting an arrow?"

"That's the plan Jerome and I discussed while you were at the vending machines."

Jerome leapt to the car's rooftop and glared at Allie and Zachary Brion. "Sadly, Allie, we can't go into The Greaser and walk around with hundreds of yards and many pounds of rope over your shoulders. We need it to come to us. And Zachary can do that, I hope."

Jerome wheezed once. He wrinkled his nose and examined something stuck on the roof of the car. Stopping, he swiveled his head around and said, "Think you're gonna have to do it without that scope, too. It's too dangerous to go back and get it, Zachary."

Zachary scratched thoughtfully at his forehead. "Jerome, allow me. There's an old business truism: One should control what one can control."

The cat laughed.

"I need my scope. My scope!" Zachary said sharply. "Imagine everything going smoothly, which it won't, and then you have no way to exit the building."

Jerome shook his blocky head. He sighed. "Fine. We'll go survey the scene. If your house checks out, we'll fetch the scope. But if it doesn't, we walk."

"That is all we can reasonably do." Evidently satisfied with the remainder of his supplies, Zachary closed the trunk and snapped

J. Scott Fuqua

his case shut. "Now, follow me," he said, leading them silently off the roadway and along a neatly hidden asphalt trail between two grand homes. They walked in silence, stumbling over fallen branches and unexpected inclines and declines. Over the course of twenty to thirty minutes, they ascended a ridge covered in elegant mansions, traversed a narrow brick lane, and dipped into a dell, where they passed more gargantuan homes of pale stone and broad verandas. They started back up a hill that rose quickly to a blunt summit.

Allie, who was breathing hard, said, "Zachary, what are these secret trails for?"

Zachary stopped. "They were designed for the residents. They're walking paths that the developer of Roland Park built throughout the neighborhood in order to inspire foot traffic."

"They're really dark," Allie said.

"They *could* use a few lamps."

Jerome slipped ahead of them, wandering down the path a few short steps before stopping and raising his large head like a little lion. "There's your house, Zach. How's it look from here?"

Zachary crouched and searched the entire row as well as he could, considering there was a grove of young trees and the roof of a nearby home blocking his view. "From here, it looks perfectly fine. Granted, it's very dark."

Jerome moseyed forward a little farther. "All right, then, before we rush down there, I'd better go scout the place."

"Careful."

"Always am," Jerome said as he dashed down the hill, slipped between two large houses and across the narrow lane. Scampering beneath parked cars, he arrived at Zachary's front walk and disappeared into the dense shadows of decorative shrubbery. A moment later, he followed the same route back and reappeared.

Materializing in front of Allie and Zachary, he said, "Boy, that Herman doesn't miss a trick. As I suspected, they've been here, probably earlier today. Lucky for us, their bad breath lingers like the odor from a diaper pail. Anyway, here's the deal: Allie, you stay hidden up here. Don't even think of coming down. If something happens, you need to run, scram, bolt. You should get to the professor's office, gather your clothes, some money Zach has stowed in a pocket of that big bag he was carrying yesterday morning, and head for the hills. Leave! Understand?"

Allie crouched down, took charge of her nerves, and said, "Yes."

"Let's make this fast," Jerome said to Zachary. The old business professor followed the cat down the dark trail and to the roadway. They skulked across, bent, and stooped in the shadows cast by the assemblage of parked vehicles. Slowly, carefully, they made their way through the darkness, until they were positioned in front of Zachary's home. Jerome stepped out onto the brick front walk and studied the entire area like a skittish forest animal. Apparently satisfied, he said something to Zachary, who rose and strode up the sidewalk as if he was simply returning from work. Casual as can be, he unlocked the front door, and they both disappeared behind it.

Allie took a deep, calming breath. She sat down on the large hard case that held their supplies. She peered around her for a few minutes, listening to the chirps of insects, the crunch of small animals moving through dry leaves, and the distant whir of cars traveling on University Parkway. She felt, as she usually felt, that someone with bad intentions was watching her. She felt scared. Her gaze arrived back on Zachary's door just in time to see her friends rush out madly. Heads bent, they sprinted down the walk and dove like two swimmers into the lineup of parked cars.

Confused, Allie stood.

J. Scott Fuqua

At once, Zachary's home, and all of the objects and memories it contained, were consumed by a massive exploding fireball. Housewares and well-crafted building parts rose high into the nighttime sky, like debris on the crest of a tornado.

Amid the sound of crashing glass, wood, and metal, a powerful shockwave struck Allie, flapping her shirt and lifting her hair as if she was caught in a downdraft. Nails, splinters, and slate roofing whizzed by her, clattering against tree trunks and sheering the limbs off of saplings. There was a sudden odd hum in the air, like a nest of hornets rocketing toward her. Then, with a thud, a broken dinner plate struck the side of Zachary's case. Covering her face with her arms, Allie raced toward the mayhem. She was sure her friends were injured and refused to leave them.

Flames licked and illuminated nearby homes. The attached houses on either side of Zachary's had partially collapsed. Realizing this, Allie worried for Zachary's neighbors—that kids and families were injured and in need of medical attention. But it was her friends she was most concerned about. The lineup of cars they'd tried to shield themselves behind was scattered. Auto alarms were going off up and down the block, while the side of each vehicle facing the explosion had crumpled inward like an empty soda can. "Jerome!" Allie screeched frantically. "Zachary!"

Out of nowhere, her friends appeared, their eyes huge and panicked. One side of Jerome's fur was charred and blackened. Similarly, Zachary's white hair was toasted across his forehead, his Ravens tee-shirt torn in half a dozen places.

Zachary hugged Allie and chanted her name until she stopped yelling theirs. Behind them, two more explosions wrecked the row of houses. Ducking against a hailstorm of crushed rubble, Zachary prodded the small velvet bag in his hand. Then he took hold of Allie's

hand and gently
directed her up the
trail. A few minutes
later, a wail of fire
engines and police
sirens built slowly in
volume.

Four blocks away,
Allie, Jerome, and
Zachary scurried down
into a thicket of weeds, where
they collapsed on a cement culvert beneath
a nameless University Parkway bridge.

Panting, Jerome said to Allie, "The place was rigged to explode."

"How'd you know?" Allie said, listening to the trickle of the little
stream they were near.

"They left a calling card, didn't they, Zachary?"

"What?" Zachary nearly shouted.

Jerome repeated himself.

The old man slumped forward and began reaming out his ears
with his pinkies. Hollering, he told her, "There was a can of Gristle
Brand Meat Parts on the kitchen counter! I . . ." He threw his head
around as if water were stuck in his eardrums. "I suppose it was the
last thing they wanted us to see."

Jerome glowered as a series of rescue vehicles roared by on the
bridge above. "Well, I for one can't believe it. They blew the house
up. They rigged it so Zachary and whoever happened to be with him
would be blown to smithereens. Why would they do that? I can see
them discreetly gunning you down, Allie, but they destroyed a whole
block, and injured who knows how many innocent people. As far as

211

J. Scott Fuqua

we know, Zachary, they weren't even aware that you were the getaway driver." He stopped short. "That is . . . unless they found something in your house related to your research."

Zachary raised and lowered his shoulders. "Maybe I left a paper or an article behind. It's possible."

"It is," Jerome agreed, looking sternly at Allie, who, upon seeing his expression, instantly recalled the photograph she'd swiped of her father. Last she'd seen it, it'd been on her nightstand at Zachary's house.

☙❦❧

Twenty minutes later, as they drove out of Roland Park, they watched a half dozen news helicopters hovering in the black skies above what remained of Zachary's street, their navigation lights blinking, their rotor blades chopping irregularly at the air, which sounded like dozens of individuals beating carpets clean. Zachary, for his part, drove very slowly, his eyes fixed. For all Allie knew, it was the first time the old man had ever operated a car with such moderation, and she was sure it was the result of his loss. She found it heart wrenching.

In Charles Village, they found a new space and parked. As they opened the car doors, Jerome, who'd been silent, unexpectedly clicked his tongue, which was a noise neither Allie nor Zachary had ever heard him make before. "You know," he said distantly, more to himself than to them, "I just realized something. For tonight, just tonight, they have no idea whether Allie's alive or dead."

"You gotta speak louder," Zachary said.

The cat extended toward the old man's hairy right ear. "Tonight, Marvin and Herman have no idea whether we're alive or dead."

"Correct!" Zachary bellowed.

"For at least the next six to eight hours," Jerome continued, "we have the upper hand. And come seven tomorrow morning, we know where Midge, Arnold, and Rena will be."

Allie sat forward. "They'll be in the kitchen making breakfast."

"And we're going to join them."

They scampered from the vehicle and cautiously walked back to the business school, where they gathered some items together, piled up Zachary's boxes of research, and reviewed the details of their strategy, or lack thereof. Finally, Allie said, "Are we just gonna slide to the ground on Zachary's rope?"

"Nope," the cat said. "This time I don't plan on going straight down. The building is now surrounded by men on Herman's Rendering Team. They'll be waiting for us at the bottom. Therefore, we're gonna try a new way in instead."

Allie smiled. "What?"

"Zip line," Jerome said.

25

During daylight, Greaser's Blight marred the skyline like the black cinder cone of a volatile volcano. At night it blotted out a vast quadrant of the cityscape like the expansive dark sail of a pirate ship. Whole sections of stars were obscured. It hid the moon in whatever phase it was in.

Worst of all, emanating from it was a sensation of inexplicable malice. Every so often, drunken stragglers were known to stumble beneath it, only to be struck by falling debris, as if aimed by unseen hands.

A few weeks before, late in the orange-tinted afternoon of a regular day, a city bus had somehow been damaged out in front of the old building by what the driver described as a "feline monster" and a girl. Of course, the driver, who was clearly in shock, was placed on medical leave, but his ridiculous story only added fuel to the building's sinister reputation. For most citizens of Baltimore, the blocks surrounding The Greaser Hotel were to be avoided at all costs.

During the drive from Charles Village all of the way downtown, Allie wished she could do just that—avoid The Greaser. Then again, if she avoided the area, she'd never save the only friends she'd ever known other than Jerome and, now, Zachary Brion. They were the lone reason she'd ever return to the building she hated so profoundly.

It was nearly two in the morning. The littered sidewalks and glittering roadways of Baltimore were mostly empty, except for an occasional pedestrian and a few rodents high-tailing it to and from garbage cans and dumpsters. Shops, or what Allie could make of them at the excessive speeds they were traveling, appeared closed, their lights off. Bars and restaurants had shut their doors. Residences appeared silent and settled. In the car, Allie tilted into screeching turns and braced herself for collisions that never occurred. Between buildings and down streets, she could see a looming void where The Greaser Hotel was located, and she hoped that somewhere high above, in the darkness, her friends were unharmed and locked in their rooms, either asleep or wishing they were.

She bent forward and began retying her boots for about the fifth time. They hit a curb, causing her head to slap the metal frame of the front seat. Wincing, she finished the job and checked the zipper of her pants and the thick belt she'd been instructed to wear. In a pocket, she found a rubber band and tied back her hair, which, she sadly realized, was beginning to feel unwashed.

Zachary slowed and the Plymouth Valiant hovered like a prowling animal. Careful about the parking spot he chose, the professor stopped once, checked something, and backed the automobile down the block, pulling into another space. Satisfied, he turned off the engine.

None of them spoke, not for at least a few minutes. Finally, Zachary said, "Well, I for one am awfully glad that Stella is not here to see the dark affairs I have gotten myself mixed up in."

"Come on, old man," Jerome said. "Don't you go worrying about Stella right now. I remember her, too, and she had a streak of adventure inside her. She'd want you to help others. She was an

involved lady. Of course, she wouldn't want your house blown to bits, but more than anything else, Stella would want you to be careful tonight. So I'm telling you: Watch your back, Zach."

Zachary tugged at his wattle. "I will make sure my back is watched. I suggest that you keep a vigilant watch on yours."

"I'll be watching everyone's," Jerome assured him. "By the time we get back, the four of them will think I'm a proctologist."

"What's a proctologist?" Allie asked.

"They are doctors who concentrate their education, research, and practice on digestive track diseases and disorders," Zachary said.

Allie had no idea what he was talking about, but she said, "Oh."

Zachary continued to stare at her. "You understand how to work the carabineers, my dear?"

"I do." So that they wouldn't jangle, Allie placed the three of them on different belt loops. Shaped like a single, large, oval chain-link the size of a bracelet, each carabineer had a little spring-loaded gate, allowing a person to clip securely to something, or clip something securely to them. "Zachary?" Allie said.

"Yes?"

"Before I go," Allie said, "in case we don't come back, I've got something to tell you."

"What's that?"

Allie blinked a few times, puckered her mouth in personal exasperation, and spoke quickly, "I might've left a picture of my father on the bedside table in my room at your house."

Zachary smiled sweetly. "Allie, are you trying to say that you are responsible for a bunch of miscreants destroying my home, that the picture you left on the table was the sole reason it was blasted? Well, it isn't. It isn't. So please, my dear, you didn't blow it up, and the fact that it was blown up is not your fault."

"I took the picture from your collection."

"Sweetheart, I saw it in your room. I knew it was there."

She turned red. "I was going to give it back."

"Enough with the confessions," Jerome said. "We've got miles to go before we sleep, so we better get onto the first one."

"And so you should," Zachary agreed.

Jerome, frowning, placed his front paws on the back of the seat and examined Allie sternly. The stripes running down his forehead bunched up and appeared to connect like the top of a drawstring bag. "You understand the compass?"

"Yes."

"Got everything else?"

"Yes."

"Then let's go save a few people."

Sliding a book bag over her shoulders, Allie didn't know how to say goodbye to Zachary. "Ah, thanks for being nice to me," she said.

Zachary nudged at something with the toe of a running shoe, then he strode forward and thoughtfully put his long arms around her. "Please, dear, it has been my honor and pleasure to get to know you. Now, you make sure that cat brings you back safe and sound."

Jerome said, "Be a real miracle if I do, Zach." And with that apocalyptic comment, he started forward.

☀ 26 ☀

Jerome could enter The Greaser without being seen—he'd done so thousands of times before. However, with Allie on his back or at his side, he'd be unable to employ his usual routes into the wrecked building. He wouldn't be able to get small and stay small. Allie's presence would slow him down.

Half a block from the gloomy building, Jerome crept forward and pointed at a homeless man a short distance down the street. The guy was warming hands the size of pasta bowls over a tiny fire he'd built in a coffee can placed in the child's seat of a shopping cart. He wore filthy rags, but his hair was perfectly brushed and parted on one side. He also possessed the strapping frame of the sort of wrestler Allie had seen on television, not the

219

J. Scott Fuqua

softer form of someone who rarely, if ever, got three square meals a day.

"One of Herman's boys," Jerome said, but Allie had already guessed.

The man spit a plug of chaw on the sidewalk and slowly turned his back, searching in the general direction of the harbor. At once, Jerome and Allie rushed from one shadow to the next. Sufficiently concealed, they hurried along, pressing themselves flat against the wall of an abandoned department store that had been extremely popular during Baltimore's halcyon days. They rounded the corner and squeezed into a recessed doorframe located directly across the street from The Greaser Hotel.

Right away, Jerome located a second guard seated on the curb near the hotel's sealed entrance. Playing the role of a destitute, the guy had the gargantuan build of a silverback gorilla and an incongruously well-maintained set of mutton sideburns along his jawline. It was his location, though, that wholly gave away his identity. No sane man or, for that matter, any insane homeless man would intentionally locate his bed at the foot of Greasy Blight, where he'd surely be struck by a stray building fragment or two . . . or three. Maybe even four . . .

Jerome searched in the other direction and, at the end of the block, caught sight of a third man inspecting the roadway and hotel. The fellow turned, and the glow of a streetlight caught the highlights of his polyester leisure suit. "Allie," Jerome hissed, "it's Privet."

Without uttering a word, Allie studied her ex-tormenter—the way he moved like a male model marching down a fashion runway. She found herself aching to club the man to the edge of death. The Friendlys' cruelty had denied her so much. Joy, love, warmth, confidence, and a sense of self-worth had all been stolen from her. As if from a distance, she heard herself say, "Why don't you go tear him to shreds?"

"Can't."

"Why?" she asked irritably, gritting her teeth.

"No one must know we're here. Not yet. We need to enter the building in absolute secrecy. They'll know we're here soon enough without leaving behind a trail of slashed and battered security specialists."

Trying to suppress her disdain for Privet, Allie closed her eyes contemplatively. She felt her lips twitch into and out of a snarl and recalled her waking nightmares, in which she was being chased or cornered by various members of the Friendly clan. She silently counted to ten, and began taking deep breaths just as she had during her panic attack in Zachary's office.

Slowly, she swept back her lids and found that Jerome was now the size of a Bengal tiger, yet quite a bit meaner-looking, as if he was a rabid stray visiting from the nearest gate of Hell. Everything about him was outsized, including the large region of fur that had been charred when Zachary's house had exploded. His mere presence radiated a barely tethered ferocity. "Climb on my back," he said sharply, watching her.

She slid onto the wide area just below his shoulders.

"Hold very tightly to my scruff and be prepared for me to leap."

Leaning forward, Allie secured her fists tightly in the loose skin around the nape of Jerome's neck. At once, the giant cat paced forward, froze, and concentrated on the dark shadows behind the phony bum still seated by The Greaser's entrance. Momentarily, Jerome flipped a soda can across the street, and it clanked and rolled forward until it fell off the curb and into the road.

The sentry was on his feet in an instant, a nasty firearm drawn from the folds of his coat. As he approached the shadows where the can had started its journey, Jerome bounded forward and across the street. Not ten feet from the man, whose back was turned, the massive cat sprang upwards with such force that Allie nearly tumbled from his back like a clown in a rodeo. Without making a sound, the cat alighted on an extremely narrow coursing of stone surrounding the second story of the hotel.

Below, the guard kicked at the shadowy debris surrounding The Greaser's broad base. Eventually satisfied that the can was just a can, he ambled back to his spot, his thighs so muscular they got in the way of each other. Sitting down, he tugged his grimy coat back around his great deltoids. Never once did he scrutinize the building.

Jerome, with Allie atop his shoulders, began inching slowly along the ledge. It was a difficult route, with gaps where the stone coursing had, over the last twenty years, dropped to the sidewalk. Still, he didn't

The Secrets of the Greaser Hotel

encounter any unsound footing, and about halfway to the building's northeastern corner, Jerome carefully leaned his gargantuan shoulders into a loosely boarded window, forcing a small entry into the hotel. Quick as a mouse, Allie slipped through the crack. In an instant, she was followed by Jerome, who was suddenly cat-sized again.

Inside an apartment she had never cleaned, Allie removed her book bag, fumbled through its contents, and found a bottle of water. She drank deeply, relieving the dryness in her throat. She placed the bottle back and felt around until she located a small flashlight. Flicking it on, she shined it around the absolutely destroyed apartment to find, not ten feet away, a writhing mass of winged cockroaches of the type that had attacked her only weeks before. Inadvertently, Allie squealed.

"Love," Jerome said softly, maneuvering his suddenly large form toward the door, "I know you hate those things, but you've got to control yourself. If you don't, we won't be checking out of this hotel alive."

"S-sorry," she said, shuddering.

They stepped vigilantly into the hallway, gently closed the door, and scampered down the extended and confusing corridors, searching for the stairwell entrance. All the while, they passed abandoned residence after abandoned residence, scarred steel doors, and a hodgepodge of door knobs, from cut glass to chipped porcelain. These were the apartments where Baltimore's poorest residents had once been stowed away and forgotten in public housing.

Allie, who had never been allowed to clean below the fourth floor, was surprised by the abject neglect of the building. The upper stories were thread-worn and crumbling, but they appeared structurally sound, while the second floor was littered with rusty steel joists that had fallen through the ceilings or sagged dangerously into the hallway.

At the end of one corridor, they came across a huge vertical girder that, from compression and stress, had evidently burst through a plaster wall.

"Is this place going to fall?" Allie asked.

"It's not just steel and stone that holds it up," Jerome said.

Furtively, they skirted the lens of a video camera and stepped over two well-concealed trip wires. They followed passageways in strange directions that ended at dead ends or, somehow, deposited them back in the very place they'd started. After quite some time, they rounded a corner and located the entrance to the stairwell.

Cautiously, Jerome sniffed at the door. He even ran a claw down the crack between it and the peeling wooden frame. Satisfied, he directed Allie to draw back the lock and step forward.

She did so, and entered into the otherworldly passage that housed the building's extensive and quite unstable wooden fire escape. Just peering at it tested Allie's desire to return to The Greaser. Each tread shook when they deposited their weight on it, while joists and planks appeared consistently out of alignment with the ones preceding them. During their escape weeks earlier, they'd simply ignored the booby traps and cameras, but now, Allie could see nails stuck up everywhere, like the hackles on a porcupine; nets set every few flights; as well as something Jerome called a "Bouncing Betty"—a landmine designed to leap into the air and blow off a man's genitals. Meanwhile, the walls at that level were painted a drippy pink and red, like the wet and inflamed lining of an animal's esophagus.

Every few floors, the minimal lighting and bare, hot bulbs created strange shadows, many of which resembled men rushing down upon them, causing Allie to flinch and her heart to misfire. For his part, Jerome appeared completely unperturbed and indescribably dangerous, his great jaw cracked open, his disturbing choppers exposed like rows of pale spikes.

They snuck around dozens of vacillating video cameras and gingerly stepped over poorly hidden pressure sensors. The stairway's shoddy construction, combined with all of the newly installed intruder surveillance equipment, and the yawning shaft that ran right down between the flights, began to wear on Allie. She grew hot and dizzy. Twice, she went through a step, and it was only by luck that she avoided snagging her ankle on nails. Spent and slump-shouldered, she began to wish, over and over, that their climb would end.

Both lost count of what floor they were on, but felt confident all the same that they were approaching the Friendlys' suites.

Then Jerome slowed. He cocked his dish-like ears and froze as if struck by a stun gun. Gradually, he looked back at Allie and indicated for her to put an ear to his mouth, which, given how frightening he looked, was a slightly disturbing thing to do.

"There's a guard above. Maybe four flights," Jerome said softly. "I can hear him snoring. We need to backtrack a few floors and get out of this stairwell." Pausing to think, he began muttering to himself, "Can't take the stairs anymore, and the elevator's too loud . . ." But then he looked up, fresh inspiration washing over his face.

Without another word, Jerome put his weight against a hallway door. As he leaned forcefully, the wooden frame cracked and splintered until, with a snap muffled by the fabric of Allie's nylon backpack, the door came open. They entered the hallway and carefully closed the door behind them. Still feeling dehydrated, Allie drank more from her water bottle. After screwing the top on tightly, she paused and, curious, checked to see if her deodorant was still working. It wasn't, and she found herself standing in the middle of the world's most dangerous hotel wishing she'd brought the little, pink dispenser.

"My God, it's hard to believe we're only on the fourteenth floor," Jerome said, staring at the numbers on a door. "I'd have bet a good plate of fish that we were up in the sixties." He paused and thought. "What's the time, Allie?"

"Ah . . . what's this say?" She tapped the watch face.

"Almost six. Very late." He tilted his head, which was roughly the girth of two to three cinderblocks. "We need to locate the elevator."

"You told me it would be too loud," she said.

"Yeah, but since then, I've had an idea."

Finding the elevator wasn't so simple. It was actually more confusing than higher math. Above, the vibrating and wildly clacking elevator motors awakened to shake the entire building but gave no hint as to the shaft's location. They could even hear the elevator car screech down and up, up and down, yet the sound seemed to emanate from everywhere as opposed to any specific point. Meanwhile, Allie led Jerome to the place where she recalled catching the lift at least a few hundred times before. Unfortunately, either her memory had gaps or the lobby had somehow been repositioned.

"It was here," she said.

"It's not now," Jerome said matter-of-factly.

Desperate, they started jogging, at which point a wall sconce swung down and clocked Allie on the head. It took at least another forty minutes after that, but at long last, they located the elevator lobby. Above, the tremor-inducing motors stopped. "Hope we're not too late," Jerome said.

Jerome stood in front of the dented chrome elevator doors. "This, my dear, is the safety door to an old Otis elevator. Don't ask me how I know this tidbit of information because I couldn't tell you," said Jerome. "High above, there is a rotating winch run by antiquated motors. That winch raises and lowers the passenger car by reeling in a cable. Located on the opposite end of that cable, after it has passed through the winch, is something called a ballast, which is a very heavy counterbalance that rides on a track parallel to the elevator car. Basically, the elevator car and the ballast are like two kids of equal weight on a seesaw. They offset each other's load, making it a lot easier to move them both up and down. Therefore, when the elevator goes down, the ballast rises on its track. When the elevator goes up, the ballast drops. So we're going to ride the ballast till we can jump ship onto the elevator car. We have no other choice," he said, noting her expression.

She rubbed at the knot on her temple caused by the wall sconce. "Does the ballast have a seat or something?" she said.

"No seats. It's not meant for passengers. You're going to have to stand on the top of it and, using the belt around your pants, carabineer yourself to the cable." Sensing her hesitation, he smiled reassuringly.

J. Scott Fuqua

"Are . . . are you trying to smile?" Allie asked.

"Yup, trying."

"Don't, okay? It makes you look dishonest."

Jerome's upturned black lips flattened. He stalked to the chrome doors, which reflected back a peculiar likeness of him, as if he were more Chinese dragon than cat. He rose and placed his front paws against the doors. He slid a few huge claws into the narrow fissure between and, growling, gradually forced both sides of the door open, then directed Allie to leap onto a distant cable.

"But . . . what if I miss?"

"You'll fall."

"Oh." She pondered. "Well, how are you going to hold on without hands?"

"I'll be riding on your shoulders," said Jerome. "Quickly, dear. We're in a bit of a hurry. Put on those gloves Zach gave you, and off you go."

She hesitated. "The cable looks hard to grip."

"It is. Now scat."

Her heart sledge-hammering blood to the far regions of her small body, Allie put the gloves on, then took one huge breath, planted her feet, and jumped.

The sensation of dropping caused her to wonder if she'd somehow miscalculated where the line was located. Then, to her horror, she realized that she had closed her eyes. She opened them just as her face struck the greasy ballast cable. Her adrenaline-fired brain instinctively informed her hands to hold tight, which they did. At once, she began sliding down and away from Jerome, unable to stop herself. "What do I do?" she called to him.

"Be prepared for me to land on your shoulders," Jerome said, leaping through the elevator doors, which rumbled shut behind him, causing the windowless shaft to fall into gray twilight. An instant later, soft as a bird, a humorously tiny version of Jerome landed on Allie's shoulder.

"I'm . . . I'm still sliding," she said.

"Cable's slippery. I expected that. Keep going until your feet hit the ballast, dear. I'm here. You're fine. We're both fine."

They dropped and dropped, past thin slots of weak light that outlined the bottom of each safety door. The purple, gray darkness seemed to wrap about them like a blanket, and they descended for so long that it seemed certain they were far below Baltimore's gritty streets, even nearing the earth's molten core. Warm air swept up the shaft from below.

Allie began to sweat. Her hands, even in the gloves, grew raw and blistered as they rubbed along the thick cable. At least the elevator wasn't being used and it was fixed in the same spot for the moment. She fought back a rising desire to scream.

At last, Jerome said, "I can see the counterbalance below, dear. Prepare to make landfall."

"But," Allie said, "it's too dark to see."

"Then I'll tell you when you're about to land. Be ready, Allie. One, two, three. Now!"

Allie cringed. Her jaw tightened. Then her feet slammed painfully into the top of a narrow object. She wobbled, exhausted, and rested her overworked hands by crossing her arms around the cable. She slumped forward like a rag doll.

From his place on her shoulder, Jerome said, "I know you're whipped, Allie, but you must now take a moment to carabineer your belt to the cable. It will free up your hands so that you can rest them a bit more conveniently."

Too tired to reply, she coaxed her nearly paralyzed fingers to operate the carabineer's small spring-loaded latch. It took a few minutes, but when she finally managed the task, she draped over backwards and allowed her belt to hold her weight.

A few moments later, she rasped, "I don't ever want to do that again."

"The need to ride an elevator's ballast doesn't actually come up that often, love."

"Good."

Time passed, and Allie's feet, positioned as they were on the narrow shelf, began to ache. She adjusted as much as possible, but the pain only grew worse. To ease it, she bent to a crouch atop the ballast and even gave a thought to sitting. But before she could situate herself, the building trembled as if it might tumble inward, reminding Allie of the bent beam somewhere on the second floor. High above, elevator gears and sprockets groaned to life.

They were about to start moving.

"Okay, Allie," Jerome said, "you need to stand up and unclip yourself from the cable."

Silent and footsore, Allie did so, even as the ballast grudgingly rose along its steel tracks for an indeterminate amount of time, as a diseased-looking wall, swallowed up in shadows, passed invisibly beside her cheek. Then, with a loud, miserable grind, the ballast stopped moving.

In a soothing voice, Jerome said, "Be prepared to step in the direction of the doors. That's the side the elevator car will pass on. Wait till I give you the word."

Even though she wasn't sure he could see her, she nodded.

Once again, the ballast reluctantly started rising. Above, the chilling sound of metal tearing at metal grew steadily closer until it overwhelmed the ballast's comparatively soft screech. As the elevator car approached, Allie could hear, above the duet of squealing parts, the clanking of loose rivets and the arrhythmic bang of the car striking the powdery walls surrounding it.

"Here it comes," Jerome said. "Get ready."

The horrendous combination of noises grew so loud that, in reaction, Allie's clothes fluttered against her.

"Step now!" Jerome yelled.

27

Allie toppled painfully onto the lift's irregular rooftop.

Jerome leapt from her shoulder and balanced on a truss. His eyes glowed like two penlights. "Ignore the awful racket this sorry thing is making. It drowned out our awkward transfer."

A few floors down, the elevator bounced to a halt and the doors cranked open. Allie could once more discern the shake of the suffering elevator motors high above. They started rising. She shut her eyes for a while, nearly falling asleep.

Then she was startled to alertness. The elevator had stopped again. Underneath her, someone's muffled voice barked out an unhappy command. Then the elevator doors labored to close. At once, the lift began wobbling upward toward the Friendlys' suites— and, more specifically, the kitchen and Allie's friends.

When, at long last, they stopped rising, Allie shined a flashlight down on the roof to locate the escape hatch. In silence, they listened as the double doors groaned wide and someone shoved someone else out, calling them, in the process, a "fly."

Below, the doors shut. It sounded like a bag of aluminum cans getting crushed. Then the elevator car was empty.

"Must've been Midge," Allie whispered.

"Okay, let's assume we've stopped at the kitchen level and go," Jerome told Allie, who yanked back the heavy steel hatch, allowing the cat to leap down. She propped the barrel of her flashlight between the hatch and its frame, leaving a narrow crack to look through. When she was settled, Allie began tapping against the top of the elevator door.

In the room beyond, somebody said something.

She tapped some more.

There was a good deal of noise and shouting. Somebody pressed the elevator button and the doors wrenched open.

Allie stopped.

Two men, both wearing dark military combat clothing and carrying similarly tinted assault rifles, stormed into the elevator car, only to find a tiny Jerome, seated calmly and looking up at them. He

J. Scott Fuqua

meowed, which sounded more like a person replicating a cat than an actual cat.

"What the hell?" the hired gun on the left said. Located on his right shoulder was a half-round patch that said "Rendering Team B."

Allie worked to get a better angle on the room beyond, where, a couple of feet in, a third Rendering Team member stood behind a wall of sandbags. He worked the trigger of a colossal machine gun trained on the elevator.

"What is it?" the machine gun operator asked, looking perplexed.

"It's a cat—the grubbiest damn one I ever saw."

"Looks like he's got grease all over him," said the gunman on the right. "If I was starving, I'd eat a leather couch before putting my mouth 'round this fella."

The machine gunner adjusted behind his gun. "Oda said it was a cat-like thing that helped the girl escape."

"Oh, yeah, well, it wasn't this here tatty thing, Sullie. She said it was huge."

The guy on the right tapped the guy on the left's shoulder with the knuckle of an index finger. "Shoot it dead so Sullie doesn't worry it's gonna scratch us."

Nodding, the gunman on the left shuffled forward and began sighting his rifle. In an instant, Jerome skipped up the barrel and unfolded like an ever-expanding origami masterpiece. A now massive Jerome slammed into the man, driving the man's head into the hardwood flooring with a sharp whack. In a blur, Jerome launched himself at the machine gunner. It was a beautiful rainbow of a leap. Arching his brawny body mid-flight, he unleashed a sweeping blow across Sullie's Neanderthalish brow, dropping him like a bag of charcoal. The guy whose head was nearly twisting off his shoulders made one quick sound, like somebody had stepped on his foot, and then he was out.

Impossibly quick, Jerome bounced off the man's chest and back over the sandbags, slapping the third operative's automatic weapon sideward as a single shot rang out. The cat reared back and plunged scythe-like claws deep into the man's right forearm. Yanking him forward, Jerome delivered a vicious head-butt that knocked him out cold.

The cat swung about and glared directly down the hall, toward the huge dining room with its bone chandelier. A second ticked by and Shoat Friendly shuffled out of the dining room, his hair styled so that it resembled a patch of matted straw.

"Sweetie, jump down," Jerome whispered to Allie. "Grab a gun—even if you aren't going to use it—and follow me." Without looking back at her, he commenced, as if propelled by thrusters, down the hall, stopping right in front of Shoat, who, noticing him for the first time, drooled down the front of his shirt.

"Hey," Jerome said.

Shoat's nose dripped. He pulled out a tiny pistol from the pocket of his pants.

Jerome said, "You're downright disgusting. Did you know that?"

Shoat pointed his weapon at the cat, but shook so much that he dropped it to the floor. "I . . . I remember you. I ain't forgotten what you done to my hand."

"Whatever."

"I . . . I got a bigger gun," Shoat said. "And . . . and, cat, this here place has armed guards looking to plug any and all trespassers, specially you."

"You must be talking about the guys I just trampled."

Shoat glanced down the hall, where, even from that distance, he could make out two of his men strewn about casually across the wooden floor. "There's more security still."

"Call them," Jerome growled.

J. Scott Fuqua

Nervous, Shoat dabbed his nostrils with the sleeve of his leisure suit.

"Tell me: Are Midge, Arnold, and Rena in there?"

Shoat glanced into the dining room, toward the kitchen. "Cooking, yeah." Shoat's rather anxious gaze flicked sideways and fixed on a space behind Jerome as Allie approached. "Rat?" he said in a high voice. "Ah, gosh, it's good ta see ya, Rat. Real good."

Allie stared at her foster brother.

"Rat, ya . . . ah . . . brought your kitty back, huh? We was . . . ya know . . . worried for ya and all the like. We was looking all over the city, scared the big cat had . . . ah . . . eaten ya or something." He smiled, a truly gruesome sight considering the state of his gums and teeth, and bent to pick up his pistol.

The Secrets of the Greaser Hotel

Allie, glowering at Shoat, felt her whole personality swallowed by a dark creature. Her emotions scattered in a flash similar to molten stone touching ocean water. If, in that moment, she had been asked her own name, she would no more have understood the question than if it had been posed in Latin.

"Real slowly now," Jerome said, "stand and take that other pistol off your hip and place it on the floor."

Shoat labored to reclaim some small composure. He peered at his pistol and the cat a few times. "I . . . I ain't gonna do it." He placed his hand on the pistol grip and looked back at Allie.

Allie was sighting him down the barrel of a large automatic weapon, her hands glowing brilliantly.

"What'cha doing, Rat? Ya . . . ya think ya gonna shoot me?" The remnants of his small composure evaporated. "After all I done for you? Ain't fair. Just ain't."

Allie didn't reply. Gripped by toxic ire, she sought the weapon's trigger, her index finger blindly searching the multiple knobs and levers along the gun's stock, her mind a pool of fire. She could only imagine the satisfaction she'd feel in dropping the man.

Shoat suddenly slumped forward, his rocky knees thumping the floor like misplaced xylophone notes. Having glided forward and set himself, Jerome had crumbled the man with a vicious uppercut to the groin.

Gurgling loudly, Shoat toppled to his side, his hands between his legs, his mouth producing mouse-like chirps.

"I believe I just saved your life," Jerome told him.

Allie lowered her rifle. She visually located the trigger, then slung the weapon over a shoulder. Dizzy from diminishing rage, she passed into the dining room, around the large dinner table, and stopped at the kitchen door.

Behind her, Jerome jammed a claw into Shoat's holster and flicked his pistol into the air. It gained some altitude and ricocheted off the buffalo skull chandelier before crashing into Marvin Greaser's ancient silver tea service, notable for its unattractive motif of snarling hyenas and poison ivy. "Keep your mind on the task," the monstrous cat said to Allie.

Jerome passed by her and into the kitchen. Allie followed. She found herself in the room she disdained more than any other, where she'd cooked so much meat, stacked so many plates, and opened too many industrial-sized cans of protein. Not fifteen feet away was pale-faced Rena, her limp hair brushing against her shoulders.

Gripping a spatula, the little girl examined Jerome from atop a wooden box positioned against the familiar griddle, which was covered now in heaps of Gristle Brand sausage and melting white strips of Gristle Brand pork fat, all of which was crackling and sputtering so loudly it was no wonder they hadn't heard the various commotions by the elevator and in the dining room.

Behind Rena stood Midge, wonderful Midge, tough as nails but kindly, and a second mother to Allie. Midge looked to Jerome, then to Allie and back. She didn't recognize either one. On her narrow face, Midge sported such a brilliantly swollen eye that it could have been mistaken for a pirate's patch or a monocle. Gripping a broom tightly, she appeared older, skinnier, and greatly fatigued.

Off to her right was Arnold, his back to them. He was working the sinks and humming a goofy tune, unaware that Allie and Jerome were in the kitchen.

Midge leaned, took time to focus, and exclaimed, "Oh my God . . . Allie! Allie, is that you behind all that grease and clean hair?"

Nodding, Allie smiled.

Midge's broom fell from her hands and slapped the floor. She rushed across the wide tiles to throw her emaciated arms around the young woman. "Allie," she moaned. "Allie, you idiot. Why'd you come back, sweetie?"

The muzzle of Allie's rifle clanked against her ankle and the floor. "Midge, we came for you," she explained. "We're here for you and Rena and Arnold," she said. "We're getting you guys out of here right now." She tried to sound strong but wasn't sure if she'd pulled it off.

Midge let go of Allie and gave her a hard examination. "Who's taking us?"

"Me and Jerome." She indicated the cat.

Midge smiled. "I was hoping you knew him." Tears welled up in her eyes. "You came back for us?" Wiping at her good eye, Midge Darlington stooped and adjusted Allie's hair so that it was out of her face.

"We need to go," Allie said.

Midge nodded, snorted harshly, and composed herself. "Yes, let's. Rena, Arnold: Come on! We're leaving!"

Rena's small nose wrinkled and her bottom lip protruded farther than normal. "What're we gonna do?"

J. Scott Fuqua

"It's Allie, dear. You remember Allie from a few weeks ago? She's going to help us escape."

"But . . . but, Midge, I don't want to leave."

Midge glared at her. "No arguments, Rena."

"But I want to cook for Mr. Gristle and the Friendlys," said Rena.

"Get off that box and get over here, Rena Duchamp!" Midge ordered. "Now!"

Irritated, Rena slowly stepped down. "Mr. Gristle's food is gonna burn," she said. "You're gonna make me ruin his breakfast."

"I hope I do."

Allie studied Arnold Armstrong, who, finally, had turned around. His expression was impossible to read.

"Hey, Arnold," Allie said.

He squinted. "Allie, dear."

"We're leaving now, okay?"

Voice quavering, Arnold replied, "Allie, I have been quite upset with your actions of late. Do you know why?"

"No."

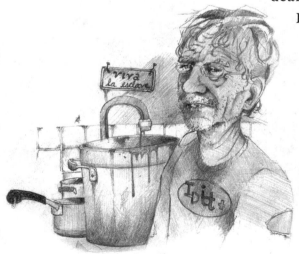

He looked at his wet hands. "Well, dear, when you left, Mrs. Friendly got in awful trouble. She got in awful trouble, that lovely woman did. I felt so bad for her. She treats us nice and works hard herself, and you gave her all the grief she could handle."

"I'm sorry, Arnold."

"She isn't even allowed to eat in the dining room till Mr. Gristle leaves. That's what Mr. Gristle told her. Nice as he is, he makes her eat the scraps after the boys are done." His head commenced to bobbing quite insanely, as if he was agreeing with his own story. "Guess what?"

"What?"

"That Mr. Gristle, he loves the pig fat more than anyone I ever knew," said Arnold. "You didn't cook much pig fat, but Rena does, 'cause he gobbles it up like blood pudding."

"That's really cute. Now we've got to go."

"Allie, you should see how Mr. Gristle cleans his plate. He swabs the fat with a chunk of meat, like pork chops or steak or muskrat or—"

"Arnold, we need to scram," said Jerome. "I'll drag you out on your butt if you want, but I'd rather not have two reluctant travelers."

Arnold's jowls loosened perceptibly. He blinked as if suffering a minor seizure. "The cat, Allie . . . it just spoke. Did . . . did you see that?"

"He speaks," Allie said. "He's my friend."

Midge jabbed at her filthy gray hair and addressed Arnold. "Dear, don't you want to go visit Oda? You haven't seen her in a few days, have you?"

"Ah . . . no. We're going to visit her?"

"That's right. Oda wants to check up on you."

Arnold, surprisingly light on his feet, came forward.

Midge grabbed Rena's hand and refused to let go.

28

Together, they all followed Jerome out through the swinging doors and into the dining room.

Allie paused to take out her compass. She held it steady in front of her and found east on the floating dial. "It's this way," she said, her words nearly drowned out by the elevator motors thundering to life.

Jerome pursed his mouth. "Someone's coming!" he hollered over the rumble. "Give Midge that gun and lead us!"

Allie passed over the rifle and trotted out into the shadowy hallway. Her eyes zipped from the compass dial to the well-maintained passages in front of her. She recalled how the Friendlys' plush sitting room had contained a series of extremely striking windows overlooking the city.

Impossibly, though, the room wasn't where Allie or Midge remembered it, throwing a wrench in Allie's sense of direction. Instead, they arrived at a wide-paneled wooden chamber, the hub of a three-way intersection. They looked up and down. Their options were limited to a northwest or southeast route—or they could go back the way they had just come. Understandably, Allie chose southeast, took two strides, and tripped on a wrinkle in the carpet. Rena, dragged along by Midge, toppled onto Allie from behind. The two of them scampered up, dusted themselves off, and started along once more.

Shortly, the corridor ended at a junction of hallways that went either north or south. Allie checked to make sure she hadn't broken the compass when she'd fallen. Holding it out in front of her, she watched the dial find north. It seemed to be working fine.

"Okay?" Jerome said.

"I think we are." She went south with everyone following her.

From far away, they heard shouting. In time, the elevator motors chugged, sputtered, and stopped firing. That noise was replaced by the pounding footfalls of large men. Allie felt panic rising inside of her. The five of them seemed to be helplessly circling the center of the building. They hurried past an endless number of closed doors and eventually came to a large room filled with bronze sculptures of hyenas and vultures standing heroically in well-tended tufts of poison ivy. They turned and hurried along a corridor heading east.

A wall switch somehow gashed Midge's elbow, but she ignored the pain and continued hauling Rena along. Every so often, the girl put up a terrible fight. At one point, an exasperated Midge turned, tugged with both hands, and shouted, "Stop it!"

Ahead, the hallway appeared to end at a vast chamber. Sadly, the whole thing was unlighted, which alarmed Allie. She could only imagine that it was booby-trapped or inhabited by ferocious, hungry animals and a large number of armed guards.

However, far off in the distance, she could see the hallway beyond glowing softly in the early morning light. She squinted but couldn't detect any obstacles in-between. Turning, she waited for Midge and Rena to catch up. Having lost the bounce in his aged step, Arnold had fallen dramatically behind. Thankfully, Jerome guarded the old man's heels.

When everyone had gathered together, Allie pressed forward, flicking on her flashlight when darkness closed around them. Far across the room, she noted a lineup of bowling alleys. Then, glancing down, she followed the compass's softly glowing dial east. In the shadowy gloom, she stumbled over a series of carpet wrinkles and a few wobbly floorboards but didn't go down. As they rushed, the lighted hallway slowly, slowly drew closer. Impatient, Allie increased the length of her stride and immediately felt something catch her ankle.

At once, Allie, Midge, Arnold, and Rena were lifted upwards and slammed against the ceiling, located a good fifteen feet above the floor. Jerome, quick as a cat, easily avoided the trap. Allie unintentionally dropped her flashlight, which clanked to the floor

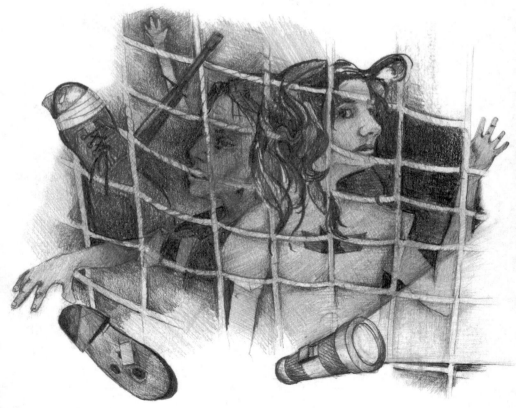

The Secrets of the Greaser Hotel

and glowed beneath them. They'd been snared. Thick netting held the three of them tightly against the ceiling as if they were flies pressed against the flat side of a swatter. She heard Midge cursing beside her. A few feet away, Rena struggled to free herself and return to Herman's breakfast.

"Jerome!" Allie called.

"I see you," he said.

"I'm caught in an awkward position," said Midge.

"We can barely move," said Allie. She struggled to turn her head toward Midge. "Midge, in my backpack, there's a knife. Can you get it out?"

"Where's Mrs. Friendly?" Arnold asked.

Jerome leapt upwards, his monstrous claws catching on the net. Dangling from one paw, he slashed through the tightly woven bands one at a time.

Allie felt Midge's hand struggle at the edge of her backpack. She toiled to draw back the zipper and strained to search the insides. Allie noticed, between the large twangs created when Jerome slicked through a band, that Midge was breathing as if running a marathon.

The woman grunted, moved, and pressed the small pocketknife into Allie's grasping hand.

Right away, Allie started cutting.

Jerome worked away separately, growling harshly from exertion. They could hear their pursuers gaining on them. Time passed, and Jerome bit through one of the remaining cords on his end of the net. The enormous snare sprang free.

Cartwheeling through the air, Allie hit the ground like a skipping stone and came to a rolling stop on the third bounce. She breathed in and coughed. She opened her eyes and saw that Midge and Rena were beside her. In a darkness broken only by the dropped flashlight and the small amount of light radiating from the exit halls, Midge said, "Is that you coughing, Allie?"

"Yes."

Jerome materialized. "Any injuries?"

"Don't know." Midge wiggled her sore arms and legs reasonably well.

"Rena?"

"She's fine."

"Arnold, you okay?"

"Yes, Mr. Cat."

Jerome's glowing eyes darted about the chamber, skipped across the bowling alleys and shimmering bowling balls, and focused on the far away hall from whence they'd come.

In the darkness, Allie noticed that Arnold was already on his feet, circling as if he was riding on a carousel. As he went, he called softly for Mrs. Friendly, over and over, as if she'd birthed him. Allie got up and gimped over. Softly, she took one of his liver-spotted hands and led him along.

"We can't keep dragging you if you fight us every step of the way," said Jerome to Rena, looking angry. "Can you carry her, Midge?"

"I don't want to be carried," Rena announced.

"I'm way too weak anyway," said Midge. "Sorry."

Jerome studied the area ahead. The lit section was closer, but still a good distance away. Midge picked up her assault rifle and slung it over a shoulder. Then, as a group, they passed into a lighted passageway after what seemed like ten minutes of geeky hobbling and tugging, all to the soft rhythm of Jerome's steady paws brushing the floor. Beyond the first few glowing wall sconces, the hallway made a hard left turn.

"Hard to believe," Jerome said, "but I think we're near the eastern corner of the . . ." His voice tapered off. He whipped about and studied the distant hallway, far across the dark chamber, with its bowling alleys and carpets. That's when he saw Marvin's men enter the wide, dark chamber and reach the middle in miraculously few strides, another mystical complexity of The Greaser. "We're not going to make it," Jerome stated flatly.

"I don't think we will, either," Allie said, gawking at their pursuers.

Jerome tilted his head, adjusted his ears, and rushed at a door that Allie hadn't even noticed. It yielded instantly. "In here," he said.

Allie led Arnold into the small, noxious-smelling room. Midge dragged in little Rena, still struggling.

Jerome curled about. "Rena," he said, "I will have Midge tie you to that bed if you don't sit still."

Rena glared at him but stopped fighting.

Jerome slammed the door shut and Midge helped the monster cat and Allie shove a huge dresser—cans and glass bottles toppling off of it—in front of the closed threshold. Once that was done, Allie went to the window and pulled back the heavy curtains. She almost laughed.

Ethereal morning light poured in, illuminating the hideous room. They were surrounded by grinning, gazing, snarling photographs of Scratch Friendly in a tiger-skin tank top, in leather underwear, and in a blue blazer sans pants. There were hundreds of photos and, overhead, the ceiling was covered in mirrors. "Of all places," said Allie.

"Scratch's room," Midge mumbled. Using the tip of her assault rifle, she stirred the scattered canisters and bottles of male cosmetics that had tumbled off his dresser. "Look, he's got Midge Darlington hair thickener, which never actually worked. The company lied."

Outside, the floor groaned under an ever-increasing load. Allie, lost in thought, hardly noticed. Exhausted and sporting a pounding headache after being thumped to the ceiling, she rubbed her temples but found them caked with oil and grease from her ride up and down the elevator shaft. All of their early morning efforts had been such a waste, she thought. She'd failed everyone and, worst of all, Jerome, who wouldn't even have been there if she hadn't insisted on a rescue attempt.

Jerome seated himself calmly in the center of Scratch's gaudy room. "It's not over, Allie. Don't act like it is," he said.

Allie sniffled and dabbed at her nose with dirty fingers. "I . . . I really thought we were going to save everyone and get out. I'm so dumb, aren't I?" She licked her dry lips. She swayed against the wall beside the door they'd entered and mashed a hand against her eyes to check her tears.

Loud clanking noises emanated from behind the door. It sounded as if Herman's men were rolling a battering ram, or maybe even cannons and tanks. A bullhorn crackled to life.

Jerome waited.

The Secrets of the Greaser Hotel

There was some wrangling, and then a familiar voice boomed off the walls and ceiling. "Hello, intruders!" Oda Friendly barked. "I am the gosh-darn caretaker, constable, and fuzz of this here lovely hotel establishment, and you're illegally trespassing, meaning I got every right ta blow ya ta kingdom come."

Arnold perked up. "Mrs. Friendly!"

Midge raised the rifle to her shoulder, aiming at the blocked door.

Allie rubbed filthy hands through her hair, grabbed it, and tugged as if the strands were the fraying ropes of a drifting vessel. Scooting sideways, she unconsciously knocked five unsightly photographs of Scratch to the floor. Feeling trapped and cornered, she began to breathe hard. Then a pure, wonderful rage began to overtake the canals and levy systems of her mind. So many years of abuse, of cruelty. Oda had taken her childhood, stolen her possibilities, and convinced her that all there would ever be was The Greaser and endless, endless labor.

"Now, pony up!" Oda said. "Who'm I dealing with? Ragpickers from Duchamp Security, come ta swipe Hammerhead back and save the day? Well, as soon as Mr. Gristle arrives, he's gonna let me and the boys use ya for target practice, Friendly-style."

Unexpectedly, the glass fronting every single photograph in the room shattered outwards.

"Allie, sweetheart," said a calm Jerome, "you need to maintain control."

But Allie didn't recognize the giant cat or understand what he was saying. White heat emerged from her fingers and swirled like glowing moths about her hands, bleaching her skin and pupils even as it crackled like radio static.

At once, the heavy dresser scooted across the floor, spilling Scratch's remaining cosmetics. Its drawers, as if propelled by tiny charges, rocketed outward, tossing polyester leisure suits, thick belt buckles, and animal-patterned briefs into the air, all of them fluttering down like streamers from the ceiling.

The wall Allie was leaning against crunched loudly and toppled outward, landing on a writhing mass of triggermen. Allie's power effortlessly stabbed into the corridor now lit by generators and large spotlights. It made a beeline toward Oda Friendly, striking her like an onrushing train, slamming her ferociously through the opposing wall.

Concurrently, a shimmering blaze crashed into the ranks of armed men to her right, throwing them down the hall as if they'd been struck by a giant pinball bumper. Guns fired somewhat randomly. Teeth were knocked from jaws. Bones snapped like the narrow parts of porcelain gravy boats. Allie's living anger snapped and hummed like a power station. It gathered Oda up and dragged her back to the energy source.

Allie was hate. She was malevolence. She was violence and power.

Still conscious, the leathery Oda snagged the howitzer-like pistol she kept holstered at her side and aimed it in Allie's general direction. Immediately, it was torn from her grip and crumpled like a tin can under a boot's heel.

Behind Allie, Rena, pulled along by Midge, stumbled out of Scratch's suite and headed east down the hallway, away from the fray. A few of Herman's boys attempted to gun them down, but Jerome was on them in an instant, begetting a bloody mess.

Allie noted the closeness of bullets as they whined inches from her elbow and neck. But she didn't flinch. Instead, her power, like the thick entanglement of electrical animus, rose against Oda, pinning the ugly woman's head to the hardwood floor in the hall.

The atrocities exacted upon Allie by Oda Friendly and her boys flashed like snapshots across her mind: Starvation. Grease burns. Blisters. Cold. Feverish heat. Backhands. Forehands. Knuckles imprinted on her cheeks, neck, temples. Slashes. Crunched fingers. Shoves. Plates in the kisser. A steak knife through the hand. Broom handles across her narrow shoulders. Kicks. Two bites that left her bleeding. And so, so much more!

Oda groaned. "Allie, please. Please calm yourself," she said. "If ya looking for an apology, I got one. I see what I done ta ya. But I didn't wanna. I was directed ta do it by the . . . the bosses. They's responsible. I was a pawn . . . just like ya was . . . de-dearie." The angry energy, leaping and popping, lifted Oda and brought her up face-to-face with Allie.

Eyes smoldering, Allie said, "Beg me." A curl of energy, like a writhing sunspot, forced Oda's head around, pried her jaw open, and sought her tongue.

It was wonderful, Allie thought, to have so much control. The power she wielded felt both divine and magnetic. The closer she came to realizing its potential, the more she wanted to keep it stirring inside. Why should she accept frailty and pain? She'd never be anyone's slave again. Instead, she'd take! Possess! "Beg!" she shouted at Oda.

"Hease. Hease, don hur me," said Oda, pain and fear warping her voice.

A trail of bullets veered away from Allie's shoulder, as if deflected. Seven slugs dug into the wall behind her. Allie grinned.

Someone over her shoulder was calling out. The voice was weedy, annoying, and distant. "Allie!" it said. "Allie, listen to me!"

How she despised her name. She no longer wanted to hear it. It was analogous to weakness, and she wasn't weak anymore. As she stepped mechanically about, her flaring power snatched at the

J. Scott Fuqua

old man. Holding him, she glanced down the hallway, her attention drawn to a huge, familiar cat shredding two knife-brandishing men.

"Allie, you're hurting Oda!" the old man behind her said frantically. "You're hurting Oda!" A bullet whizzed past, lacerating the skin of his brow and knocking him unconscious. He toppled to the messy floor.

Pirouetting about, Allie again smirked wickedly at Oda, who was trying desperately to crawl away. Allie lifted her, brought her close and, a second after grinning at her, an impossibly powerful explosion shook the halls, firing dark shrapnel at Oda, tearing her clothes, grabbing at her boots, slicing her skin. "No, you don't," Allie said, supernaturally drawing her back.

Then everything went dark.

The Secrets of the Greaser Hotel

29

The thrum surrounding Allie diminished and silence fell over all the combatants.

A silvery beam flickered on in the large chamber where they'd been pinned to the ceiling by one of The Greaser's endless traps. The light adjusted and shined across the bowling alleys and toward the combatants. It then swelled and illuminated its source—a man who stood dressed in a fancy bathrobe and leather slippers. He had a plush blue towel across his shoulders and a hand casually placed in a pocket. His thick hair was brushed upward and his eyes were laser keen. "Allie," Herman Gristle said, his voice unnaturally loud, "you have the audacity to disturb my bath. How brave."

A second beam of light flicked on. Its beam honed in on Allie.

"My, you're filthy," he continued. "Not at all as I imagined you'd be if ever I caught up with you." Herman Gristle casually rubbed one of his cheeks, clearly admiring the smoothness. "Well, it is a relief to see you. It will be, like many family reunions, a short, painful visit."

Allie leveled her dangerous gaze at him.

"Allie, are you angry with me? Is that what I sense? Do you think yourself my equal?"

She didn't reply.

"Tell me, tramp, do you think I'd allow you to pillage unchecked amongst my security staff?" asked Herman. "I am not Marvin. I don't put on airs, or scheme and plot, or play too much with people's heads. I simply get rid of problems. And, currently, you are just that."

A bowling ball, as if remote controlled, lifted from the far alleys and jetted forward at the speed of a high-powered bullet. It slammed into Allie's chest, sending her to the floor, where she struggled for air. Pain gripped her ribcage and lungs, but pain was something she was familiar with. Pain didn't muddle her brain. She got up and raised a hand. Light crackled and raced outward like a harpoon closing in on the man in the bathrobe.

The Secrets of the Greaser Hotel

Herman waved a hand, and the attack burst like water against steel. With the subtlest twitch of his head, dozens of weighty bowling balls lifted in the air, rifled forward, and circled above Allie like planets around a star. With a second twitch, they struck from every direction. She tried to shield herself but lacked the strength.

She staggered like a drunk before dropping to the floor and scattering various male cosmetics about. Out of breath, her mouth bleeding, her legs throbbing, her nose swelling, she smiled.

Herman released the bowling balls from his control, and they bounced loudly to the floor. With a mild wave of the hand, he levitated Allie. Then a blood-red light shackled her neck. It carried her sideways and pinned her to a wall above the floor.

Allie gripped tight to the manacle, holding it back, keeping herself from being strangled. She tried to break its clutch but, sadly, recognized that her strength was only a small fraction of Herman's. Anger sizzled in the air about her.

Herman, clean from his bath, casually approached, tapping his coif into place and checking his fingernails. He was only a dozen feet away when something tan and grubby zeroed in on him.

Jerome struck before Herman could react. Four huge gashes marred the Baron of Carrion's cheek, the very one he had been admiring seconds before.

Cursing loudly, Herman released Allie and circled to meet the animal.

He was too slow. Jerome slammed into him, clawing his back, tearing brutally at his shoulders and then the hands Herman had raised to protect himself. Herman lurched forward as if he might go down. He wobbled under the weight and ferocity of his assailant but, somehow, maintained his footing. Eyes rolling back, he directed two prongs of power above his head. Gleaming red, they seized Jerome, indelicately prying the cat away. Incensed by pain, Herman banged the animal to the floor once, twice, three times before flicking a finger and throwing him, ablaze, at Allie.

Jerome landed at her feet, his burning fur snuffed out by his tumultuous landing.

Allie worked to find focus. She remembered Jerome. She remembered that he was her friend. In a rush, the poisoned floodwaters

of her mind were drawn down a secret drain, and Allie's searing anger subsided, taking with it her power.

Herman's anger, however, did not subside. He heaved his hands skyward, and parts of Scratch's destroyed bedroom wall raced forward and pelted Allie. Herman staggered toward her, his once well-groomed hair askew like a worn toilet brush. His shoulders were in terrible shape, bleeding and gashed, while his plush blue towel was stained. His elegant leather slippers had fallen off.

Swaying, Herman reached down and pinched one of Allie's cheeks. Sounding delirious, his face marred horribly, he said, "I always knew that, if you were still alive, you would come back. It's obvious you want what I have, and if you were stronger and more loyal, Marvin would take you under his wing. That is the insult. But . . . I am the boss of me! *I am the boss of me!*"

Allie felt tears come to her eyes.

Herman grinned chillingly, the gouges in his face pumping blood down his neck. "You have no idea who you are, do you? You just want, and you don't know what. You just want power. I know. I know." He reached into the shredded pocket of his bathrobe and withdrew the photograph Allie had left on the bedstand at

J. Scott Fuqua

Zachary's house. Herman snickered and, in that moment, an old, weathered board materialized out of the darkness and delivered a devastating shot across the back of his head.

Allie, stumbling weakly, worked to refocus on the space in front of her. And there, behind Herman's fallen form, was Arnold Armstrong, who was loosely holding onto a thick wooden joist from the collapsed wall. Arnold leaned and lowered the tip of his impromptu

The Secrets of the Greaser Hotel

club to the floor. "Run, Allie," he
told her, huffing, his small body
shivering like a tuning fork.
"Get away, child."

Groaning, Jerome rolled
over and scurried to all fours.

Allie hugged the big cat,
yanking him forward by the
scruff of his neck.

"Go!" Arnold shouted.
Bobbing feebly, he dropped
to a single, fragile knee.

"You're coming, too,"
Allie said.

"Go," he repeated.

Smoke had filled the hallways, but no sign of flames was to be
found. "What's burning?" said Allie.

"Smells like Gristle Brand pig fat," Jerome said.

"Go," Arnold said, as if it was the only word he could speak.

Beside them, Herman groaned and moved his head, his hair mussed
with blood.

Allie and Jerome hobbled
away, into the darkness
and debris, past the
remains of Herman's
battered and
injured Rendering
Team, eight brawny
men shredded and
fileted by the big cat.

J. Scott Fuqua

They veered down the hallway and arrived in warm, refreshing daylight flooding through a large window in front of them. Somehow, it wasn't even boarded.

Braced in a corner, Midge trained her rifle on Allie and Jerome. "Warn me next time," she said. Trapped behind Midge's legs was Rena, who was trying to break free. In a flat voice, Midge told Allie and Jerome, "We aren't getting out of here. They've got people everywhere. Rena ran to the window to call for help—not for us but for Oda and Herman—and somebody shot an arrow at her. Nearly got her in the arm. We don't stand a chance."

Even before Midge finished her statement, Allie had located the arrow and was pulling on the braided fishing line tied to the back of the arrow. She tugged and tugged until there was a large pile of string at her feet.

Down the hall, they heard a second loud crack of wood. "Arnold just gave Herman another shot," Jerome said. "I can't imagine he'll be allowed a third."

The string seemed to extend for miles. Allie could feel it getting heavier and realized that the climbing rope was somewhere on the other end. Regardless, it didn't seem like it would ever reach them. She accelerated her motion. The room and the hallway were filling with dark smoke that carried the promise of burning meat.

Abruptly, outside the window, the bright tip of the climbing rope appeared.

"Midge," Jerome shouted, "shoot out the glass but don't hit the line!"

Midge sprayed the window with bullets.

They reeled in the rope and tied it to a radiator. Moving quickly, Allie grabbed a small length of rope from her backpack, wrapping it around Midge's legs and waist as she explained what they were going to do. She slapped a carabineer on the former maven of homemaking.

Smoke was everywhere now, and Midge, apparently willing to do anything to escape Greaser's Blight, clamped her carabineer onto the line and, without the slightest indication of thought, took off over the terrifying abyss.

Allie didn't even watch her progress. She was busy wrestling with Rena, struggling to get a cord of rope around the little girl.

"Do as you're told," Jerome said, "or I will knock you unconscious, girl, and don't think I won't."

Momentarily, Rena was zipping down the long climbing rope, across Baltimore's pigeon-and-buzzard-populated skyline, before roughly landing what seemed like miles and miles away, on the roof of a building across the street.

J. Scott Fuqua

The hallway suddenly exploded, causing large fragments of The Greaser's roof to drop to the floor. Meanwhile, Allie carefully tied the rope around her legs and waist.

Herman, they supposed, had risen to his feet. The hallway was suddenly engulfed in a web of flames and swirling, writhing power that licked about the building.

Allie rushed to the window and fixed the carabineer to her new belt. "How about you?" she asked Jerome.

"Go," he said. "I'm coming."

"No!"

"Allie, I have no intention of dying here. I'm coming! I'm coming! Now go!"

She climbed up on the sill and attached herself to the rope. Without looking down, she jumped.

Jerome sprang after her, his enormous form shifting, creasing, and folding until a small cat dug deep into Allie's shoulders to keep from plunging to the streets so far below—streets that, from that altitude, resembled satellite imagery.

Together, Allie and Jerome gained speed and descended as if they were in free-fall. It was hard to imagine that anyone could have gotten an arrow so far. It was amazing. The rope started to bow, slowing their speed as they approached the patchy tar roof of a once posh department store. Allie could see Zachary's face, his wattle, and a shirt that said, "Fighting Irish." She saw that he still held the big bow he'd fired the arrow from. It had another arrow on it, and he was aiming it up at the window they'd just exited.

Then the entire downtown was lit with a flash of crimson, and the windows and upper floors of The Greaser exploded outward, sending stone, glass, plaster, boards, and glossy photos of the Friendly boys into the morning sky.

The rope snapped.

Allie and Jerome's momentum carried them the remaining distance—just barely. Allie landed on her behind, tearing the seat of her pants. Rising, she unclipped herself, and as soon as she was free, Zachary snagged her hand and ran with her, Jerome riding atop her shoulder like a parrot, to the far side of the building, where Midge and Rena were waiting.

Zarchary had spent his time wisely. He had tied off a second zip line that ended at a tree beside Stella Brion's old Valiant. Midge, who'd blistered her fingers on the ride down from The Greaser, ignored her pain and rocketed down the rope. She landed gently beside the old car and unclipped herself. Rena, eyeballing Jerome and Allie, followed.

"Zachary," Allie said, clipping on, "you should ride with me."

"No need," he said. He gave Allie a surprise shove, and the weary girl drifted gently down through the crisp air.

Sirens converged on The Greaser Hotel from every direction. Zachary gave a thoughtful look back at the impossible shot he'd made. He smiled.

Smoke puffed gently upward from The Greaser, but it wasn't mounting. On the contrary, it seemed to be fading fast. Regardless, there existed in the side of the monstrous hotel a blast hole, a cavity shaped like an enormous fang.

Turning, Zachary placed one of the deep notches of his compound bow over the rappelling line. Heaving his tired legs over the lip of the building, he pushed off, making it look far too easy considering he was a seventy-three-year-old professor emeritus of business history and ethics at Johns Hopkins University.

The Secrets of the Greaser Hotel

Somewhere above the Mason-Dixon Line, a Plymouth Valiant rocketed down a serpentine Pennsylvania highway, where, off to the side, large fragments of pale stone ruptured a hard green field like the bony spine of an immense animal.

Allie mourned Arnold. She'd once loved the old man. When she'd first met him, he'd been a kindly and resilient character who resisted the Friendlys' daily cruelties. Like Midge, he'd offered Allie help, humor, and a certain amount of parental love, or at least as much of those things as he could sneak in while cooking and cleaning in Friendly-imposed silence.

J. Scott Fuqua

What truly saddened Allie were his final years. If it was mortification and subservience that Mrs. Friendly sought to inflict on her captives, she had achieved it with Arnold Armstrong. He'd become a court jester—somebody to kick around and insult whenever she felt the urge.

"I'll miss Arnold," Allie said.

"I've missed Arnold for some time," Midge replied softly. "But, in the end, he returned to us. He did what he'd always wanted to do. He rocked Herman Gristle's world pretty good." She rolled down the window and cool air streamed in. "Once, I had a vacation home about an hour from here," she noted.

"Tell me," Zachary said, his eyebrows arched, "do you still own that home?"

"It's gone, just like my old life." Her gaze roved the lush countryside.

Rena, seated between Allie and Jerome, whined, "Do I have to go live with my parents now? Do I?"

"We'll see," Jerome said, the look in his intelligent eyes revealing concern for the child.

Allie rubbed at the dirt on her hands. She closed her eyes, and even though she missed Arnold, she felt free—truly free!—for the first time in years. Her life was in front of her, not restricted to the world of The Greaser or the whims of the Friendlys.

Yet a small, troubling thought existed somewhere inside the folds of her mind. As pleased as she was, she wondered about the violence she'd so easily dispatched at the top of the old hotel, and at the joy she'd felt when she'd torn away all of the sentiment and all of the ridiculous chains keeping her from being who she was meant to be. She was more than a girl. She was—the distant, distant thoughts hissed—meant to have everything. She was meant to subjugate and exhaust.

Allie suddenly shook her head, terrified by the prodding murmurs of her mind.

"You okay?" Jerome asked from the front seat.

Tears suddenly rolled down her face. "I think," she said. "I hope."

"Allie," he said, "enjoy the moment. Enjoy the quiet. It won't last forever. It can't. But I have plans. I won't allow them to hunt you, dear. I won't allow that."

"Even if Marvin becomes president?" Allie asked.

Midge sat up. "What?"

Zachary, cranking his head around toward Midge, explained, "Believe it or not, Marvin Greaser has officially thrown his ancient black bowler into the race for the presidency of the United States."

"Oh my God!" Midge said, slumping against the back door.

Allie sighed.

Purring, Jerome rose on his toes and rubbed his head against Allie. "Hold onto this moment, dear," he said. "See the birds, which, of course I'd enjoy eating. See the hills and the sun and the road. See us, your friends."

Zachary interjected, "Yes, we are your friends. And don't you forget it."

Jerome told her, "And feel the hope. Feel it."

Allie nodded distantly, struggling not to hear the soft rants of her mind. "Okay."

"Do you feel it, then?" Jerome asked.

Midge hugged her and said, "Do you, sweetheart? Because we're free. You saved us—even Arnold, in a way."

Breathing hard, Allie worried for herself and her friends. "I feel it," she said. "At least I think I do. Maybe somewhere."

Jerome said, "After all you've seen and been through, 'somewhere' is good enough, Allie Argos. Hold onto it, too. Hold it tight, because

J. Scott Fuqua

this is a journey. Everyone in this car is on a journey that will entail green pastures, dark woods and, of course, bandits. These, dear, are all of the things that accompany risky travel."

Zachary snickered and took a turn way too fast. The wheels screeched sharply.

Midge raised a hand and gently rubbed Allie's back.

Rena peered straight ahead, still troubled.

And then Allie smiled. Jerome was so persistent, so sure, like a father. Allie looked at her friend, her mind suddenly free of the appalling darkness that had for so long enveloped her deepest self. Her soul was as clean and clear as the endless Pennsylvania sky above. She laughed. "Jerome, did you really say we're on a journey with bandits?"

The cat nonchalantly rotated his head away from Allie, so that he appeared to be staring out at the road ahead. "And hopefully with fish," he said. "I like fish."

Acknowledgements

I started *The Mystery of the Greaser Hotel* about six years ago, so it's amazing to finally see it on the page. It started, first, as a book about the narcissism of people who seek total self-satisfaction at the expense of others; then the entire world changed in the blink of an eye.

The economy tanked—completely tanked. And as it became clear why, I, like so many others, grew disgusted. The health of the nation was shaken by simple greed. Pure greed. Ugly greed.

The economy and so many modest dreams were laid waste by people who believed that their lives were of greater value than the lives they were destroying. They believed that they owed nothing to the greater community. There's no other way to justify so much personal gain amidst so much personal loss.

Anyway, I began to see a harder and more all-encompassing narcissism in their actions.

And so *The Greaser* morphed.

This is a fun book, an emotional book (I believe), with three amazingly cool protagonists, a confused girl on a journey of self-discovery and emotional growth, a magic cat, and a retired former professor of economics (physically based upon my father-in-law).

It is not a dirge against the only economic system that has proven to work, that has ushered the middle class into the world, and that has raised the standard of living for all. However, it is an indictment of the greed that grows in the darker and more complex corners of the economy.

The Mystery of the Greaser Hotel is about the old and new robber barons that seek six homes, fifteen cars, political power, and societal influence—people who harbor a basic disdain for anyone and everyone. It is about people who want to increase and keep what they have without losing one single biscuit off their huge plates or a single coffee cup in their cupboards. It's about people who will trample anyone for their own gain. Yuck!

Personally, I wish and hope for a nation that cares for all, that seeks to better all, that wants to raise everyone's boat. I seek a nation that would function better if the captains of capitalism were moral and ethical and cared for the greater community from which they take. Hail Bill Gates!

Okay now, sorry for all the yammering. Really. Let me thank the many people who contributed:

I can't express enough appreciating to Bruce Bortz, my publisher, who allowed me to construct a story with an odd voice, with over one hundred pieces of art, and an undercurrent of social commentary. Of course The Greaser is supposed to be fun, humorous, and exciting, but, please, the guy is brave and relentlessly seeks excellence no matter the cost. That's unheard of in the industry.

I can't say enough about Susan Mangan, the book's graphic designer, into whose hands I dumped all of my illustrations and told her to put them together "right." Of course, I had no idea how to do that. She did, and the results are a joy to see. I am profoundly grateful.

Thanks to the Voos family, who provided reference for all sorts of characters, from Allie to Midge to Marvin and more. I specifically thank Halle, who had no idea what the heck I was doing when I shot about five hundred pictures of her faking all sorts of actions. In fact, it was a little hard to get her to look furious or troubled, for she smiles a lot.

Thanks to Doug, a wonderful soul willing to act despicable in order to capture Herman Gristle's personality.

Thanks to the family cat, Jerome, who passed before the book was finished.

And thanks to all my neighbors, many of whom gawked or happily participated when I said, "I wanna draw you for a book, but I'm gonna exaggerate everything about your face and body. Okay?"

Finally, and most importantly, I thank my wife, whom I love deeply and completely during some beautiful part of every day. She's a great and total gift.

I thank my indescribably lovely children, too. They stir my heart. There's Calla, who's a spectacular artist (musical theater) in her own right. I secretly watched and observed her in order write Allie.

And thank you to my son, Gabriel, who, like a pixie, inexplicably spreads joy and enthusiasm to almost everyone he comes in contact with.

Finally, I thank everyone I left out. Writing this book was a long journey, and involved nearly every interaction I had with folks for about six years. I expect the next book will be finished in much, much less time.

Be well, and always hope.

Jonathon Scott Fuqua (please, just call me Scott)

2014